THE

MUSEUM

MURDERS

Dawn Brookes

THE MUSEUM
MURDERS

Carlos Jacobi PI
Book 3

Dawn Brookes

Oakwood Publishing

Paperback Edition 2023
Kindle Edition 2023
Paperback ISBN: 978-1-913065-85-0
Hardback: 978-1-913065-86-7
Copyright © DAWN BROOKES 2023

Cover Images: Adobe Stock Images
Cover Design: Dawn Brookes

Prologue

The biting wind cut through Henry Cutter's tattered clothes like a knife, chilling him to the bone as he shuffled through the deserted streets. The city centre, once familiar and comforting, felt alien to him. Henry longed for better days; the warmth of his wife's embrace, the joyful laughter when he threw his baby son into the air and the camaraderie of his fellow soldiers. He had once been a proud man serving his country, with a happy family and the security of a roof over his head. But those days were long gone, swallowed up by the relentless tide of time.

A group of youths had laid into him as part of their night's entertainment, waking him up and hurling abuse, followed by empty beer cans. When he hadn't responded, they got bored and scurried away into the darkness. But their cruel words hung heavy in the air, weighing him down. There was a time when he could have flattened the lot of them.

'Stupid kids,' he muttered under his breath as he pulled the collar of his threadbare coat tighter and trudged forward. He caught a glimpse of himself in a car's wing mirror and was shocked at how old he looked. Some things the kids had shouted rang true. He sniffed the air, recoiling at his own smell. He was desperate to find shelter from the chilling wind and pouring rain, but knew it wouldn't be easy. The rain shower caused his straggly long hair to stick to his cheeks. His clothes were riddled with holes and his feet were soaked because the soles of the shoes he'd found in a bin were hanging off. He needed to keep moving to avoid freezing to death, but every step he took carried the weight of his regrets.

Henry turned into an alley. The Jewry Wall Museum with its Roman wall towered on one side, while the eerie and depressing graveyard of St Nicholas Church was on the other. Shivering when he glimpsed the ancient tombstones through the fence, Henry kept his head down. Some vagrants slept in the graveyard when they were desperate, but not him. He was superstitious and didn't believe in disturbing the dead for fear of rousing angry spirits.

Henry focused instead on the museum. Faint memories of happier times when he and his Lori had visited it together. She had always marvelled at the artefacts and rich history they represented. Rain bounced off the stones of the ancient wall and he looked up, allowing the water to wash his face, but Henry's heart soon ached with an overwhelming sense of loss. Each raindrop was like a tear from heaven. He had been brought up by devout Baptist parents who would be ashamed to see what had become of him.

The alley offered a little relief from the storm, and the prospect of finding a dry nook among the ruins gave him a glimmer of hope. He stared at the wall again, imagining the horrendous and good things it had witnessed through the centuries. That wall had seen plenty, but then so had he.

Henry continued along the dark alley. Guided by distant streetlights, he clung to the hope of finding a place to sleep among the ancient ruins of the bathhouse. He climbed over the fence and clambered through overgrown bushes and trees. The branches clawed at his worn clothes and tugged at his hair, but he persisted, driven by the need for shelter.

When he reached the dugout foundations, they were eerily quiet. The wind seemed to whisper through the exposed stones, laughing at him, as the rain pattered softly on the surrounding grass. Despite the spine-chilling atmosphere he sensed from the graveyard on the other side of the alley, Henry pressed on, desperate for a place to rest his weary bones.

He slogged through the excavated ruins, his eyes slowly adjusting to the darkness. His feet dragged as they crossed the forgotten path, mud and dirt caked his soles. He felt his socks getting wetter and heavier by the minute. Henry felt the icy embrace of the early hours creeping across his skin, unsettling his heart. He fixed his eyes on the ground, not wanting to fall into a trench or trip over the excavated rocks.

Henry stopped. Something had caught his eye. A glimmer in the darkness. He had walked these grounds many times before, but something seemed out of place. Squinting to make out what it was, he couldn't. The night was too dark and the lights inside the grounds weren't switched on. Henry needed glasses, but couldn't afford any.

He stepped closer to what seemed off. That's when he saw a pair of eyes staring endlessly into the dark sky. The woman had been beautiful, that much he could see. She looked like a forgotten angel. Her pale face, and the once vibrant eyes were cold and empty. A silent scream seemed to be eternally frozen on her lips.

Henry had seen death before. Lots of people he'd met on the streets had died, more than he cared to remember, but no experience was worse than when he'd held his darling wife in his arms as she passed away. Though this was something else. It was different. This woman had met a violent end, and he'd witnessed enough of those in the army to know.

Henry checked the surrounding area, gasping when he felt his heart lurch with shock and horror at what he was contemplating. He stumbled back, confused and frightened. Who was she? What had happened to her? And why was she here in these ruins?

Summoning every ounce of courage he had left in his heart, Henry approached the body again.

'God rest your soul,' he murmured, crossing himself despite it being years since his last prayer. Forcing his feet to move, Henry stepped closer and knelt down, his breath slow and shallow, trying to control the pounding heart within his chest. It filled his head with fear and confusion.

The woman's clothing was intact, but mud-stained, her bright red hair matted and wet. Henry reached out and touched her arm, but recoiled at the ice-cold sensation permeating his leathery skin, hardened from years living on the streets.

He caught sight of a sack lying next to her. Henry hesitated, debating with himself whether he should go through it. The gnawing hunger in his stomach urged him to take a peek – perhaps there would be food or something valuable inside. He wrestled with his conscience, arguing with his former self, who told him what he was contemplating was low, even for him. Still, the rumbling in his stomach argued the opposite.

Finally, his hunger won out, and he reached for the bag to check the belongings. He pulled it open and rummaged through its contents. A few coins clinked at the bottom and he pulled out a photo of a man before dropping it again.

'I can't do this,' he whispered, horrified by his actions. He threw the sack down and left it beside the lifeless body. The thought of robbing the dead filled him with guilt and disgust.

Henry stood up slowly and backed away from the body, feeling sorrow for a life cut short. He held back tears, remembering his own loss once more before stumbling out of the museum grounds and into the night, his heart heavy with sadness and guilt. His feet slipped in the mud as he tried to make sense of what he had just seen. With every step he took, the weight of the mud clinging to his shoes slowed his progress.

But then something made him stop in his tracks. Henry looked back at the place where the body lay and knew he had to do something. It was important to tell someone. He couldn't leave her lying there like discarded trash.

Swallowing hard, he headed along the High Street. It was deathly quiet other than the distant hum of street cleaners working through the night. He didn't envy them their task of clearing up the mess left behind by Saturday night revellers. The rain continued to pour, each drop stinging his face.

As Henry walked, his mind raced. Something about the girl was familiar. Had he seen her at the shelter? If only his memory functioned better. He couldn't stand the thought of the poor woman's death going unnoticed. He would do right by her, but he wouldn't wait around to be accused of having anything to do with her death.

Hunger continued rumbling in his stomach, pulling him out of his thoughts. He spotted an overflowing bin. Some contents had spilled onto the rain-soaked pavement. Though he was no stranger to rummaging through bins for food, each instance was a blow to his pride.

Hunger overcame dignity, and Henry started digging through the discarded waste. To his relief, he found a half-eaten kebab, wrapped in dripping wet paper. It wasn't much, but it would do.

Finding shelter in a doorway, he sat down, huddling against the elements as he tore into the cold, wet meat. It wasn't appetising, but at least it was something to satisfy the gnawing emptiness inside him. As he ate, his mind continued to race. Thoughts of the dead woman intertwined with memories of his wife and the life they'd shared before it all fell apart.

Once he had finished the meagre meal, Henry searched the ground for cigarette butts. Desperation had long since robbed Henry of any qualms about smoking discarded fags. He collected a few of the dryer half-smoked butts, storing them in his tattered coat pocket.

Casting one last glance around, he ventured further up the High Street, as far as the clock tower, where he turned right. From there, he shuffled towards the single black telephone box, standing like a sentinel, promising anonymity. If he could get to it unnoticed. He looked around to check before slipping inside the booth.

These modern booths had no doors for kids to kick in, but he felt secure enough. Even without a door, stale smoke filled his nostrils. He took a deep breath to steady himself before lifting the receiver, his numb fingers hovering over the buttons as he dialled 999.

The line rang with a shrill echo that drilled into Henry's skull. He pressed the receiver against his ear, straining to hear any sound amidst another relentless downpour starting up outside. He was in two minds whether to drop the receiver when the operator's voice came through.

'Emergency. Which service do you require?' Her tone sounded professional and detached.

'Police… I-I found a body,' Henry stuttered, fighting to keep his voice steady.

'Just one moment.'

Another voice came onto the line. 'Police, how can I help?'

'I found a body,' he repeated. 'A young woman. She's lying in a dugout at the Jewry Wall Museum.'

'Are you sure she's deceased, sir?' The question sounded clinical, lacking emotion.

'Yes, I'm sure.' Images of the once beautiful face flashed before him, making his stomach churn. He hesitated for a moment, considering whether he should divulge more information.

'Thank you, sir. Stay on the line.' The woman's voice remained calm, betraying no hint of the urgency Henry felt. 'We're sending officers to the scene immediately. Can I have your name and contact information?'

Henry bit his lip before putting the phone down. He heard loud ringing as he hurried away.

It was risky returning to the museum. But something compelled him to go back. He felt responsible for the girl.

Steeling himself, Henry climbed over the gate into the graveyard of St Nicholas Church, pushing down his fears and superstitions. He sought refuge behind a large tombstone, apologising to the interred inhabitant.

'I'm trying to do good here,' he said, as if that would ward off any retribution from the deceased. Crouched behind the weathered tombstone, Henry waited, his breath sounding ragged as he watched the museum grounds. The rain pattered against the stone, adding even more chilling dampness to the place. A coil of tension wrapped itself around his chest and squeezed.

'You can't stay here for long,' he whispered, his fingers holding onto the rough, moss-soaked surface of the tombstone. 'Just need to see what happens next.'

The sound of tyres pulling up on the wet pavement reached his ears, and Henry's heart skipped a beat. Two police officers emerged from their vehicle, torches dispelling the darkness. The rain muffled their voices, but the urgency in their movements was unmistakeable. Minutes later another car arrived. A man got out, donning white overalls before going over to the scene.

'Pathologist's here. You did the right thing,' Henry muttered, trying to reassure himself.

As the officers moved to search the grounds beyond the Roman wall, yet another car pulled up, this time outside the church. The car door opened, revealing a priest in a black cassock. Henry's heart missed a beat as he recoiled his head behind the tombstone. He was relieved to see the priest walking around the church grounds and into the ruins.

'That was close. Time to go, Henry,' he told himself. 'Let them do their job. You've done your bit.'

Henry stole away from the scene, avoiding the pools of light cast by the officers' torches, and slipped into the night.

Chapter 1

The pounding bass vibrated through the hull of Fiona Cook's narrowboat as the hands of her clock flickered past 3am.

Fiona groaned, dragging a pillow over her head in a futile attempt to muffle the noise. In the early hours of this Sunday morning, a throbbing headache forming behind her eyes was evidence she had a day off. She shouldn't have had that last pint of lager before leaving the local pub.

After tossing and turning for over an hour, Fiona threw back the covers.

'Right. Enough is enough.'

She pulled a creased t-shirt over her head and put on a pair of trousers. Fiona stomped to the rear of her boat where she slipped into her wellies, opened the hatched doors and jumped onto the towpath. Torrents of rain pelted down, stinging her face as it hit. She was soaked by the time her trampling led her to where the noise was belting out from the neighbouring vessel. Fiona pounded a fist on the roof.

Her breath was visible in the chilly night air. Everything except this lit-up boat was in blackness. There was no reply from her thumping.

Fiona shouted, 'Hey! Do you mind?' Still no response. She banged again, harder this time on the roof and the window.

The music cut out abruptly, followed by the sound of breaking glass and raucous laughter. A dishevelled man she knew as Graham, who was in his late forties, stumbled out of the hatch and blinked at Fiona in surprise.

'Sorry, love, didn't realise we were keeping you up,' he slurred. Fiona stepped back to escape the strong whiff of beer and cigarette smoke. 'Party got a bit out of hand.'

Fiona folded her arms, unimpressed. 'No kidding. Now do us all a favour and pack it in, would you?'

The man gave a mock salute. 'Yes, ma'am, Detective Inspector, sir!' His friends erupted into giggles behind him.

Fiona bit back a retort, too tired to argue.

A big bloke from the boat two moorages down emerged through his door wearing flip-flops and boxer shorts. He waddled like a sumo wrestler and his muscular arms, covered in tattoos, tensed as he approached.

He glared at Graham. 'Are you gonna stop the racket or am I gonna come inside and stop it for yer?'

His arrival wiped the smile off of Fiona's drunken neighbour's face and all behind him went quiet.

'No need for that, mate. We're finished. Sorry.' Graham disappeared quickly below.

The burly guy in the boxers flashed her a grin. 'That should put a stop to it, love.'

Fiona had recently moved her boat from north Derbyshire to its new mooring in Leicestershire and hadn't got to know her neighbours too well yet. The party guy, Graham, was usually quiet, and they'd passed the time of day a few times, but she hadn't met boxer shorts man before. Now wasn't the time for introductions.

'Thanks,' she said.

The guy gave her a nod before trundling back to his boat looking ridiculous in his drenched boxers. Not that she looked much better, but at least she had clothes on. Fiona squelched back to her own domain and climbed inside to dry off.

As the sounds of the party finally died down, she collapsed onto her bed with a groan, her head still pounding. Being a detective was rewarding, but some days, the job felt like it was too much. She'd lost count of the hours she'd put in this past week, and having a Sunday off was something to look forward to. As Fiona tried to drift off to sleep, she longed for a normal 9 to 5 and a decent night's rest.

'It's 4:37am,' she groaned, glancing at the old clock on her bedside table. 'How can I be still awake?'

The boat rocked gently on its mooring, and the rain was pitter-pattering on her roof rather than hammering, a slight comfort. She squeezed her eyes shut, trying to will herself into some much-needed rest. Fiona felt herself drifting, but as if on cue, her mobile phone buzzed, its screen illuminating the cramped space.

'You've got to be kidding me?' She snatched the phone and swiped it open.

'DS... I mean, Acting DI Cook,' she snapped.

'Sorry to bother you, ma'am. We've got a body at the museum – possible suspicious death.'

Fiona shook sleep from her head. 'That sounds like a film title. Which museum?' There were four that she knew of and most likely more that she didn't.

A chuckle at the other end of the line. 'Nice one, ma'am.'

Fiona pinched the bridge of her nose, stifling a groan. She could feel the weight of her eyelids, weighing down like lead anchors, when she threw her legs over the side of the bed.

'Tell me what happened.' Fiona put the phone on speaker and rubbed her temples.

'Right, ma'am. The body of a young Jane Doe, assumed homeless, has been found in one of the trench dugouts of the Jewry Wall Museum. We had an anonymous phone call from a telephone box in the town centre. A man – probably another vagrant, but he's long gone. We've got two officers on the scene. One of them is new and wants to make a name for herself,' Fiona could imagine the eye roll at the other end of the phone matching her own. 'They called the pathologist – also new – and… well, there's a priest who's proving to be difficult.'

'Great, just great,' Fiona muttered. Her lack of sleep was making her more irritable than usual. 'Am I hearing you right? There's an ambitious police officer, a troublesome priest and a rookie pathologist at a museum in the early hours on Halloween?'

'Strictly speaking, ma'am, Halloween's not 'til tonight.'

'Well, I hate to imagine what that holds in store for me! Hang on a minute. Is that the museum with the ancient wall which houses ruins of a Roman bathhouse?'

'That's the one. The body's in one of the dugouts.'

It was starting to make sense. 'Next door to a church and a graveyard, hence the priest?'

'You've got it.'

'Shame they didn't just bury the body and save me going out there,' she said. Morbid humour might keep her going right now. 'Tell them I'll be about forty-five minutes.'

'Right you are.'

Fiona ended the call and threw her phone onto the bed.

She hurriedly pulled on some clothes, not bothering to straighten or tuck them in properly, and grabbed her beloved mac. The cold air hit her face as she stepped onto the towpath. But at least it had stopped raining. She resisted the temptation to bang on the windows of the boat next door and shout *good morning* as she passed, instead muttering it under her breath as she walked along.

Fiona's phone rang while she was trudging along the towpath. She stared at the display in surprise. 'Sir?'

'Morning, Fiona.' The DCI's cheery voice usually meant trouble.

Fiona tried to sound bright and awake, even though she felt like a zombie. 'Good morning, sir. I'm just heading to the scene now.'

'I'll save you the bother. There's no need for you to attend this homeless case. Father Crane called me and I was nearby, so I'm here. You go back to bed. I know you've had a lot on lately.'

Fiona stopped in her tracks. Terry Masters could be okay, but it was usually when he wanted something, plus, he was inherently lazy. This felt like she'd entered a parallel universe and was speaking to his alter ego.

'Are you sure, sir? I can be there in half an hour.'

'Quite sure. There's nothing suspicious about it. Looks like the poor woman took a fall, but we'll do all the relevant checks just to make sure. I know Sebastian… erm… Father Crane. It's better if I handle it.'

Fiona felt suspicion creeping through her. Apart from it being unusual for her boss to do anyone any favours, as far as she knew, he wasn't religious. Now he was interfering with a case in the early hours of a Sunday morning without a lackey! His dismissing her presence so casually was weird. She wondered if there was something more going on behind the scenes.

'If you say so, sir. Let me know if you need me to do anything.' Fiona clenched her jaw, trying to suppress her mounting frustration.

'Have a good rest, Fiona. I'll see you tomorrow.'

'Okay. Thanks.'

With that, the call ended, leaving Fiona standing on the towpath, confused. The abrupt ending of the phone conversation was more in keeping with the DCI's character. Fiona concluded this priest must have friends in high places if he could drag Terry Masters out of bed at this hour. Still, she was happy to leave him hobnobbing with the bigwigs and would gladly go back to bed and forget about it.

THREE WEEKS LATER

Chapter 2

Carlos Jacobi's eyes moved methodically over the last of a stack of files. Six cases concluded. Boring they might have been, but they paid the bills. He prided himself on attention to detail, a trait that had served him well both in his military career and as a private investigator.

The Leicester town centre office was a reasonable size with a flat upstairs where he crashed more and more often these days. He had lined the walls with filing cabinets and filled the shelves with crime-solving and forensics books. There was also space to see clients and a second desk for his assistant, Julie Stacey.

'Julie, can I have the file on the Thompson case?' Carlos looked up from his desk. 'I've finished with these. You can send out the bills tomorrow.'

'Here you go.' Julie handed him a file, taking the pile back to her desk. He had been fortunate to inherit Julie along with the office after the previous PI had been murdered. The late PI's wife had offered Carlos the lease after he had tracked down her husband's killer. He was trying to wind down his London office where a partner managed the day-to-day business. Julie was thirty, trustworthy and reliable. He had kept her on when he took over the office for those reasons, plus she loved his faithful dog.

'Thanks.' Carlos flipped open the folder. It was another mundane case which involved tracking down a man avoiding maintenance payments for his two children. It irked Carlos when people tried to shirk their responsibilities, especially with looking after their own family.

While Carlos examined the documents, Lady, his beautiful liver and white Springer Spaniel, lay at his feet, with her head resting on her paws. Her head pricked up every time there was a movement outside. Lady had been a police dog, but when her handler emigrated to Australia, she was too quirky to continue in that role, so his friend had asked Carlos to take her on. She was an important part of his life. Her sixth sense and the additional training he had given her came in handy when he was investigating.

'Our guy's been hopping from job to job to avoid detection,' Carlos said, scanning the employment records in the file. 'Anything more on his current whereabouts?'

'I've got the numbers of a few of his old friends which his wife brought in this morning. Would you like me to ring them?'

'Please do,' Carlos replied, his brow furrowed in concentration. 'And see if you can find any connections between the companies he's worked for – there might be something in there that can tell us where he's moved on to. Can you get me an appointment with his most recent boss?'

'I'm on it.' Julie finished prioritising the files he'd given her and dialled the first number on her list.

Carlos knew it wouldn't take long to track this guy down now. Getting him to pay up was another matter altogether. He set about typing new information onto the computer. His preference was to have as little paperwork as possible, but some things he and Julie just had to file, such as receipts, contracts and evidence.

Lady jumped up suddenly, sniffing at the door. Carlos glanced at her, a smile tugging at the corners of his mouth.

'Easy, girl, it's just someone walking past.' She returned to his side, and he reached down to give her head a comforting stroke. Her tail wagged briefly before she resumed her place at his feet.

Julie cleared her throat after putting the phone down.

'Any luck?' Carlos looked up from his computer.

'The first guy said he doesn't know where he is, but the second, an old friend, mentioned he saw him visiting a pub near his old workplace.'

'Good work, Julie,' Carlos said encouragingly. 'Could you write down the name of the pub? I'll drop in.'

Julie scribbled an address down on a piece of paper and handed it to him. 'I'll see if I can get you an appointment with the last boss.' She picked the phone up again.

Carlos watched her for a moment, appreciating her efficiency. She was growing in confidence, having had it knocked out of her by a failed relationship where her ex left her with a three-year-old. He didn't pay maintenance either, but Julie wanted no contact with him, so had turned down Carlos's offer to help. Instead, he helped by offering her flexible employment enabling her to fit childcare responsibilities around her work. Something she had not once tried to abuse.

Lady jumped up again, this time with her tail wagging. Carlos grinned as he recognised the silhouette through the frosted glass as that of his friend, Fiona Cook, an acting detective inspector based in Leicester. He opened the door.

'Fiona, good to see you.' Carlos leaned in to hug her. Lady ran in circles around his visitor, tail spinning. 'As you can see, Lady's pleased to see you as well.'

'Hey, Lady, missed me?' Fiona chuckled, bending down to give the overexcited dog a stroke, nodding to Julie at the same time.

'Come on in,' Carlos gestured towards a seat. 'We've got fresh coffee brewing.'

'Perfect.' Fiona brushed past him to take a seat next to his clutter-free desk, giving it a wipe with her finger. 'You've missed a bit of dust,' she said, grinning widely.

It was no secret he had OCD when it came to order and cleanliness, which made their friendship even more interesting, given Fiona's dishevelled appearance and love of junk food. She had on the light blue mac she always wore, and her hair looked wilder than usual.

'Hilarious.' Carlos smiled before turning to Julie. 'Coffee?'

'No thanks. I'll be off in a minute. I need to collect Freya from the nursery. Mum's got a dental appointment.'

'How is young Freya?' Fiona asked.

'Speaking in complete sentences now. She's really coming along.' If there was one thing that caused Julie's chest to puff out, it was speaking about her daughter. As she put her coat on, she added, 'I can't get hold of Thompson's boss, but I'll get onto it in the morning.'

'No problem,' said Carlos.

Once Julie left, Carlos poured Fiona and himself mugs of filtered coffee and took a seat opposite her. Her eyes met his, serious yet warm.

'So, what's the latest on Nicolae? Any progress?'

'Unfortunately not,' Carlos admitted, frowning. 'He's proving to be as elusive as ever since we let him off the hook.' He scowled, but it was unfair to blame Fiona. When hired brawn connected to the organised crime boss had threatened her brother's life if she pursued Nicolae, she had been placed in an impossible position. Plus, neither Carlos nor Fiona had any evidence that would be enough to charge him. 'We'll get something on him,' he added.

'Too right we will,' Fiona agreed. They both wanted to track this man down and build a prosecutable case against him.

'Anything at your end?'

Fiona shook her head. 'I wish I could formally investigate, but I don't want Masters knowing anything about it.'

Carlos felt his muscles tense at the mention of his nemesis, Fiona's boss. 'He's not on Nicolae's payroll, is he?'

Shrugging, Fiona stopped smiling. 'I don't think so, but I can't trust him on this one. Plus, he's up to something.'

Fiona tried to remain as loyal as she could to her DCI, who had given her the opportunity to work in a senior role, so it worried Carlos when she said anything negative about him.

'What?'

'I wish I knew, or perhaps I'm glad I don't. He's in the process of gathering a cliquey team around him. I don't like it.'

Carlos grimaced. He hoped Masters wasn't involved with Nicolae. It would make their job even harder if he were.

'Anything we should be worried about?'

'Who knows? I've got enough work on my plate with cases up to my ears. I shouldn't worry about it at all, except…'

'Go on,' Carlos encouraged.

'The guys and girls he's huddling up with are arrogant, ones who might be tempted to blur the lines.'

Carlos had stood up to refill their mugs, but grabbed hold of his desk, lightheaded.

'Good grief, Carlos. Are you all right?'

'Fine. Low blood sugar, probably.'

Fiona's knowing eyes were fixed on him. She didn't believe a word.

'If you ever want to talk about it.'

'Thanks,' he said. Terry Masters and Carlos had both been serving in the forces when Carlos's best friend had been killed while they were on patrol. Everyone there that day knew deep down Masters was responsible, but because he had gathered a team of wannabe alpha males around him, they closed ranks. None had been willing to admit to what had happened.

Carlos almost tripped over Lady while handing Fiona another drink. 'Watch it, Lady!'

'She knows what's up, and she also knows bull when she hears it,' said Fiona. 'But don't worry. I get it. Maybe you'll be able to talk about it one day.'

'Yeah, maybe.' Carlos stared into space. Would he ever be free of this?

'And if you have got low blood sugar, it's your own fault. You should eat more… and I should eat less.' Fiona chuckled, patting her expanding middle. Carlos appreciated the change of subject.

'I haven't got far with Nicolae, but I took a trip to Edinburgh last weekend and found out something about our lawyer friend.' Seeing Fiona's eyes widen, he added. 'Don't worry, your brother's okay. I scoped the address where he lives with the guy's daughter. He seems happy enough.' Carlos didn't mention the people going in and out of the house who looked like stereotypical drug dealers.

Fiona exhaled. 'Tell me more about the lawyer.'

'They call him Alastair "The Crooked" McTavish. I asked around, pretending to be on the lookout for a lawyer who didn't mind bending the rules.' Carlos rubbed Lady's head as she pressed against his leg. 'His name came up every time.'

'Be careful, Carlos. If he thinks you're poking around in his business, he'll be after you.'

'I've never been one to shy away from a fight, especially with scum like him and Nicolae, but for the sake of discretion, I used a false name and a heavy disguise. I look good with long hair and a beard.'

Fiona laughed. 'Did you take Lady?'

'I'm not stupid, Fiona. Of course not. Rachel looked after her for the weekend.' His heart missed a beat like it always did when he thought of his girlfriend. The woman he hoped to marry one day.

'That's good.' Fiona was visibly relieved. 'We can't give him any inkling we're investigating him; not until I can figure out a way to get Steve out of there.'

'What if Steve doesn't want to get out of there, Fiona?'

'Then I'll do what I have to do. Getting him arrested will be better than letting them use him as leverage. I can't be a crooked cop, whatever the outcome, but I'll do everything I can to coax my brother out of their clutches. In the meantime, we'll keep working on this, off the books. We can't let these people continue to exploit innocent lives, but we have nothing we can use against them. Alastair The Crooked McTavish is also The Clever McTavish. He gets others to do the dirty work for him. I don't know what I'll do if I get any more threats.'

Carlos nodded, grateful for her bravery. He knew how hard it was for her to pursue this, and it wasn't just her brother's life on the line, it was her career. If they could turn her through any means, they would.

'We'll get them before that happens.'

Fiona looked less certain. 'Let's hope so,' she said, her voice heavy. 'Anyway, I should go. I've got a pile of paperwork waiting for me back at the station.'

'Yeah, and I've got a pub to visit,' Carlos replied with a smirk. 'Don't worry about your brother, Fiona. He's a grown man. You're not responsible for him. In the meantime, keep your own head down and be cautious.'

'Always,' she assured him, standing up.

Lady raised her head, eyeing Fiona with a soft wag of her tail, but not getting up.

'Bye, Lady,' Fiona said, bending down to give the dog a quick head rub. 'Be good and look after him, okay?'

Carlos chuckled as Lady thumped her tail on the floor in response. He was sure she understood every word. Fiona left the office, the door closing softly behind her.

As Carlos sat back in his chair with Lady curled up at his feet once more, he contemplated his next move. The stakes were high, and the danger ever-present. But he couldn't let Nicolae and a corrupt lawyer continue unchecked. What their partnership was, he hadn't yet fathomed.

'Right, Lady,' Carlos got up, 'fancy a drink?'

Lady leapt up and ran to the rear door which led to a small carpark.

'Clever girl. Let's get the mundane out of the way.'

Chapter 3

Carlos parked his classic Ford Capri in the back carpark, admiring the vehicle while he let Lady out. He entered the corridor leading to his office via the back door, humming a tune. The door swung shut behind him with a thud. Lady padded on ahead.

He heard voices coming from inside. He wasn't aware he had any appointments pending, but Julie might have booked someone in and forgotten to mention it. When he entered his office, Julie looked up from where she was sitting with a couple, offering Carlos a warm smile. The couple stood up.

'This is Carlos Jacobi,' Julie said. 'And this is Mr and Mrs Sand.'

Carlos's gaze shifted to the couple, and he put his hand out. 'Pleased to meet you.' Both appeared to be in their mid- to late-fifties, dressed in clothes that shouted wealth and privilege. Mrs Sand dropped his hand quickly, but her husband's grip was firm and confident. As they returned to their seats, Carlos noted the pot of tea on the small table in front of them.

Carlos took one of the vacant seats.

'Mr and Mrs Sand might like to hire you,' Julie said, bringing him a cup of tea and retaking the fourth seat, armed with a pen and pad.

'Please call us Rose and Harry,' said the woman.

Lady wagged her tail, but sensed the couple weren't dog-friendly, so she didn't do her usual thing of demanding fuss. Instead, she helped herself to a drink from the bowl kept at the side of Carlos's desk.

'That's Lady. She's our third investigator.' Carlos noted a look of disapproval from Rose as Lady slurped her drink, dribbling the contents on the mat.

Rose was a tall, elegant woman with short blonde hair framing a tense face. She was striking. A gold necklace gleamed against a cream blouse worn under a lime-green jacket, emphasising a slender neck. Her expensive perfume filled the room. In contrast, Harry was overweight with friendly, although slightly worried, eyes and a receding hairline. He was wearing a brown tailored jacket.

The couple both looked uncomfortable.

'We must apologise for not making an appointment,' said Harry, clearing his throat. 'We wanted to check out the place first.'

Carlos nodded, understanding. People came to see a private investigator for all kinds of reasons, many of which were embarrassing or painful.

'What can I do for you?' he asked, offering a friendly smile before taking a sip of the hot tea.

'This might sound odd, but we'd like you to find our daughter, Christina,' Rose said, her hands folded neatly in her lap.

Carlos raised an eyebrow.

'It might be nothing, but we've just returned from a six-week cruise around Southeast Asia. We keep in regular contact with her – every Sunday, in fact. But the last call was three weeks ago and on a Saturday. Since we got back yesterday, we haven't been able to reach her.'

Harry chimed in after a furtive glance at his wife. 'We've tried calling her multiple times, and there's been no answer. The message on her mobile says it's switched off, and the landline goes straight to the answerphone. On rare occasions, she misses calling, but she doesn't go completely silent.'

Rose's lips pressed into a thin line, her eyebrows knitting together. 'It's not unheard of.'

Carlos set his cup down on the table, suspecting it was Harry, rather than Rose, who was the reason for them being here. He leaned forward.

'You say it was three weeks ago when you last spoke to her?'

'Yes,' Rose answered hesitantly. 'She mentioned she was busy with work, but didn't give any specifics, so when she didn't call again, we assumed she was preoccupied.'

'Did she seem anxious or upset during that conversation?' Carlos asked, observing their reactions.

Rose glanced at Harry before answering. 'Not that I could tell. She seemed her usual self. A little distracted, perhaps.'

Julie scribbled down notes on her A4 pad while Carlos continued.

'You say you usually speak on Sundays. Who calls who?'

'Is that relevant?' Rose snapped.

Carlos shrugged. 'I'm just trying to get a feel for her state of mind.'

'She calls us,' said Harry. 'We don't like to disturb her.'

'So you didn't try calling her on the Sundays she missed?' Carlos asked.

'No,' said Rose.

'I tried once,' Harry interjected.

'You didn't mention that.' Rose glared at her husband.

'And can you think of any reason she wouldn't be returning your calls now? Any recent conflicts or changes in her life?' Carlos probed.

Harry shifted in his seat, looking uncomfortable. 'Christina has always been independent. Perhaps she needs some space, but complete silence is unusual.'

'I'm sure that's all it is.' Rose's lips tightened again, but there was a tremor when she picked up her tea. She was more worried than she was letting on.

'Tell me what you can about Christina. Is she married?'

'No, she's not married. She goes under the same surname as us. She's twenty-eight, attractive—'

'Takes after my wife in that respect.'

'What's her routine, social circle, boyfriends?' Carlos wanted to understand the context of Christina's life and whether this really was a missing person case or just a daughter taking a break.

'Christina is a lecturer at the University of Leicester,' Rose informed him. 'As for her social circle, we don't know a great deal. She keeps her personal life private.'

'There might have been a boyfriend, but he could have been a colleague,' Harry added. 'She stopped mentioning him.'

'Do you know his name?'

'I'm not sure she gave us a name.' Harry shifted again, uncomfortably.

'Which department does she work for at the university?'

'I'm not exactly sure. Genetics, I assume.' Rose tensed again. 'Our daughter likes to compartmentalise and always says when she isn't at work, she wants to switch off. But her degree is in genetics.'

'Have you met any of her friends or co-workers at the university?'

'Unfortunately, no,' Harry glanced at his wife, a tinge of regret in his voice. 'She's never invited us to her workplace or social events. As far as I'm aware she only lectures at the university some of the time. Her main job is based at a separate place, not far away, the Institute for Evolutionary Genetics and Research. She has a best friend, though. What's her name, Rose?'

'Bethany. I don't know her surname and they *were* best friends. I don't know whether they still are.'

Do these two know anything about their daughter? 'Thanks.' Carlos hesitated before asking, 'Have you contacted hospitals or the police?'

The tension in the room mounted as the couple looked at each other. 'We don't want to involve the police just yet,' Rose explained, her voice barely hiding her anxiety. 'Christina values her solitude and independence. We don't want to cause any undue stress or be accused of parental interference.'

Harry shifted in his chair, his right knee bouncing up and down. He cleared his throat before speaking up. 'That being said, we haven't ruled out contacting them if necessary.'

Carlos noted the tense exchange between the couple and suspected that Harry would prefer to go to the police sooner rather than later.

'We didn't think to check the hospitals, but we're the next of kin, so would have heard if she'd been involved in an accident. You could phone around later, Harry.'

Carlos moved the conversation forward. 'I understand your concerns, and I'm sure you're right. If anything had happened to her, the next of kin would be informed. Let's focus on gathering more information about Christina. Do you have a recent photo?'

Rose reached into her oversized handbag and pulled out a photograph, handing it to Carlos. In the picture, Christina was smiling, her striking brown eyes shining with happiness. She was beautiful, with gorgeous wavy red hair.

'Thank you. Could I have her telephone numbers and address, plus the date of birth?'

'I thought you would need basic details, so I brought along a list.' Rose reached into the handbag again and passed him a sheet of paper containing sparse details. He noted the address was in Stoneygate, a wealthy part of the city. 'She has an apartment in one of those new-builds,' Rose added. 'She bought it a few years ago after starting work.'

Harry intertwined the fingers of both hands. 'Our daughter has money, Carlos. A trust fund left to her by my father, which she can access whenever she wants to. We would hate for anyone to be taking advantage of her because of that.'

'Has anyone tried that before?'

'Plenty of times,' Rose snapped. 'But Christina's not stupid. She wouldn't fall for a scam. I'm sure this will be a pointless use of your time.'

Let's hope so, Carlos thought, but said, 'And you have received no telephone calls or letters?'

'Kidnapping ransom demands, you mean?' Harry said. 'No. Nothing.'

'Does Christina live alone?'

'As I've said, she's not married.' Rose was clearly losing patience with Carlos's questions.

That's not what I asked, thought Carlos, but opted not to go down that road just yet.

'We've tried to leave messages,' said Harry.

'I'm sorry to ask this, but how would you describe your relationship with your daughter? Are you close?'

Harry and Rose exchanged a glance, Rose's expression stiffening further.

'We have a… respectful relationship,' Harry said cautiously.

'Respectful?' Carlos raised an eyebrow. 'What does that mean, exactly?'

'It means we don't interfere in each other's lives,' Rose explained. 'Christina is very independent, and values her privacy. We have different interests, therefore we try to give her the space she needs.'

Carlos observed their body language, noticing how they avoided each other's eyes and seemed almost embarrassed by the topic. He was also curious about how little they seemed to know about their daughter's life, particularly her work.

'What are your interests?' Carlos asked.

'We travel and attend functions. Harry plays golf,' said Rose.

'Christina went through a phase a few years ago where she disapproved of the life she'd been born into. Wanted to make her mark. We've taken a step back to allow her to grow out of it.' If Harry was looking for approval when he checked with his wife, he didn't get it. Her look could have frozen hot coals.

'Every family has its difficulties,' Rose snapped.

'I've got enough to be going on with. Have you decided whether you would like to hire me?'

Rose gave Harry a cursory nod.

'Yes,' Harry replied, his shoulders relaxing. 'Money is not an issue. We're prepared to cover whatever fees you charge, including expenses.'

'I'll need to ask you to sign a contract, but hopefully I will track her down soon,' Carlos said.

Rose placed the teacup back on its saucer. 'Please tread carefully with your investigation, Mr Jacobi. As I mentioned earlier, we don't wish to be intrusive if Christina is simply taking some time for herself. We just need to know she's safe.'

'Of course,' Carlos assured her, understanding the delicate balance they were trying to maintain. 'I will proceed with discretion. My priority will be to ensure Christina's wellbeing and to provide you with any information I can.'

'Thank you,' Rose whispered, her voice wavering ever so slightly as she dabbed at the corner of her eye with a handkerchief.

'In that case, let's get the formalities over with.' Carlos nodded to Julie, who handed the couple duplicate contracts mounted on a clipboard.

'Please take your time, our fees are clearly laid out on the other side,' she said. 'Your details go at the top of the first page. Please complete and sign both copies.'

The couple reviewed the terms of service briefly before filling in the required information. They signed the contracts and handed the clipboard back to Julie who handed it to Carlos. After Carlos had signed both copies he gave one to Harry.

'I'll keep you updated,' Carlos promised, shaking their hands again with the meeting concluded. 'Could you let us have the details of the trust fund your daughter has access to?'

'Yes, of course. I'll phone you later. Thank you,' Harry said, his eyes filled with anxiety as if he was just realising what was happening. 'And can I just say, I'm sorry in advance if this turns out to be a waste of your time.'

Carlos tried to give a reassuring smile, but couldn't bring himself to offer false comfort, not knowing yet why Christina had fallen off the grid.

He escorted them to the door, watching as they stepped into the bustling High Street. As the door closed behind them, Carlos turned to Julie, who had been silently observing the exchange during her note taking.

'What do you make of it?'

'Seems like a classic case of money can't buy happiness to me,' Julie replied, her eyes focused on the signed contract in her hands. 'I mean, judging by their clothes and demeanour, they're well-off. But there's definitely tension between them and Christina. Well done for coaxing some of that out of them.'

'Rose wasn't pleased about it, though,' Carlos said, his brow furrowing as he thought about what Harry had said. 'The way they talked about Christina needing solitude and not wanting to cause her undue stress. It sounds like they tread a fine line in the relationship with their daughter. Maybe even distant.'

'Not close, that's for sure. It doesn't seem like they know much about her life, either. Rose couldn't even tell us what she teaches at the university and clearly didn't know — or didn't want to know — about her work at the other place.'

'Does your mum know what you do here and who your friends are?' Carlos asked, pacing back to his desk.

'Apart from the confidential details, yes. And she knows all my friends. In fact, I think they like her as much as they like me.'

Carlos smiled, but was thoughtful. 'The first step is background, and then I'll visit Christina's apartment. I'd better not contact the university or the institute she works for until we know if she's really missing. I'll see if we can find any leads from her home.' He paused for a moment, deep in thought. 'Can you run a background check on Christina Sand and her parents? There might be something in her past that could help us understand why they are so concerned, yet reluctant to involve the police.'

'Got it,' Julie replied, immediately getting to work on her computer. 'Do you want me to look into the genetics department at the university, see if she's a listed lecturer? Anyone can do that.'

'Good idea. Let's leave the place Harry mentioned for now. Keep me updated if you find anything,' Carlos said, grabbing his jacket and heading for the door. 'First, I need to let Mrs Thompson know I've tracked down her errant husband. When I come back, I'll start on Christina's social media accounts. With any luck, we'll find her safe and sound, and this will be a case of overanxious parents.'

'Feeling guilty for not knowing what's going on with their daughter,' Julie murmured.

Chapter 4

It was no surprise when Christina Sand's landline went to voicemail, nor that her mobile was still switched off. He couldn't find much of a social media footprint for her. And she was sensible enough to keep any accounts she held private. Carlos had a contact who could hack through the privacy setups, but he didn't want to call him or invade her privacy without justification.

He logged in to LinkedIn to see what information he could gather from there. She definitely worked at the Institute for Evolutionary Genetics and Research, and Julie had already confirmed she was a part-time lecturer at the university. Christina was a lecturer and a researcher, but apart from that, the LinkedIn profile told him nothing he didn't already know.

Carlos parked across the road from the new-build apartment block. The carpark entrance was barrier operated with visitor access controlled by residents inside.

Tapping a search into his phone, he checked whether the apartment building had a concierge or something similar. It did, but they finished at 4pm and it was now 6:30.

'Come on, Lady, this is getting us nowhere. Let's see if we can get inside.'

Hearing her name, Lady sat up and, as soon as he opened the door, she leapt out. They walked across the road and waited close to the entrance. A few people parked up and entered the building and a couple came out, but he was able to remain unseen in the shadows. It was a freezing, frosty night, and he stamped his feet up and down, trying to keep warm when nobody was in sight. Carlos's breath formed white plumes while he waited.

Lady sat patiently by his side, oblivious to the temperature. She was used to this kind of work and no longer whined like she had done in the early days. He leaned down and stroked her head.

'Good girl.'

Big brown eyes gazed into his as she gave a satisfied grunt.

Finally, his opportunity came. A young woman with her arms full of shopping walked towards the door. While she put the bags down and fumbled around in her handbag to find her key, Carlos ambled along, talking to Lady as he went so as not to frighten the woman. She swiped the door, and it clicked.

Carlos moved swiftly.

'Let me get those for you,' he said, picking up the bags.

'Thanks.' The woman didn't give him a second glance.

Once inside, Carlos handed over the bags, and then moved to the post boxes on the wall. With the woman out of sight, he checked the box for number B30. The name C. Sand was etched beneath. His heart sank. It was chock-a-block.

Carlos sifted through the post, checking the date marks. The postmarks went back over three weeks. This wasn't looking good, but neither was it definitive. Christina could still have taken a break without telling her parents. It sounded like something she might have done.

He stood in the foyer, perusing each letter one at a time without opening any. There was a genetics magazine in a clear plastic wrapper; a pile of junk mail; credit card statements; a postcard from Rose and Harry, short and impersonal.

Then he came to one that interested him. It had a *Leicester Mercury* stamp. Carlos thumbed it for a minute or two before opening it. Inside, he read.

'Dear Miss Sand,

Further to your personal advertisement, there have been no responses since our previous contact. Please let me know if you would like to rerun the ad, or whether I can be of any further help.

Yours sincerely,
Tony'

Carlos pulled the phone out of his pocket while climbing the stairs to the second floor.

'Carlos? Long time, no speak.' Tony Hadden answered straight away.

'Sorry about that. How are you?'

'Bearing up. I can't move as fast as I used to, but at least I'm alive. I doubt you're calling to check on my health, though. What can I do for you?'

Tony Hadden was a reporter for the *Leicester Mercury*, whose car had been forced off the road while he was pursuing a lead to help both his own ambition and a case Carlos had been working on. He'd spent a long time in intensive care, followed by extensive rehab. Just before the incident, Tony had called Carlos, saying he had important information. He never got to share that information because he had ended up in hospital. When Carlos had asked, Tony said he couldn't remember, but Carlos knew Nicolae's men had got to him. They still shared information now and again, but Tony had lost a chunk of his ambition to be an investigative journalist for one of the big nationals.

There was now an unwritten rule between them. Carlos wasn't to mention the accident.

'I'm holding a letter in my hand. One you sent to a Christina Sand. Does that ring any bells?'

There was a shuffle of papers in the background and the sound of voices. Tony was still at work.

'Yeah. Are you helping her find her boyfriend?'

'Sort of. Can you tell me a bit about him?'

'Not really. She contacted me about a young guy who she said had gone missing. She wondered if I might be interested in writing a piece about it, but there was nothing to write. No body, no crime. He just fell off the grid. I figured he didn't want to be found. It happens. But I liked her, so I suggested she take out a personal ad in the paper asking for sightings, that sort of thing. She did and, against my advice, added the offer of a reward.'

Carlos was well aware rewards had their place, but they could also bring lots of time wasters.

'It's not like you to get involved in personal ads, Tony.'

'I felt sorry for her. She was desperate to find this bloke and suggesting it when I told her there wasn't really a story to write eased the blow. Must be getting soft in my old age.'

'Good to hear,' said Carlos, smiling. 'The letter suggests you had a few responses. Who were they from?'

'She should be able to tell you that... hang on a minute, Carlos. What's going on?'

Tony's mind was still as sharp as a razor, and Carlos didn't want to waste time trying to fool him.

'Off the record, Tony, Christina might be missing herself.'

A breath blew in Carlos's ear. 'No way! Now that might be a story worth writing. She's rich, that girl. Kidnapping, do you think?'

'No. Look, Tony, this might be nothing, so don't go shaking any branches yet, okay?'

'Fair enough. I've got a lot on anyway covering a city centre gang fight.'

'Can you send me a copy of the ad she put out, and the responses you got from it, including the dodgy ones?'

'Sure. As long as you promise me first dibs on any story.'

'You have my word,' said Carlos. 'But I hope there won't be one.'

'Me too, in this case. I like her.'

'Did you ever meet?' Carlos was still trying to get a feel for the Christina Sand he was searching for.

'No. It was all done over the phone and via email, but she was polite, respectful, you know? We don't get too much of that as journalists.'

Perhaps you would if you didn't go prying into people's lives was what Carlos wanted to say, except he was doing the same thing, albeit for different reasons.

'Thanks for the help, Tony.'

Carlos stuffed the letter in his overcoat pocket and put the others back in the mailbox.

Chapter 5

By the time he got to Christina's apartment, his phone had pinged with a message from Tony. He'd look at it later. Standing outside the flat, he pointed to the door.

'Search, Lady.'

Lady sniffed and snuffled at the door, but gave no signal.

'Good girl. Sit.' Carlos gave his dog a treat, satisfied there was no dead body on the other side of the door. He knocked. Surprised when the door opened, Carlos took a step back.

A young woman with jet black hair was holding a long-haired cat in her arms. It hissed as soon as it saw Lady.

'Can I help you?'

Carlos took the ID from the pocket inside his coat. 'I'm Carlos Jacobi, a private investigator. Is Christina Sand home?'

The woman's eyes widened. 'Have you found Simeon?'

'Do you mind if we come inside and talk?' Carlos flashed a reassuring smile.

'Let me put Jemmy in the bedroom first. She's not keen on dogs.'

Carlos and Lady waited outside the closed door, which opened a short time later.

'That's better. Come inside. Lovely dog.'

Lady was already piling on the charm, snuggling up to the young woman and being rewarded with the fuss she loved.

'Her name's Lady.'

'Hello, Lady. Gorgeous girl.' The woman looked up from dog patting. 'I'm Bethany. Christina's away, but I'm expecting her back any minute. I thought she'd be here by now. She knows I've got something on tonight. I've been cat sitting.'

Carlos let out a relieved sigh. 'Have you heard from her recently?'

Bethany bustled around in a high energy sort of way, gesturing for Carlos to take a seat. 'No. But she warned me I wouldn't. She's due back at work tomorrow, though. Can I get you a coffee?'

'Thanks, that would be nice. Where has Christina been?' Carlos tried to sound casual.

'No idea. It was all last minute. I assumed it was to do with her work. She'll be delighted to hear you've got news. Did she hire you? Sugar?'

'Milk, no sugar, thanks.'

Bethany finally sat down and Lady settled herself in for lots of strokes, sensibly avoiding eyeing the cat food across the room. Carlos grinned and inwardly congratulated his dog for resisting the temptation.

'So where's Simeon?'

Carlos took a sip of coffee. 'I'm sorry, Bethany, I don't know. Is Simeon Christina's boyfriend?'

'Not anymore. I'm not even sure he ever was. She keeps that kind of thing to herself, but she's been worried sick about him. Whoa! If you're not here about Simeon, why are you here?'

'I'm looking for Christina.' Carlos checked Bethany's reaction.

Shaking her head, brow furrowed, she stopped stroking Lady for a minute. 'Why?'

'Because her parents are worried about her. She hasn't been in touch for just over three weeks, but if she's due home tonight, it's obviously a misunderstanding.'

The colour drained from Bethany's face as the realisation sank in. 'She always calls her parents. Every Sunday without fail. It's what they do.'

'Her mother suggested it has happened before, that Christina has missed calls. Christina's mobile is switched off.'

'Rose can be funny. Memory like an elephant. Christina only stopped calling once, and that was years ago. She wanted to see if they would phone her for a change, but they never did.'

Carlos swallowed a lump in his throat. 'But if she was on some sort of assignment, might she have got distracted? For instance, she last called them on a Saturday rather than a Sunday.'

Bethany nodded. 'That might explain it, but she would usually have told them, like she does if she's going abroad and might lose the signal. Maybe they were out of signal when she tried. They're on a cruise.'

'They got home yesterday. Her father says he's left messages on the answerphone.'

'He can't have. It's full. I didn't want to answer her phone and I wouldn't check her messages. Christina's a private person.'

'So I've heard. This sudden trip. Did she say anything about where she might go?'

Bethany rubbed her forehead. 'No. She just called to say she needed to go away and could I look after Jemmy. I agreed to do it, but only until today because I've got a big job on. She won't let me down.'

'But you think the trip has to do with her work?'

'I thought it was, but maybe it was something to do with Simeon.'

That name again. 'Do you work with Christina?'

'No, she lectures at the university where I'm based but works mostly for a fancy research institute. I'm not as bright as Christina. Photography's my thing.' Bethany handed him a business card as if by rote before checking her watch. 'Look, I've got a really important commission at the Jewry Wall Museum tonight. There's a film crew scouting it for a major deal that would bring a tonne of money into Leicester and the university if it goes ahead. I'm doing the photos.'

'In the dark?'

'They want to see some night scenes, and then we've got an all-day shoot tomorrow. I'm going to have to go. I've left Christina a note on the kitchen table.'

'Do you mind if I look around?' Carlos asked, frustrated he couldn't ask her more about Simeon.

'I guess it would be all right if Christina's parents have hired you, but you're wasting your time. She'll be back any minute.'

Carlos forced a smile. 'I'm sure you're right. Good luck with the photo shoot.'

Bethany hopped up and down. She looked like she might change her mind any minute.

'Okay. But please lock up after you and don't go in her bedroom. She'd be furious with me if you did that.'

'Which one's hers?'

Bethany nodded towards a closed door. 'Jemmy's in there. Don't let her out either until you leave. I've been sleeping in the other one, but there's nothing in there. I've stripped the bed and cleaned it. It's just a guest room.'

'Noted. Here, take my card so you know who to report if Lady breaks anything.'

Bethany chuckled. 'You're on. Maybe when she gets back, Christina will hire you to look for Simeon. I guess she never thought of hiring a private investigator.'

'In that case, I'll stick around,' said Carlos. 'Do you have a suitcase I can help with?'

'It's already in the car. Give Christina my love if you see her.'

'We will, won't we, Lady?'

Carlos waited a few minutes in case Bethany changed her mind and came back. He thumbed her card, which had a University of Leicester logo in the top left-hand corner: Bethany Jiggle, Professional Photographer. There was a mobile and a landline number.

Now there's a name that suits its owner.

He and Lady sat in silence for a little while. Carlos watched the door, hoping Bethany was right and that Christina would walk through it any minute.

Chapter 6

Carlos felt concerned that the answering machine had a remote access facility, yet it didn't appear to have been checked. Feeling like an intruder, he bagan listening to Christina's messages from the most recent. Most of them were nothing but gaps left by callers hanging up without leaving a message, a sure sign of telesales. There was a message from the concierge letting Christina know her answerphone was almost full and he had taken in a few parcels for her. As he worked backwards he scribbled down a couple from those who had left names. One was the optician letting her know her glasses were ready for collection, and another was from someone called Paul, but he withheld the number. More telesales gaps followed.

A call from her father a week ago asked Christina to ring her parents when she got the time, which confirmed what Harry had told him earlier.

There were no messages from friends, but there was one from a man Carlos assumed she worked with.

'*Christina, Ronald here. I've just found out you're on leave. We could do with you coming back early if you're in the country. Let me know when you get this message.*'

Carlos was almost finished with just two left to listen to, frustrated that none of the callers mentioned Christina being away, apart from Ronald, the colleague. Nonetheless, Carlos remained poised, pen in hand, when the next person spoke.

'*Hello, Christina. It's Hazel Jarvis here. Sorry I wasn't able to help when you came to the shop. You said to contact you if I remembered anything. I might have something relevant for you. Please give me a ring. You've got the number.*'

The caller number was withheld, but Hazel had left the message at 9pm two weeks before Christina last spoke to her parents.

The more he listened to the voicemails, the more concerned he became. How long had Christina been away? He'd assumed it was just since the last time she'd called her parents.

Bethany didn't appear to have checked Christina's post, or spoken to the concierge about her. But that fitted with the privacy-loving person he was trying to trace. Carlos tried calling Bethany's number, but it went straight to voicemail.

'Bethany, it's Carlos. We met at Christina's earlier. I wonder if you could give me a ring on this number when you have a minute. Thanks.'

He would also need to speak to Hazel Jarvis before thinking about going into Christina's workplace.

Carlos sat in one of Christina's leather chairs and brought up the information Tony had sent him. He scrutinised the missing person article Christina had paid for.

MISSING
Has anyone seen this man?

Below the header, there was a photo of a man with fair hair and a world-worn face. He wore a thick curb chain around his neck.

The ad continued:

Simeon Vasili was last seen walking along the High Street on the night of the 10th of September. He's around five foot nine inches tall, with fair hair down to his shoulders. If you have any details, please call the number below.
£500 reward for information leading to his whereabouts.

Carlos dialled the number at the bottom and got through to the *Leicester Mercury* helpline. It must be one Tony had provided, so he got first knowledge of anything newsworthy before passing information on to Christina. Either that, or he was doing his good citizen bit and protecting a single woman from the weirdos that sometimes phoned in response to personal ads.

Carlos looked at Lady. 'Do you get the feeling this is not a waste of time after all, girl?' Lady was sitting up on full alert, sensing his tension.

Next, he checked the names and numbers of people who had contacted the *Leicester Mercury*. One of them jumped out: Hazel Jarvis.

'Now we're getting somewhere.'

He noted she worked at a newsagent's on the High Street. Carlos called the telephone number, which went straight to the shop's voicemail. After a quick internet search, Carlos found the right shop and its opening times. That would be his first call in the morning.

His heart beat faster as he tapped Harry Sand's number. Something bad might have befallen his clients' daughter.

'Have you found her?' Harry's voice shook.

'Not yet. I'm at her apartment. Her friend Bethany was here when I arrived. She's been cat sitting. The thing is, Christina is due back today, but is later than expected. It might be nothing, and I've got a few leads to follow, but I recommend if she doesn't return home tonight, you file a missing person report with the police.'

'You think something's happened to her?' The voice at the other end sounded flat.

'If I'm honest, I don't really know. But your daughter's disappearance is out of character, from what you and her friend have told me. The police can move things forward faster than I can.'

Carlos heard a muffled conversation at the other end of the phone as Harry passed the information over to his wife. He came back on the line.

'We'll do as you ask if nothing turns up, but if her friend is expecting her back tonight, we can afford to wait. Please continue with your enquiries and we'll discuss it again tomorrow afternoon.'

'Of course. Would you be happy for me to call someone I know in the force off the record? She's a detective inspector.'

'As you wish. But we don't want the police upsetting Christina and would be grateful if you did keep it off the record for now.'

'Just one more thing. Have you ever heard Christina mention a man called Simeon Vasili?'

Harry paused at the other end of the line, conferring with Rose again. 'My wife thinks they were at university together, but lost contact. Is he involved?'

'It's hard to say yet. I'll keep you informed.'

'Fine. And remember, Mr... erm... Carlos, off the record.'

Harry ended the call. Carlos hoped his concern had got through, but that he hadn't shattered their hope too soon.

Things would move much faster with Fiona on board. He could trust her to be discreet. He just hoped she wasn't too bogged down to discuss a missing person case with him.

As he sat back in Christina's chair, Carlos tried to piece together what he knew about her so far. It appeared she was isolated, studious and kept to herself, and as far as he could gather, there were just two people she cared about: Bethany and Simeon, plus a cat. There was also this guy, Paul. Who was he? The woman was a mystery and he wanted to find her.

'Right, Lady. Let's see what else we can discover while we're here.' Carlos strode through a door and stood in what was obviously Christina's home office, taking a moment to orientate himself. He perused cupboards and drawers, approving of her love of order and organisation. Carlos could sense the pulse of her work life, just not her personal one. Most of what he found related to genetics, cancer treatments, research and diagnostics.

He moved away from the desk and browsed the bookshelves. A shelf above her desk seemed to house a snippet of her life beyond science. He looked through photo albums from her childhood, a file containing certificates and some personal bank account details. From the outer edge, he selected an unlabelled box file which stood out from the rest. He lifted the lid.

Christina looked out at him from a stack of photos. She was happy. These photos showed her standing next to a man who wore a graduate mortar cap and gown, and had a twinkle in his eyes. Carlos was staring at a younger and happier-looking Simeon Vasili, the subject of the personal ad he'd discussed with Tony.

Carlos sat in Christina's leather office chair – she clearly liked leather furniture – and tried to get more of a measure of the woman. He ran his hand along the shelf beneath the desk and pulled out a small pile of leaflets. They were A5s and a mirror image of the article from the *Leicester Mercury*, but in larger print. It wasn't his job to find Simeon Vasili, but he had the feeling that if he did so, he would find Christina. Hopefully both were alive and well somewhere.

It was getting late and Carlos had been in the apartment for a few hours with still no sign of Christina. He told Lady to sit by the door while he broke Bethany's rule and entered Christina's bedroom. The cat was fast asleep on the cotton-covered duvet. He closed the door just in case Lady took it into her head to have one of her quirky moments and disobey.

The bedroom was as tidy as the rest of the apartment. Some would call it sterile, but to him it spoke of an ordered, minimalistic life, although even he liked to have a semblance of the social around his home and office. There was nothing like that here.

Christina's wardrobe was stacked with office clothes first, and then more casual outfits and dresses. The chest of drawers was much the same; even her underwear was folded inside a compartmentalised drawer. Carlos didn't linger and moved back to the wardrobe. Christina's shoes were arranged in a similar format, from the official to the informal on a three-tiered pull-out shoe rack. Lastly, he moved over to the bed, being careful not to disturb the cat. Carlos ran his hand under the mattress. Nothing hidden.

He opened the drawers of her bedside table on the side it was obvious she slept on from its contents. Her mobile phone was in the top drawer, switched off. Either Christina owned two phones, or she didn't want to be found. That could be good if she had located Simeon and the two of them had run off together. But from what her parents had told him, he couldn't imagine Christina would be afraid to go against their wishes if that were an issue.

Carlos replaced the phone and left the bedroom, closing the door behind him. Time to ring Fiona.

Chapter 7

Fiona was finishing up paperwork in the office she had been given after taking on the role of acting detective inspector. She perused the messy desk containing half-eaten packets of crisps, a half-drunk cup of coffee and a chocolate bar waiting to be munched. That would be the reward for getting everything typed up on the computer.

The room wasn't a bad size and even had a window, which she hadn't worked out how to open. Until she knew for certain she was staying, she didn't want to make it home. It still belonged to her predecessor. Fiona hated the painted beige walls and hadn't been able to rid the office of the faint smell of emulsion lingering from a refurb just before she took it over.

She stopped typing for a minute and leaned back, stretching her arms in the air to relieve the tension from sitting for too long. Her mobile jigged about on the desk, buzzing into life. She saw who was calling and checked through the glass separating her office from the communal one beyond before answering. DCI Masters held a vindictive hatred of Carlos, and she didn't want any of his cronies knowing they were friends.

It was okay. Her door was closed and there were only a few people still working.

She swiped the phone. 'Hello, Carlos. What can I do for you at this time of night?'

'Are you still at work?' he asked. There was tension in his voice.

'Yes. Just finishing the mountain of paperwork that goes along with modern policing. You know how it is.'

A chuckle came from the other end of the line. 'And I know how much you love paperwork. I'm surprised you don't get one of your DCs to do it for you now that you can.'

'I would normally, but I've assigned them other tasks and my sergeant's had to leave early for a dentist's appointment. Not to mention…' Fiona paused before continuing, '…your best mate's in the Maldives. Anyway, I take it you're not calling to check the police are doing their job?' Fiona lowered her voice. 'Have you got something on Nicolae?'

'Nothing like that. I just wanted to give you the heads up on a missing person case I'm getting a bad feeling about. If she doesn't turn up, her parents will report it sometime tomorrow.'

Fiona had been half-listening, resuming her work on the computer, eyes concentrating on the keys while Carlos spoke. She stopped, crossed her legs and leaned back in the chair.

'Okay, you've got my attention. Tell me about this missing person.'

'I don't know too much, to be honest. Her name is Christina Sand. She's twenty-eight years old, works at the Institute for Evolutionary Genetics and Research and lectures at the university, she also has access to wealth. Her parents are Rose and Harry Sand. He's some sort of business executive. They came by the office and hired me today because she hasn't been in touch for just over three weeks when she normally phones them once a week.'

'So why are they worried now? And why haven't they contacted the police?'

'I asked the same question. They're just back from a lengthy cruise and assumed – still do – she was busy with work. I think Harry would have contacted you first, but Rose didn't want to waste police time.'

Fiona laughed. 'Whereas wasting a PI's time is fine.'

'I'm well paid for my time,' Carlos said.

'That you are. She's rich, you say. Has there been any hint of kidnapping?'

'None. At first, I thought they could be right and it might be one of those investigations that turns out to be a complete waste of time. You know the sort where a diva daughter winds her parents up to get their attention? But now I'm in her apartment, I'm not so sure.'

'I won't ask how you got into her apartment.'

'Legally, I assure you. Her best... maybe her only... friend has been cat sitting while Christina's away.'

Fiona scrunched her eyes. 'So if she's away, why the concern?'

'A few things that are jumping out at me. First, her friend has a big thing on tonight at the Jewry Wall Museum and was expecting Christina back earlier in the day. Bethany – the friend – is a photographer and there's a film crew scoping the ruins as a location for some film or other.'

'Hang on. Did you say the Jewry Wall Museum?' Fiona wracked her brains, trying to remember where she'd heard that name recently.

'Yes, is that significant?'

Fiona squinted. 'I don't think so. Go on.'

'Well, Christina not being back isn't all I'm worried about, although we'll know for sure by tomorrow if she's genuinely missing. According to Bethany, she's due back to work tomorrow. What's most intriguing is that Christina has been on the search for an ex-boyfriend... or friend... I don't know which yet. A guy called Simeon. She took out a personal ad in the *Leicester Mercury*. I've got a few leads to follow up from that tomorrow.'

'Does this Simeon have a surname? And is he a missing person too, or is she someone who can't take no for an answer?'

'I got some information from Tony Hadden. The man's name is Simeon Vasili. He looks around the same age as Christina. The ad is on my phone, I'll send it over to you.'

There was a pause at the other end of the phone and Fiona took the opportunity to pull up a search program on the computer.

'Anything your end?' Carlos drew her out of her reverie.

Fiona entered Vasili's name in the system using various spellings in case of a wrong entry. 'There's nothing about him in our system, so it doesn't look as if she reported him missing. Just hold on a minute, Carlos.' Fiona lifted her head and beckoned one of her DCs, Gary Munro, into her office. Gary looked as though he was about to leave and she noted the sigh as he opened the door.

'Yes, ma'am?'

'Does the name Simeon Vasili mean anything to you?' Fiona spotted the DC's face flush the instant he heard the name. His eyes were another giveaway when he feigned a shrug before answering.

'Not really.'

Fiona narrowed her eyes. 'I'll need more information than that, Gary. Either the name means something, or it doesn't.' Sometimes Fiona wondered whether Gary was thick or lazy, or perhaps a bit of both. He had started out with such promise. Now he was avoiding eye contact, umming and ahing as if frightened to say anything.

'Out with it, Gary.'

'It's nothing, ma'am. A guy called Simeon Vasili was reported missing a month or so back, but we found him not long after, alive and well.'

'And why am I only hearing about this now?'

'DCI Masters dealt with it, so I didn't think to mention it. Besides, there was no evidence of anything dodgy, and the case was closed.'

Fiona's hackles were rising; her lips felt taut. What the heck was the DCI doing tracking down a missing person? And how come her DC knew about it when she didn't? No doubt DCI Masters had told Gary not to mention it.

'So where is he now?' she snapped.

'He's in the Maldives, ma'am.'

'Give me strength, Gary! Not the DCI. Simeon Vasili?'

Gary shook his head. 'No idea. As I said, the—'

'Get me the file.'

'Now, ma'am? I was about to go home.'

'Yes please. NOW!'

As soon as Gary left her office, Fiona picked up the phone again, exasperated.

'Did you hear all that?'

'I did. Why would Masters be interested in a mundane missing person case?'

'That's what I'd like to know. Trouble is, the guys look up to him like he's some sort of god, and never question what he does and doesn't do. They all want to be one of his in crowd.'

'Is your Gary one of his band of brothers?'

Fiona thought about it. Gary had been acting strangely recently. She'd believed it was down to his partner being pregnant and first-time baby jitters, but now she wasn't so sure.

'He's got the makings of a good DC, but maybe he's vying to be like Masters. Who knows? I'm just a lowly acting DI who doesn't carry the same weight... or charisma.'

'You're a good copper, Fiona. And I'm grateful you're nothing like Terry Masters.'

'Me too if I'm honest, but I have to work with him, Carlos. And the rest of them.'

She heard a heavy sigh at the other end of the line. 'Let me know if you get a whereabouts of Simeon Vasili. Perhaps I'm wrong about her being in trouble, and Christina's with him,' Carlos said.

'Will do. Let's hope there'll be no need for Mr and Mrs Sand to come in tomorrow.'

'I'd be happy if that's the case. Speak soon.' Carlos ended the call.

Fiona stared into space, wondering at Gary's behaviour. Then she slapped her head as it registered where she'd heard the Jewry Wall Museum come up before. It was where the homeless woman had been found dead three weeks ago.

'My God! Was that Christina Sand?' Fiona frantically bashed keys on the computer, bringing up the homeless case, her heart racing. She blew out a breath when the name of the deceased appeared on screen: Carrie Clark. A priest, Father Sebastian Crane, had identified the body when no living relatives were found.

Fiona recalled the conversation with Masters and how he'd told her the priest had rung him. The desk sergeant that morning had said there was a new PC.

Who else? she thought. *That's it!* A new PC, a troublesome priest and a rookie pathologist. The coroner's case was opened and closed. It looked from preliminary reports like he concurred with DCI Masters's theory and didn't take it any further. The homeless woman apparently fell backwards and bashed her head on a stone on the way down.

Fiona was still reading the report when Gary returned, flustered.

'Sorry, ma'am, there doesn't seem to be a file, and it's not on the system. It could be locked up in the DCI's desk.'

And pigs might fly past my window, Fiona thought. 'I see,' she said. 'You can go now.' Gary turned to leave. 'Wait! Have you heard the name Christina Sand?'

Gary flushed again, looking uncertain. She glared at him, waiting for the reply.

'That was the woman who reported Vasili missing. Is something wrong, ma'am?'

'I don't know yet. See you tomorrow, Gary.'

Fiona watched her DC hurrying through the outer office towards the exit. What did she have here? Incompetence or something more sinister?

'Please, God, let it be the former.'

Fiona turned her attention to the initial pathologist's report, followed by the post-mortem on Carrie Clark. As she read down, her heart dropped to her stomach. She swallowed hard before settling in for a few more hours' work.

Chapter 8

The newsagent's shop wasn't too far from Carlos's office. He parked his car in the back carpark, leaving Lady in the office with a generous bowl of water, and walked the short distance. The High Street was quiet, apart from the sound of people heading to work and the smaller shops pulling their shutters up. The Highcross Shopping Centre wouldn't be open for another hour, which was usually when the city centre got busy.

Carlos mulled over what he knew about Christina Sand and had to admit it wasn't much. She was a woman who liked her privacy and, from what he'd gathered from her apartment, she was a dedicated professional with a brilliant career ahead of her. Somehow, a desire to trace Simeon Vasili had disrupted her ordered life. Why was that? Judging by the photos of the two of them, they had been close in the past.

Although Fiona's detective constable had said Simeon was no longer missing, Carlos hadn't been able to track down his address. Fiona should be able to help with that, but she hadn't got back to him last night. Before leaving the office, Carlos had left a note for Julie to check graduation records from the University of Leicester and to find out where Simeon worked.

Carlos arrived outside his destination and studied it from across the road, watching people going in and out. He could just make out a woman behind the counter, and hoped she was the one he was looking for. He spent a few minutes checking notices in the windows, but couldn't find any sign of the A5 flyers he'd discovered in Christina's apartment. There were some listing items for sale and flats to rent, but that was it. The rest of the window space was taken up with advertising.

Carlos snapped a few photos on his phone before entering. It was a compact newsagent shop with two glass front windows and an open door in the centre. Once inside, he scanned shelves displaying daily newspapers, magazines and puzzle books. The smell of coffee from a machine close to the entrance gave it a welcoming aroma.

Carlos browsed the newspaper stand while waiting for a flurry of customers to buy their morning papers and/or cigarettes. A few purchased bottled drinks and snacks or used the coffee machine before leaving. There was a photocopier at the back of the shop which one person used after paying the woman behind the counter.

Carlos sighed in relief when he heard the name Hazel as some of her regulars passed the time of day. He was satisfied he'd found the right person. Carlos watched and listened as she chatted away to people while serving them. Her voice was soft and friendly.

After the last person left the shop, it was silent. Carlos stepped forward and approached the counter. His eyes were drawn to the cigarette lighters, matches and vapes neatly lined up on the shelves behind.

The woman at the till was in her fifties. Her face radiated warmth and kindness. She smiled. Her deep brown eyes and the gentle lines around them hinted she laughed a lot. Shoulder-length hair framed a round face.

'Good morning,' she said, taking the copies of a few of the morning's tabloids from him and scanning them through the till.

Carlos paid for the papers before starting the conversation. 'I wonder if you can help me. I'm looking for Hazel Jarvis?' Carlos held up his ID, which Hazel scrutinised.

If she was taken aback, she hid it well. 'You've found her. What can I do for you, Carlos Jacobi, private detective?' She chuckled. 'I don't get too many of those in here.'

He was surprised he hadn't been in here before with his office being so close, but he tended to pick papers up while out and about. 'I wondered if you could help me in relation to a case I'm working on. Without going into detail, it's important that I trace a woman called Christina Sand. I believe you tried to contact her.'

Hazel's eyes widened. Her round face revealed a mix of recognition and concern.

'I did. But that was weeks ago. Has something happened to her? I knew she shouldn't have been there.' The words tumbled out of Hazel's mouth, but another customer entering the shop interrupted the conversation. Carlos stood aside, waiting until the customer chose what they were buying, paid and left.

'Where was it she shouldn't have been, Mrs Jarvis?' Carlos had noticed the wedding ring.

'Call me Hazel, please.'

'Okay, Hazel. What can you tell me about Christina Sand?'

'She came in here... must be five or six weeks ago, looking for a man about her age. I assumed it was a boyfriend, but she didn't say. The shop was busy at the time and I didn't have time to talk. She left me with an A5 missing person flyer and scribbled her phone number down. She asked me to put the flyer in the shop window. I'm afraid I didn't get around to it. That afternoon, I saw she'd already put an article in the *Mercury*.

'Anyway, later the same evening, I dropped some snacks that had reached their best before dates at the local homeless shelter. At the time, my daughter volunteered there some nights with people from her church. While I was talking to a few of the regulars, I saw him – the man Christina was looking for.'

'Simeon?'

'Yes, that was his name. He had a foreign surname.'

'Vasili,' said Carlos.

'That's it. I almost didn't recognise him from the way he looked. He'd obviously fallen on hard times, poor chap. His hair was much longer than in the photo Christina Sand had showed me, and his eyes were haunting, if you know what I mean?'

Carlos nodded. 'He was homeless?'

Hazel dealt with another few customers while Carlos waited patiently for the next instalment of the story.

'Where were we? Oh yes. The homeless shelter. As I say, the young man had fallen on hard times and was in the shelter asking for a night's kip, so I'm sure he was homeless. I would have spoken to him and told him about the woman looking for him, but a fight broke out. The man running the place ushered me away while a few of the male volunteers broke up the fight. It left me a bit shaken and pleased Sian wasn't on that night, so I went home.

'I called the paper and left my number, but Christina didn't get back to me. A week later, I found the flyer on my counter, which reminded me of her quest. I left a message on her answerphone, but again she didn't get back, so I assumed she'd found him.'

'You said she shouldn't have been in that place. Was that the shelter?' Carlos asked.

'A few days after leaving the message on her phone, I'd shut up shop for lunch and gone for a walk. I try to get as much exercise as I can, despite the extra weight I carry. Anyway, I was passing the shelter and was shocked to see Christina. Tried to speak to her, but she shook her head and raced inside.'

'Do you think she'd found Simeon?'

'That's what I thought at first, but why would she be dressed like that if she had? A decent girl like her.'

'I'm not following you,' said Carlos, confused.

'She was dressed like one of them. As though she was trying to look homeless, but she stood out a mile, if you ask me.'

Carlos thought for a moment, registering what Hazel had told him. Things were falling into place.

'Did you see Simeon at all that day?'

'No, I didn't, nor since the night I phoned the paper. Until you walked in this morning, I'd forgotten all about them. My husband tells me I'm a sucker for happy endings. I guess I'd hoped it had all ended in a glad reunion. Now you're here, I'm not so sure, and judging by the look on your face, you're not either.'

Hazel had locked her concerned eyes on Carlos's.

'If you see either of them again, would you call me?' Carlos handed over his card. 'Day or night.'

'I'll keep an eye out. I'd ask Sian to do the same, but she's packed it in. It was getting rough – soul destroying, she said, what with so many of the young 'uns disappearing.'

Carlos didn't get the chance to ask what Hazel meant by the last sentence as another batch of customers entered the shop with some queuing at the counter. At the same time, his phone rang out from his pocket. He waved to Hazel on his way out.

'Fiona? I assume you got the email with Christina's photo.'

'Meet me at your office in thirty minutes.'

Carlos's heart sank. 'I'm just around the corner. See you soon.'

Chapter 9

The post-mortem room was already buzzing with staff preparing the next body for examination when Fiona arrived. She bypassed it and knocked on Tabitha Swinson's office door. Fiona had got to know the senior pathologist well over the past twelve months after a rocky start. Tabitha had annoyed Terry Masters in a previous case by informing a murder victim's wife of his death before the police got the chance to rule her out as a suspect. It turned out Tabitha was a neighbour.

'Come in.' Tabitha was nobody's fool, and she was already scrutinising the report they had discussed over the phone when Fiona arrived.

'What do you think?' Fiona asked, taking a seat across from the pathologist.

'Good morning to you too, Acting DI Cook.' The attempt at humour didn't fool Fiona. Tabitha was seething beneath the cool exterior. The pursed lips and hard stare as she looked up were dead giveaways. 'What I think is that this woman's death was suspicious, but I cannot conduct a second post-mortem because the body was cremated two weeks ago.'

Fiona felt her jaw drop. 'Have you spoken to the initial pathologist?'

'I have. He says he raised doubts about the bruises, but was overruled by the police, who convinced the coroner it was an accidental death.'

Fiona tried to suppress the anger rising in her chest. 'In the police report, DCI Masters concluded the bruises were old and, considering the way she had apparently lived, could have been sustained as a byproduct of sleeping rough.' Her voice sounded weak to her own ears and she knew she wasn't convincing Tabitha or herself.

'In other words, the DCI wanted a quick result and got one.'

Fiona didn't reply.

'I'll be writing a second report and handing the case back to the coroner, but I can't do much more without a body. I'll also be raising a formal complaint about my colleague's concerns being overlooked.'

'That's your prerogative. Do you mind if I look at your report?' Fiona nodded towards the file that Tabitha had slammed shut.

'Didn't you get a copy?'

Fiona cleared her throat, embarrassed. 'I haven't got a photo of the dead woman.'

'Help yourself.' Tabitha pushed the file towards Fiona. 'And if that woman was homeless, I'm a Martian.'

Why did Fiona get the impression Tabitha was enjoying her discomfort? There was no love lost between the pathologist and the DCI, but she had never been openly hostile before. Now, she was almost crowing.

'What do you mean?'

'People who live and sleep rough don't have lily-white skin underneath their clothes. Despite the bruises from her *lifestyle*,' Tabitha's voice dripped with sarcasm, 'the deceased was well fed, had excellent muscle tone and was as healthy as you and me prior to her death. Although she may well have been beaten for living... or pretending to live... on the streets.'

Fiona swallowed hard, reaching into her pocket as she opened the file. She removed her phone, which held the image of Christina Sand Carlos had sent to her, and placed it next to the one of the deceased.

Tabitha picked up Fiona's phone. 'That's her. That's Carrie Clark.'

'Christina Sand, actually,' said Fiona. She was almost overwhelmed by rage, but the sadness at what she would have to do today was worse.

Tabitha's voice softened. 'Who was she?'

Fiona rubbed her eyes hard, still staring down at the photos in the post-mortem report, before looking up.

'You're right about her not being homeless. She was a lecturer and scientist who taught at the University of

Leicester and worked for the Institute for Evolutionary Genetics and Research. Genetics being her specialism.'

The pathologist's eyes widened as she enlarged the photo on Fiona's phone. 'I thought she looked familiar, but I was too busy concentrating on the physiology. She works with Ron.'

'Ron?'

'Professor Ronald Brooker; he's a leading light in cancer and oncological research. The institute you mention is a charitable concern with some very high level benefactors.' Tabitha frowned.

'You don't like him,' said Fiona.

'Whatever makes you say that?'

'The look in your eyes and the tone in your voice. I'm a detective, remember?'

'Let's just say he and your boss have a lot in common in terms of attitude. Both misogynistic narcissists. But perhaps I'm being unkind to Ron. He's determined to be the one to find a cure and can be very charismatic – the latter just like your DCI Masters.'

'But?'

'He can also be ruthless. For someone who cares so much about ridding the world of cancer, he can come across as unfeeling.'

'Says the woman who deals with dead bodies all day long.'

Tabitha smiled. 'It's the way I deal with them that counts, Fiona.'

Fiona chuckled. 'How well do you know Professor Brooker?'

'We're on first-name terms and our paths cross in our line of work. I share tissue samples with the institute and he's head of their genome research. He had a fallout with the university but I don't know the details.'

'Perhaps because he's a misogynist and a narcissist,' said Fiona.

'I suppose genius has its downsides. The institute is where I've seen this woman.' Tabitha tapped the image on Fiona's screen, handing the phone back to her.

'Did you know her?' Fiona asked.

'Not at all, but I've seen her. I'm just good with faces. You never know who's going to end up on the mortuary table, so I take notice. She looked very different in real life, of course.'

'If you had to hazard a guess at the cause of death from this,' Fiona tapped the report, 'what would it be?'

'The initial conclusion of subdural haemorrhage, resulting from the back of the head hitting a hard surface, is correct, but the faint mark on the chest which was mentioned by the original pathologist...' Tabitha picked up one of the photos and pointed to the mark she was referring to, '...suggests she was pushed. At the very least, it should have been a reason for further investigation. Homeless or not, the deceased deserved someone to care enough about finding out what happened to her.'

'And the other bruises?'

'I concur with your boss. They most likely occurred a few days prior to death.'

'From a beating, or a warning?'

'That's for you to find out, Fiona. If it weren't for the mark on the chest, I'd agree it was an accident. The fact is, in this poor woman's case, your colleague didn't do enough. I hope you're about to rectify that.'

'I'm certainly going to try.' Fiona had a better chance of reopening the case with her boss holidaying in the Maldives, but she'd have to act quickly and get the super on board.

There was a knock at the door, and Tabitha's assistant entered wearing blue scrubs. 'They're ready for you, Doctor.'

Tabitha looked at Fiona. 'If you'll excuse me, I've got work to attend to. Feel free to use the photocopier over there if you find anything else that's missing from your original copy.'

'Thanks.' Fiona studied the file in front of her, hoping and praying this was purely down to incompetence and the DCI's desire for quick results, rather than a conspiracy. She couldn't get the fact that this priest, Father Crane, had called Terry Masters on the morning the body was discovered and how the DCI had dropped everything to attend out of her mind. If only she had ignored his phone call and attended the scene as well. But what could she have done? Terry Masters was fast earning a reputation for solving crime quicker than any of his colleagues or predecessors, and that, in turn, saved the force money.

Like it or not, money was a key feature in modern-day policing.

Fiona telephoned the station, requesting a meeting with the superintendent, who wasn't available until 3pm. She'd need to speak to Carlos, and get the team to start some preliminary enquiries. They'd already lost enough time and this woman's parents were going to want answers.

Chapter 10

The door burst open, wind and rain swirling into Carlos's office. Fiona flew in like a tsunami, her unruly hair sopping wet and plastered to her head. Raindrops poured off her coat onto the carpet.

'Let me take that for you.' Julie intercepted her before Fiona could drip her way through the office.

'Oh! Thanks.' Fiona reluctantly allowed herself to be separated from her light blue raincoat.

'Here. Use this.' Carlos handed her a towel to dry her hair, grimacing at the mess following in her wake.

'Uh, sorry about the dirt.' Her eyes flickered to Carlos and away again, colour staining her already wind-chapped cheeks.

'It's nothing.' The white lie convinced nobody. He swallowed hard before turning around. 'Coffee?'

'Please.' Fiona flopped into a chair next to the coffee table with a groan.

As Carlos busied himself with the coffeemaker, Julie hung Fiona's mac on a coat stand. He handed her a coffee and joined her. Julie returned to her desk and resumed her task, typing up the notes he had given her outlining his conversation with Hazel Jarvis.

'Bad morning?' he asked, watching his friend gulp the coffee down.

'You could say that. I've found your missing person, but it's not good news, I'm afraid.'

Carlos had already guessed as much. 'She's dead, then?'

Fiona nodded, her face solemn, before taking another gulp of coffee, finishing it up. She set the mug down with a clatter. Carlos refilled it, leaving Fiona to rub her hair with the towel while he took in the bad news.

'I've just come from the Leicester Royal. You're right, Christina Sand is dead.'

Carlos kept his face blank as he placed the second mug of coffee down on the table. The disappointment settled on his stomach.

'Where was she found?'

'You're not going to like this story any more than I do, so I'll start from the beginning. Just over three weeks back, in the early hours of Halloween, I got a call about a homeless woman who had been found dead.'

Carlos's eyes widened. 'That explains a lot. You realised your Jane Doe was Christina, from the photo I sent?'

Fiona shook her head vigorously, holding her hand up. 'Let me finish the story, then you'll understand. No, because I didn't get to attend that scene and we didn't think the woman was a Jane Doe. That morning, Masters phoned me when I was heading to my car and told me not to go. He said he was on scene and that a priest he knew had ID'd the woman, and there was nothing suspicious to investigate.'

Fiona paused, watching him closely. Carlos felt as though someone had punched him in the stomach, but he waited for Fiona to go on.

'I didn't think any more of it until you called last night and told me about Christina Sand and her looking for this Simeon Vasili. To cut a long story short, my DC, Gary Munro, couldn't find a file on the Vasili missing person case. It was you mentioning the Jewry Wall Museum that made me remember the homeless death. And it fitted in with the timescale of your missing person, so I pulled up the records.'

'Are you saying they found your homeless victim at the Jewry Wall Museum?'

'In the grounds, yes. When I checked the file, it reassured me the body belonged to someone else. We had identified the homeless woman as a Carrie Clark. But the more I read of the report, the more concerned I was that not only had something been missed, but it might have been a case of mistaken identity.'

'Why?'

'I'm not sure. Maybe it was the age and the initial pathologist's report seeming to throw doubt on the deceased being homeless. Not to mention the dead woman had been beaten a few days prior to death. I grew even more concerned when I couldn't find a photo of Carrie Clark in the file, so I arranged to meet Tabitha Swinson, our senior pathologist, first thing this morning. Anyway, I've now seen photos of the deceased and Carrie Clark is definitely Christina Sand.'

'You say she was beaten up a few days earlier. How did she die?' Carlos felt unusually sad, but it was nothing compared to the simmering anger in his gut.

'Initially it was assumed she fell into the dugout in the Jewry Wall Museum grounds where she was found and hit her head on the rocks.'

Was it a coincidence that Christina's best friend had been going to the same place the night before? Carlos would need to look into that.

'And now?'

'There's more than a reasonable doubt about the accident theory. She was most likely pushed.'

'How was that missed?' Carlos couldn't contain his anger any longer.

'As I said, she had taken a beating a few days prior to death, and the theory was that she might have fallen because of the aftereffects of that, or even thrown herself in. Tabitha believes both theories are unlikely. The first because it's unusual to fall backwards and the second because there was a faint new bruising mark on her chest, suggesting she could have been pushed.'

'I take it Christina's parents don't know any of this yet.'

Fiona sighed. 'I thought we'd see them together. Break the news in person.'

'Right,' said Carlos, dreading the task. 'They come across as cool, but I know they'll be devastated. We should do this as soon as possible.'

'We can go when you're ready.' Fiona's phone rang. 'Give me a minute.' She went out the back to take the call.

'How awful. That poor girl... and her parents...' said Julie. 'Fancy dying and nobody knowing who you are.'

'I'd like to know why she was posing as a homeless person in the first place, and why she was using an alias.' Carlos frowned, shaking his head.

'Should I call her parents and tell them you'll be visiting?' Julie asked.

'No. Best to do it face to face without worrying them beforehand. They'll have enough of that after we've seen them.'

Fiona strode back in, an energised look on her face. 'Good news. That was the super. I've got permission to officially reopen the case as the SIO while Masters is on holiday. She wasn't keen at first. But when I pointed out Tabitha's concerns about the cause of death, the mistaken identity, and added the fact her parents are powerful people who have already hired a private investigator, she saw things my way. I'd already booked a meeting with her for this afternoon to ask for permission. She wants me to keep that appointment and give her a full report.'

'What's she like?' Carlos asked.

'She's a person who likes results, but has an impeccable background, as far as I can tell. The only issue is she and

Masters have become allies in speeding up the numbers of crimes solved.'

Carlos scowled. 'Understood, but as long as she's not like him in any other way.' Carlos and Fiona both knew that Terry Masters was bent. How bent was where they might differ.

'Did you get anywhere with your leads from the personal ad?'

'I had a useful meeting with Hazel Jarvis, a newsagent on the High Street. I met with her this morning. As well as being a person who responded to the article Christina put in the paper, she'd also left a message on Christina's answerphone.'

'How useful? What did she know?'

'Christina visited her shop a few weeks before the last call to her parents. She was looking for Simeon and gave her a flyer to put in the window. As it turns out, Hazel visits the homeless shelter with food near or past its best before date every so often, and she went there after Christina had been into the shop. She saw and recognised Simeon from the photo Christina had showed her, and the flyer. The homeless link seems to start there. He was one of the men staying at the shelter. It doesn't quite fit in with your DC's story about him, does it?'

'No, it doesn't.' Fiona pinched the bridge of her nose.

'Hazel called the paper, but got no call back, and a week later, she rang the number Christina had given her and left a message on her answerphone. I know Christina didn't listen to that, which means she's been away from home at least two weeks longer than I thought. I'll confirm that with her friend Bethany later today. She's at the museum again all day, and I'd like to break the news personally.'

'Are you okay doing that? We'll need to speak to her as well.'

'I've met her already, so it'll be better coming from me. There's a cat you'll need to place into care when you search her apartment. Can you make sure it's not rehomed until I've given Bethany the option of keeping it?'

'What about the parents?'

'We'll ask them, but I'm pretty sure Rose Sand won't want a cat cluttering up her lifestyle.'

'You don't like her?'

'I'm not saying that. She just didn't strike me as an animal person. Lady got the message straight away and didn't even attempt to go near them.'

'Unforgiveable.' Fiona laughed, stroking Lady.

'Continuing with the Hazel story, the interesting part is that a few days after leaving the message on Christina's answerphone, she spotted her at the shelter posing as a homeless person.'

'Mm, that explains why she was identified as homeless. Did Hazel say whether she was using a false ID?'

'She didn't get to speak to her. Christina warned her off and disappeared inside.'

'Do you think she'd found out Simeon was staying there?'

'There's more to it than that. I believe she was on to something.'

'Like what?'

'I don't know, but if she just wanted to track him down, she could have gone in there as herself and offered him help. Why pretend to be someone else?'

'Unless he'd gone missing again.'

'Perhaps. But that's what we need to find out, Fiona.'

'Too right. Let's go and see her parents. Might as well get the horrible bit over with first, and then we can crack on with the case.' Fiona retrieved her mac from the hook near the door. 'We'll take your car.'

'Right.' Carlos took his keys from the hook. 'Let me just ask Julie to follow up on a couple of things while we're out.' He turned. 'Julie, keep looking into Christina's background, and Simeon Vasili. See if you can find any recent addresses, or anything else to track him down. We'll stay on the case until the Sands tell me otherwise.'

'Right. I'm on it. Good luck.' Julie shot him a compassionate look.

'Thanks. Also, follow up with the university. I saw a graduation photo of Simeon when I was in Christina's apartment. They might have an address or email for him.'

'It's on my to-do list. I got your message,' said Julie, jotting down notes.

Carlos grabbed his coat and paused to give Lady a stroke, holding her head in his hands.

'Lady, you stay here. This wouldn't be one for you, girl, even if they did like dogs.'

Lady had jumped up in expectation, but sat down again, bereft, doe eyes watching Carlos and Fiona heading to the door.

Julie smiled at the dog. 'Don't worry, Lady. I'll take care of you. Maybe you'll even get a treat or two.' Lady wagged her tail as if she knew what was coming.

'You got over your heartbreak quickly.' Carlos grinned, nodding gratefully at Julie before leaving with Fiona.

'I've asked my sergeant and Gary Munro to go through the original file and for one of them to revisit the crime scene. There was an anonymous male caller who reported finding the body. We'll need to find him. I'll brief the team after we've seen the parents.' Fiona sounded grim as she tugged her coat tight.

They stepped through the back door into the rain, both bracing themselves for the difficult conversation ahead.

Chapter 11

The Sands' property was next door to a golf course south of the city. Carlos turned right into a large drive and parked next to a Range Rover.

'See why I asked you to drive,' said Fiona, smiling.

'I don't remember being asked. It was more like a command, Acting Detective Inspector Cook,' he retorted, laughing.

'Whatever,' she said. 'Either way, my car wouldn't look right parked outside a place like this.'

'Appearance isn't everything, my friend.'

The house was large, but not as majestic on the outside as Carlos had been expecting. Instead of an old stately home, the modern architecture in front of them, tall and imposing, had smooth lines and a sleek design. It could have been built yesterday.

Carlos had looked into Harry Sand's background and they had been discussing it during the drive. Harry owned a horse stud farm in Ireland, renowned for producing champion stock. Sand's Equestrian Centre bred a huge number of thoroughbred racehorses that were sold all over Europe.

'I wouldn't mind a taste of this sort of life,' said Fiona.

'You could start by investing in bricks and mortar and getting off that boat of yours.'

Fiona shrugged. 'The boat community would be hard to replicate elsewhere. I'm getting to know my new neighbours. When you live on a boat, everybody looks out for everybody else. Apart from the odd rotten apple, that is. You wouldn't get that in a place like this.' She nodded her head towards the Sands' residence.

'Good point. Now come on, Fiona. Stop stalling.' Carlos climbed out of the car. He, too, was dreading the task ahead. He couldn't imagine how Fiona coped with breaking bad news like this as often as she must have to, working in serious crime.

'At least it's stopped raining,' she said as she exited, slamming the door a little harder than he would have liked.

Carlos watched a camera following their progress as they approached the front door. 'Be careful. We're being filmed.'

'I saw,' she said.

Harry Sand opened the door before they had the chance to ring the bell. His face, full of hope, dropped as soon as he saw the grim expression Carlos gave him, warning him of what was to come.

'Sorry to turn up without an appointment. This is Acting Detective Inspector Cook from Leicester CID. Do you mind if we come in?'

Rose appeared behind her husband, tight-lipped. 'I thought I said this was to be kept off the record.'

Harry took his wife's arm. 'Let's go inside, Rose.'

The couple led the way through the interior, packed with modern fixtures. Abstract paintings hung on the walls and any furniture was minimalistic. Their home was designed to exude sophistication and wealth. Carlos and Fiona followed close behind. They arrived in a plush sitting room with not a thing out of place.

'Please sit down,' said Harry. His eyes betrayed the dread of what he was about to hear. Carlos felt a lump in his throat, not daring to look at Rose.

As soon as they were seated, Fiona wasted no time. 'I'm sorry to tell you, we have some bad news.'

Harry gasped as he took his wife's hand. She shrugged him off and turned away, looking out of a full-length window onto a large manicured lawn and beyond.

'What's happened?' Her voice was icy, but she didn't turn around.

Fiona laid out the story in as much detail as she could while Harry and Rose listened in stunned silence. She missed out the bit where her boss had told her not to attend the scene when the body of an apparently homeless woman had been discovered. Fiona merely apologised for the fact the police had misidentified the body.

Then came the bit both she and Carlos had been dreading. Fiona paused, looking at Carlos first, then said, 'Unfortunately, because your daughter was identified as someone with no living relatives, the council cremated her body.'

Angry tears filled Rose Sand's eyes as she finally spun her head around to face Fiona.

'How could you be so incompetent?'

Carlos watched as Fiona tried not to flinch. The accusation aimed at her was unfair, but she took it on behalf of the police force she remained loyal to.

'I'm so sorry,' she said.

'You said Christina's death was initially thought to be an accident. Does that mean you've changed your mind?' Harry had picked up on Fiona's breadcrumb trail. She had deftly delivered fresh information in small pieces so as not to overwhelm them.

Rose opened her mouth, looking as if she was about to have another swipe at Fiona, but this time Carlos intervened to answer the question.

'Acting Inspector Cook met with the senior pathologist this morning. The pathologist has reviewed the original file and believes someone could have pushed your daughter to her death. Whether the push was meant to kill her is unclear. She died when her head struck something hard.'

'None of this explains why our daughter would be presumed homeless when she has... had... substantial wealth.' Harry's face had turned a pale shade of grey. His wife had resumed her staring out of the window position.

'We believe she pretended to be homeless to look for Simeon Vasili. The man I mentioned last night,' said Carlos. 'She took out a personal ad in the *Leicester Mercury,* and we've since discovered that Simeon had become homeless.'

'That's not possible,' said Harry. 'He comes from a wealthy family.'

'Can you tell us about Simeon and his family?' Fiona asked.

'We know nothing about the Vasilis,' Rose snapped at her husband.

Not looking at his wife, Harry furrowed his brow. 'Will it help you find who did this to our daughter?'

'It might,' replied Carlos, gently.

'I expect you know we own one of the best horse breeding farms in Europe,' seeming resigned, Rose took over from her husband. 'The Vasili family owns a rival business in the United States. Simeon Vasili befriended Christina when they were at university. We believe his family sent him to spy on our techniques and take that information home. Horse racing can be a murky business. There's a lot of money involved.

'Christina invited him to join us for a family holiday in Ireland, and he took a great deal of interest in the farm. Our stud manager over there became suspicious and checked into his background. It didn't take long to discover Simeon was the son of a competitor. There you have it. The Vasilis are scoundrels. Frankly, Simeon Vasili broke our daughter's heart. He wasn't who he said he was.'

Fiona appeared confused. 'Wouldn't you know the names of your competitors? Was Simeon using a different name?'

'Almost,' said Harry. 'His real name is Simeon Vasili-Wright. Their business name is Wright & Hill's Thoroughbreds. Vasili was from the maternal side of the family.'

Carlos stroked his chin. 'What do you think happened to him that would make him homeless?'

'We don't know.' Rose's eyes blazed. 'And we don't care. Not satisfied with breaking our daughter's heart, he's got her killed. Probably did it himself.'

'No,' Harry said. 'Simeon wasn't like that. I believe what my wife says is true, though. They sent him over to uncover secrets, but I also believe he loved our daughter.'

'Love!' Rose spat the word out. 'What does he know about love? Face it, Harry. The son you wanted him to be was, and is, a traitor. You're so gullible.'

Harry's hand went to the side of his face, as though someone had slapped him.

'If you'll excuse me, I've got things to attend to,' said Rose.

They watched her stride from the room, holding her head high. The cool pretence at control did not fool Carlos.

'Please excuse my wife. She's not good at showing emotion, but she loved our daughter. We both did.'

'What she said just now,' Fiona said. 'I'm sorry for asking, but how much of it is fact? Maybe he showed an interest because of his background, rather than to steal secrets.'

'I'd like that to be the case. I don't deny I liked Simeon. He became part of the family. Sorry I didn't tell you this last night, Carlos, it's just that... well... we were shocked to hear his name mentioned after all these years. Christina wouldn't allow us to speak of him again.'

'What makes you believe he loved her?' Carlos asked.

'When we found out about him, and he saw the look on Christina's face, he was devastated, but she shut him out completely. It was as if he'd never existed. Our daughter inherited her mother's way of dealing with all things emotional. Pretend they don't exist. But it didn't work for Christina. She became more and more aloof. She compartmentalised everything. I always hoped that one day she would face her demons and come back home. Not home, as in here, but home as in being a happy person again. Now that's not going to happen, is it?'

Carlos felt his heart crumpling in his chest. 'What happened to Simeon after the breakup?'

'He called me one night, hoping I'd be able to speak to Christina, but I knew it wouldn't be worth the effort. I was angry with him myself. He confessed his family had tasked him with getting insider information through bribery if necessary, but that after visiting the farm with us, he realised he had fallen in love with Christina. He told me he hadn't told his family anything.'

'Did you believe him?'

'Not at the time. I told him I wouldn't speak to Christina for him, that he'd betrayed our trust and that we wanted nothing more to do with him. I said if he phoned again I would call the police. After that phone call, I assumed he'd returned to America.

'Since then, I've gone over the conversation so many times in my mind and, despite what Rose says, have concluded that he loved Christina. Whether the rest of what he told me was true or not, I don't know.'

'Do you think he could have killed her?' Carlos asked.

Harry put his head in his hands. 'Oh God, I hope not. The Simeon we met seven years ago was not a killer. Who knows what he's become if he's destitute, as you say. Are you sure it's the same person?'

Carlos removed a copy of the flyer from his pocket and handed it to Harry, who nodded.

'Yes, that's Simeon. Why would Christina look for him when she hated him for what he'd done to her?'

'Perhaps she'd forgiven him,' said Carlos.

'If he killed her, Carlos, I want you to make sure you bring him to justice.'

'This is a police investigation now, Harry. Are you sure you want me to continue?' Carlos hoped he'd say yes because he was involved now and wanted to find the killer.

'Well, it's clear we can't trust the police to do their job.' Rose had returned to the room along with the forced frosty exterior, but the redness around her eyes gave her away. 'Of course we want you to continue.'

'I'm happy to work alongside Acting DI Cook, but she's the Senior Investigating Officer, so it will only work with her permission.'

Rose looked at Fiona. 'I apologise, Inspector Cook, but I'm sure you understand our concerns. Thank you for coming here today. It can't have been easy, and I suspect from what you've told us, you weren't in charge of the original case where the failures occurred.'

Fiona didn't reply.

'Please allow Carlos to work with you. Obviously, we don't understand the ins and outs of it all, but we trust him.'

Fiona mellowed. 'I'm happy to work with Carlos. We're friends and we respect one another. I'm sorry for your loss.'

'What happens about identification?' Rose asked.

'There are dental records which the pathologist will use to confirm her identity.'

'And the ashes?'

'I've arranged for them to be kept and they can be sent to an undertaker of your choice,' said Fiona. 'I'm sorry you won't be able to see her.'

'Thank you.' Rose walked back to the window. 'I'd rather remember her alive.'

'We'll be in touch,' said Carlos. 'You've got my number.'

Harry walked them to the door, and Fiona handed him her card.

'If you or your wife hear from Simeon Vasili, please don't meet him. Contact me or Carlos.'

Carlos heard the door close behind them, but couldn't bring himself to speak until they were in the car and on the road.

Chapter 12

Fiona marched into the incident room, still reeling from Rose Sand's view of the mess she'd inherited. The sound of fingers on keyboards and murmur of voices cut short as all eyes turned in her direction. Carlos was with her, but moved away to the back of the room. She had prewarned him he wouldn't get a warm welcome and asked him not to say anything unless requested.

Fiona stood with hands on hips, surveying the board that her sergeant, Hugh Barber, had begun organising under the heading of Christina Sand. She attached the photos she had copied after her meeting with Tabitha Swinson. There were maps of the museum grounds, with the dugout the victim's body had been found in highlighted. Case notes sat on Hugh's desk.

Turning her attention back to the room where whispered conversations had resumed, she eyed her team.

Hugh ended the call he was on while her DCs Gary Munro and Kerry Gray waited for her to start the briefing. A few uniformed officers who assisted with their investigations were huddled around a desk.

'Right, listen up.' Fiona spoke assertively. She would not pander to them any longer. Not knowing who she could trust was a problem. It was time to stamp her authority down while she could. 'As you know, we have a new case involving a suspicious death. Or should I say, we're reopening a case where serious errors have been made.'

The team exchanged a few muffled murmurs and glances as they focused on her and the board. Fiona paced while she spoke, the team tracking her movements, a mixture of confusion and concentration on their faces. She felt satisfied her words had whipped them into shape.

'The body pulled from the Roman ruins in the Jewry Wall grounds three weeks back was originally thought to be a homeless woman named Carrie Clark. Photographic and dental records have positively identified her as Christina Sand, whose parents reported her missing yesterday to private investigator, Carlos Jacobi. We have since discovered that rather than being a homeless vagrant like the original investigation found,' Fiona pursed her lips, 'she was far from it, but I'll come to that shortly.'

She waited for the conversations to die down again before continuing. 'Here's an even bigger blow – the pathologist found bruising on the deceased's chest consistent with her being shoved into the dugout. So we are not looking at an accident, we are investigating a suspicious death. Someone pushed Christina Sand into that trench, and we have to consider murder.'

Chatter rippled again through the room. Fiona raised her hand for silence.

'I want theories. Why would this priest,' Fiona attached a photo of Father Sebastian Crane onto the board, 'ID our vic as someone else entirely?'

Her piercing gaze swept over the team. Gary shifted uncomfortably in his seat while Kerry stared intently at her notebook, writing.

After a pause, Fiona nodded. 'Exactly. We don't know. Therefore, we need to dig deeper into our overly helpful priest and his relationship with the dead woman. I don't need to tell you how difficult the conversation Jacobi and I have just had with Christina's parents was.'

Fiona pinned a couple more photographs of the woman in life and death on the board.

'You also don't need me to tell you how upset they were, and how angry they are the council cremated their beloved daughter without ceremony. Be thankful I managed to intercept the ashes before they were scattered over a pauper's section of Gilroes Cemetery!' Fiona glared at her team, wondering how much they had known of the case before she called them after her meeting with Tabitha that morning.

'Christina Sand was beaten a few days before she died. Who by and why? Shortly after that beating – could it have been a warning she didn't heed? – she ended up dead. Are we looking for two separate attacks or are they connected? Likewise, are we looking for one or more attackers?'

She stopped pacing. Her hands moved back to the board, where she added an arrow from Sebastian Crane to the dead woman.

'Here's what we know about Christina Sand.'

Fiona paused, looking over the sparse details listed on the board before beginning.

'She was a lecturer at the university here in Leicester but worked most of the time at the Institute for Evolutionary Genetics and Research. By all accounts, she led an ordered, private life and had a brilliant career. There don't seem to be any skeletons in her cupboard and she had few friends, from what Jacobi and I have gathered so far, apart from this man.'

Fiona stuck a picture of Simeon Vasili onto the board.

'I'll come to him in a minute. It's down to us to bring order from the chaos of the identity mix-up and the position we are now in.' Fiona shot a pointed look at Gary.

'Christina Sand's ordered life changed a couple of months ago when she became obsessed with finding Simeon. Her parents have confirmed he was an ex-boyfriend who used her and whom she hadn't been in touch with for around seven years. Simeon Vasili.'

Her gaze lingering on Gary, Fiona wondered if he would break eye contact first. She wasn't ready to reveal that Simeon had been spotted at the homeless shelter. Not yet.

'Christina reported him missing at this station and, according to DC Munro, we found him safe and well, so there was no follow up.' Fiona looked away from Gary and spoke through gritted teeth. 'The file relating to that case has since gone missing, so if anyone knows anything about it, come and see me after this meeting.'

Fiona turned to DC Kerry Gray. 'Kerry, where have you got to on the homeless setup in Leicester? Any leads on Christina or why she was considered homeless?'

Kerry straightened in her seat, always eager to contribute. 'Yes, ma'am. My background checks have identified Father Crane runs homeless counselling at his church.' She looked at her notes. 'Gracious Heart Church; it's on Fosse Road Central.'

Fiona felt her eyes widen. 'Not St Nicholas Church?'

'No, ma'am, although Father Crane has been seen there as well.'

'The counselling could be the connection between the priest and our victim,' said Fiona.

'Yes, ma'am. There's also a local GP named Dr Mishka Andreeva, who regularly visits a city-centre shelter and treats the homeless. Anecdotal evidence shows he might be recruiting young homeless adults into some kind of clinical trial run by the Institute for Evolutionary Genetics and Research.'

Fiona raised her eyebrows, impressed by what Kerry had discovered.

'What about other shelters?'

Kerry looked at her notes. 'There are dozens in the Leicester area, ma'am, but the one that jumps out because of its locality to the museum and the town centre is called Gracious Heart House, run by—'

'Don't tell me… Father Crane.'

'It certainly has connections to his church, The Gracious Heart, hence the name.'

'So we've got two links between the dead woman and the priest.' Fiona wondered what Father Crane had been doing hanging around the Jewry Wall Museum on the night the body was found, but she kept that to herself for now. 'Excellent work, Kerry. You and I will pay the GP, Dr Andreeva, a visit after this meeting. Let's see if he knows anything about Christina and what else he can tell us about the homeless community.'

Fiona made a note. Next, she turned her attention to DS Barber.

'Hugh, what's the update on revisiting the crime scene?'

Hugh shifted in his seat, looking irritated. 'There's a film crew working at the Jewry Wall site today. I wasn't able to get access.'

Fiona frowned. 'A film crew? That's inconvenient.'

'Tell me about it,' Hugh grumbled. 'I asked them to stop for a few hours, but they refused. Said they had permission to scope it out for a film and a schedule to keep. They should be finished by the end of play today.'

'Hmm, I don't suppose we'll find much now anyway. The death was weeks ago, but I'd like to get the CSI team to take another look at the dugout, if the film crew have not trampled it. It needs to be re-examined thoroughly.' Fiona tapped her pen on the board.

'I'll call Sheila and put her on alert,' Hugh offered. Sheila was the local go-to CSI team leader for gathering evidence, even when there didn't seem to be any to gather.

'Good idea.'

'In the meantime, shall I interview Father Crane about his connection to the victim?' Hugh looked hopeful.

'Carlos Jacobi is going to do that.' She pointed over to her friend. 'He's ex-military and a proficient PI. Some of you know he's helped in the past.'

Fiona noticed Hugh's jaw tighten and his nostrils flare. He wasn't happy about her decision, but tough. She understood no officer liked a civilian barging in on an active investigation, but she needed Carlos's expertise, and what's more, both she and the victim's parents trusted him.

'Of course, ma'am,' Hugh said tightly, sharing a glance with Gary, who was looking increasingly uncomfortable.

'What I would like you to do, Hugh, when you've finished your lunch…' he was spooning what looked like a home-cooked casserole into his mouth while listening, '…is interview Christina Sand's lecturer colleagues at the university, and at the institute where she worked most of the time. The latter is led by a Dr Ronald Brooker, make sure you speak to him. Take Gary with you.'

Hugh nodded, looking happier. Gary's expression was unreadable. Fiona turned to him.

'Gary, any progress on locating that missing file on Simeon Vasili? Or finding out where he's living now?'

Gary shifted in his seat, avoiding eye contact. 'No, ma'am. I think he may have returned to Europe where his parents live. The file is still missing.'

Fiona studied Gary. His body language told her he was holding something back, and she knew he was lying. Her suspicions that DCI Masters had got to him were proving more likely. She would watch him closely. There was no way she was going to allow him, or anyone else, to obstruct the investigation. The missing file might end up being a result of incompetence, or Gary could be covering for her DCI's laziness, but the elusiveness over Simeon's whereabouts, along with the misdirection, didn't sit right, unless he was trying to save face.

'What makes you think he was from Europe?'

'Erm… isn't it obvious, ma'am? The name?' A ripple of laughter spread amongst uniform. The rest of her team appeared shocked at Gary's attempt at belittling her in public. Still, now wasn't the time for confrontation. She needed to keep Gary onside or pull him back from making a big mistake. Pushing now could jeopardise that. She'd tread carefully.

'I would cast your net further afield, if I were you.' She noticed a grin forming on Carlos's face. 'Mr Jacobi?'

Carlos obliged. 'Mr and Mrs Sand informed us that Simeon Vasili is the son of a wealthy family in the United States. They are in a similar line of business to the Sands – horse breeding. Simeon dated Christina to gather insider secrets on behalf of his family.'

Fiona wrote the name of the American company on the board. 'We don't believe Simeon has left the country. It's important we track him down. For now, he's an unlikely suspect.'

'Yes, ma'am. I'll keep at it,' Gary said, face flushing just enough to show his faux pas had embarrassed him.

'Good.' Fiona turned to Hugh. 'Report back once you've spoken to Dr Brooker. I want to know if he saw any changes in Christina's behaviour prior to her taking unplanned leave, and ask why he left a message on her answerphone. Jacobi's already checked her apartment, but we'll need CSI to go over it. Can you let them know, Hugh?'

Hugh nodded.

'Let's establish a timeline leading up to Christina's death. Jacobi has determined it's at least five weeks since she's been in her apartment, probably longer, and we know she died twenty-four days ago.'

'Yes, ma'am.'

Fiona paused, deciding it was time to drop her bombshell and the homeless link. She'd given Gary enough time to reveal it, and he hadn't. She inhaled and exhaled.

'Nobody asked why we don't think Simeon left the country, so I'll tell you. Jacobi found out Vasili may have hit hard times. He was spotted at a homeless shelter – working assumption, Gracious Heart House – a few weeks before Christina ceased contact with her parents and around the time she took unplanned leave. It looks as if Christina went undercover as a homeless person to track him down.'

Surprised looks spread through the team.

'Why would he be homeless if he comes from money?' Barry King, one of the uniformed officers, asked.

Fiona shrugged. 'It happens. Remember, his parents are a long way away. Maybe they fell out. Any ideas why Christina would need to pretend to be homeless?' she asked. 'What was she looking for?'

'Drugs?' Kerry offered. 'We know they use some of the homeless as drug mules. Perhaps Simeon was involved in that and Christina got wind of it?'

Fiona nodded, impressed with Kerry's insight. 'That's one theory. Any others?'

'Perhaps she suspected Simeon of doing something else criminal?' Hugh said. 'Maybe she thought he was involved in trafficking? A friend of mine in vice tells me there's a new player getting in on the homeless action.'

Fiona's stomach lurched. She wanted to shout. Why was she only being told of this now?

'Did your friend give you a name?'

Hugh shook his head. 'No. He's secretive about it, but according to his boss, the guy's one bad dude with powerful connections.'

'Romanian?'

'How did you know that, ma'am?'

Fiona tried to stop her voice from shaking as she answered. 'Lucky guess. Anyway, both are excellent suggestions.' She scanned the room, meeting each pair of eyes. 'We need to find out more about what's going on at that shelter and dig into Simeon's background. I want to know where he is and why Christina was so intent on tracking him down after seven years of no contact.'

She straightened, folding her arms. 'This is going to be messy and I might have to bring vice in on the action if our case is linked to theirs, but for now, we work on keeping all lines of inquiry open. We owe it to Christina and her family to find out what happened.'

A more positive murmuring flowed through the team, each member nodding. Fiona smiled at them. For now, their focus was on solving the case.

Fiona looked at the uniformed officers. 'Find me this anonymous caller who reported finding the body in the early hours of Halloween. He has to be one of the homeless, or he'd have stuck around on the night in question.'

The officers nodded, getting up from their desks. Fiona waved to Carlos as he left the room. They would talk again later.

'Kerry, you're with me. The rest of you know what to do.'

Chapter 13

As he left the briefing, Carlos's phone buzzed in his pocket. Julie's name flashed across the screen.

'Hello, Julie. Did you get through?' He had texted her from the briefing room after Fiona mentioned him interviewing the priest.

'I've got you a meeting with Father Sebastian Crane. He's expecting you at The Gracious Heart Church on Fosse Road Central in an hour.'

'Thanks, Julie. I'll come back and collect Lady, then head over.'

Forty-five minutes later, he parked in the church carpark. The bright white façade and glass exterior of The Gracious Heart Church made Carlos squint. He climbed out of his car, shielding his eyes while looking up at the sloped roof. There was a lot of clear glass, interspersed with modern stained glass windows. The building's contemporary grandeur seemed out of place on the Fosse Road with its older houses and the Methodist church just a short distance away.

'How on earth did they get planning permission for this, Lady?'

Lady barked, happy to be with him and out of the car. There were just three other cars in the carpark, along with an old motorbike. They headed towards the church entrance, passing a row of newly planted trees that were most likely a condition of building permission.

'I wonder how many donations those gleaming white stones cost, girl?' Carlos moved his hand towards the door handle, but the door opened before he got to it. A slender woman with brunette hair, about his age, stopped in her tracks.

'Can I help you?' Her tone was polite.

Carlos extended a hand. 'Carlos Jacobi, I'm here to see Father Crane.'

The woman narrowed her eyes briefly before smiling, which softened her face. 'Of course, Mr Jacobi, you're a little earlier than expected. I was just heading out to get some milk, but we can check whether Father Crane is ready to see you. I'm Gloria Hallam, the church secretary. No dogs are allowed inside the church unless it's an assistance animal. You can leave it in the entrance lobby. I'll lock the door.'

'Sorry, Lady,' Carlos said, tethering her to a hook. 'Be a good girl and stay.' Lady sat obediently, but gave a whine of disapproval.

Gloria locked the door and turned back towards the inside. 'Please follow me.'

The interior of the church was as sleek as the exterior, but the high roof made it seem larger. They passed polished wooden pews and Carlos noted the absence of kneeling cushions and hymn books. The stained glass was decorated with abstract shapes rather than saints, which was a refreshing change. The altar was at the far end where a woman was hoovering. Carlos noticed that the altar and confessionals followed the modern look with straight lines and brushed steel edgings.

Their footsteps echoed back at them from the vaulted ceiling as Gloria led him through a side door into a wide corridor. The corridor was lined with framed photos. Each one featured a priest Carlos assumed to be Father Crane. In one picture, the priest was shaking hands with the city mayor; in another, he was speaking to a packed audience surrounded by adoring parishioners; and another had him with a group of businesspeople.

'Did you have any trouble finding us?' Gloria asked, making small talk while they walked.

'Not at all. It's quite a building,' Carlos replied, his gaze drifting over the modern decor.

'Father Crane had it built a few years ago. He wanted a place that would reflect the modern spirit of our congregation and appeal to younger generations as well,' she explained proudly.

They reached the end of the corridor, having passed various doors and alcoves. Gloria stopped in front of a large wooden door and knocked twice before opening it. After a brief word with the priest, she motioned for Carlos to enter.

'Father Crane, this is Mr Carlos Jacobi, the private investigator.' Gloria stepped to one side.

Seated behind an imposing oak desk was the priest from the photos. Sebastian Crane rose, and with a politician's smile, he extended his hand.

'Pleased to make your acquaintance, Mr Jacobi. We don't get many private detectives visiting our humble abode.' He winked at Gloria before giving her a dismissive nod while shaking Carlos's hand.

'I'm just going out to get some milk, then I'll be right next door if you would like tea?'

'Thanks, Gloria.'

'Thank you for seeing me,' said Carlos, not quite able to call any man other than his father, Father. He eyed the charismatic but imposing man in front of him. Father Sebastian Crane was late forties, sported a healthy tan and had a full head of dark brown hair, neatly combed back. His eyes were a striking shade of blue, and he had an authoritative air. He wore a heavy gold crucifix over his short-sleeved black clerical shirt and white Roman collar. His forearms were muscular, giving the impression he worked out.

'Not at all. I'm intrigued. Please have a seat, Mr Jacobi. That's a Jewish name, isn't it?'

Carlos flinched at the priest's quick reference to his religious background. 'It is, but call me Carlos or I'll think I'm in trouble.'

Crane laughed easily. 'Then you must call me Seb. My friends call me Seb.'

Carlos took the seat across from the priest, studying Seb's relaxed posture and genial smile. Everything about him projected modern approachability, but there was something in the eyes that suggested he wasn't a man to be crossed.

'All right, Seb. I expect you're wondering why I'm here, so I'll get straight to the point. It's about the woman who was found dead at the Jewry Wall Museum at the end of last month. The one whose body you identified as being that of a homeless person called Carrie Clark.' Carlos continued without preamble. 'It appears her name wasn't Carrie Clark, and she wasn't homeless.'

Seb's thick eyebrows shot up in surprise. 'That's unexpected, but not surprising. Sometimes those that are destitute live under a false identity. What was her real name?'

'Christina Sand. She was a lecturer and scientist. Miss Sand worked at the Institute for Evolutionary Genetics and Research not far from the university where she lectured.'

Carlos watched the priest closely. Seb leaned back in his chair, looking thoughtful.

'I see. Well, although this is rather unexpected, it's not unheard of. I could have sworn...' He trailed off, shaking his head. 'I'm sorry to hear of the error, but there was a good reason for it. How has her family taken the news?'

If it hadn't been for the defensive wording and posture, the priest's apology might have seemed genuine, but something about his manner felt off. Too smooth, too practised.

'Devastated, as you can imagine. They initially hired me to find their missing daughter, which I've done, but now they want to know what happened to her and why she was cremated in haste.' Carlos looked around the office, trying to get a feel for the man across the desk.

'How the young woman's body was disposed of was out of my hands. The Catholic Church doesn't prohibit cremation, but we are not for it. We highly recommend burial.'

Ignoring the slick response, Carlos continued. 'I'm sure you understand the implications of this development. I'm working with the police to gather as much information as

I can to help piece together what happened and why errors were made.'

'Of course.' Seb nodded, his voice and face pasting on outward concern. 'I'll do my best to assist, Carlos. Although I'm not sure I can be of much help. I'm truly sorry for the confusion and distress this must have caused Christina's family.'

'You say you had good reason to identify her as Carrie Clark. Would you mind elaborating?'

'We met at the homeless shelter I founded and she told me her name was Carrie. Do you know the shelter?'

Carlos shook his head. 'No, I'm afraid not.'

'Carrie – the woman you now inform me was called Christina – spent a few nights there. She carried photo ID – we try to ID all the residents. I expect we'll have a record of it at the shelter. She had the most beautiful red hair, although it was ragged and dirty. That was what I recognised when the poor woman was found dead.'

'Is it unusual for you to have to identify a dead person?'

'Alas, not unusual for a person in my position. Not common, but not unheard of either. When she arrived at the shelter, she told us she had no living relatives.'

'Tell me more about the shelter,' said Carlos.

Seb nodded eagerly, seeming pleased to move on from the dead woman's identity.

'We're doing great work there with the homeless from the city centre community.' He leaned forward. 'Although the shelter is an ecumenical entity in its daily running, I'm proud to say I founded it. The Gracious Heart House vision was realised three years ago when I worked with the vicar from St Nicholas Church and witnessed first-hand how many people were sleeping rough on the streets. Complaints to the council about the impression the homeless community was giving were building up.

'The mayor approached me, knowing our church likes to be out there in the community. He asked whether I could do anything to help and said the council was willing to give us a grant. We acquired a rent-free building and started small… just a few beds and a food bank, but the need grew and our reputation spread, so we quickly expanded.'

Seb gestured expansively around the office. 'As you can see, God has also blessed me to build and move into this wonderful building. The shelter isn't so grand, but it's a place where I… erm… we can offer hot meals, showers, medical care and so much more to those less fortunate than ourselves. My congregation has embraced the work and given generously to the cause.'

His enthusiasm and pride would have been contagious, but his trouble with the use of the word 'we' rather than 'I' was concerning. Seb was eager to present himself as God's humble servant, but it rang hollow in Carlos's ears.

'We have over fifty volunteers who donate their time, and our reach extends far beyond the shelter's walls. Local businesses donate food. We do outreach to connect people on the streets to health and social care services and do our best to advocate on their behalf. I'm also involved in policy changes and increased funding at city level.' Seb smiled, stroking the large crucifix. 'The Lord's work takes many forms and I'm blessed to be an instrument of His grace.'

Carlos grunted an affirmation. Something about this priest set his teeth on edge. The all-too-perfect image and rehearsed humility was annoying. Was it his cynicism or was the priest hiding behind a façade of benefaction?

'Your dedication is admirable,' Carlos said carefully. 'But I expect it's also costly. Have you had challenges making ends meet?'

Seb's grin faltered briefly before the genial mask slipped back into place.

'The Lord provides. Of course, we've had some lean times, but our community rallies around. I trust that the work is part of God's purpose, therefore the funding will come.'

Carlos studied the priest's face again. The earnest devotion seemed like overcompensation. He knew men and women of faith – his girlfriend and her father were two of them who didn't need to constantly reassert their piety.

'But it must have its challenges.' Carlos tried to look sympathetic.

'As with any non-profit organisation, there are financial hurdles. We rely on donations from our congregation and the community at large.'

'Have you ever had to turn anyone away because of a lack of funds?' Carlos pressed, watching as Seb's self-assured smile faltered again.

'Unfortunately, yes. It's never a straightforward decision, but sometimes we simply don't have the resources to help everyone who comes to us.'

'That must weigh on you,' Carlos said. 'The responsibility for so many vulnerable lives. And when tragedy strikes, as with this poor woman's death... it must be hard to bear.'

Seb's jaw tightened. 'I leave the past in God's hands. All I can do is serve those who need me now. But, of course, I will continue to pray for her soul, using her given name from now on.'

Despite his words, the priest seemed untouched by the death. Carlos leaned forward, his gaze intense.

'Let's return to the night Christina Sand was found. What brought you to that area of the city at such an early hour?'

Seb shifted in his seat. 'My work with the homeless doesn't end with running the shelter. Along with a few other volunteers, I trawl the city centre, offering assistance to those sleeping on the streets. I had several volunteers out that night...'

There was the use of I again.

'...It was cold and wet, which is when the rough sleepers are most at risk.'

'Were any of the other volunteers with you when the body was found?'

'No, I went to investigate on my own when I spotted the police car at the museum. The police were on the scene when I arrived.'

'And you were on foot?'

'Yes.'

'Why did you contact Detective Chief Inspector Masters directly?' Carlos asked. 'Surely the officers present could have dealt with the matter?'

Seb smiled thinly. 'DCI Masters is a member of my congregation. He doesn't attend Mass often, but I know he is a senior police officer. I wanted to make sure the matter was handled properly, and I thought he'd want to know about a young woman's death on his turf. He takes an interest in our charitable work.'

Carlos doubted the DCI's interest would be anything other than self-serving, but he nodded, keeping his true feelings veiled.

'Terry arrived shortly after the pathologist who examined the body. He seemed rather inexperienced, so Terry took over. I also called Mishka.'

'Who's Mishka?' Carlos pretended he hadn't heard of the doctor mentioned in Fiona's briefing.

'He's a GP who registers as many of the homeless as he can with his practice. We both made the mistake of believing her to be Carrie Clark. Terry didn't know her, but Mishka and I thought we did.'

'You both failed to identify her correctly?' Carlos said.

Seb's mask of humility slipped at the implied criticism. 'I'm afraid a transient population like the homeless isn't fond of close scrutiny, Carlos. But rest assured, we did everything we could. We can't be blamed if a person lies about their identity. I will pray for her forgiveness.'

Carlos wondered if he was being unreasonable. This man was out there in the middle of the night, caring for people with no roof over their heads when everybody else was tucked up in bed. Still, it irked him that the man of God seemed to care more about protecting his reputation than admitting to his mistakes.

'I hope what I've told you will bring an end to the matter and that the poor woman's parents can lay her ashes to rest now. Please inform them my door is always open if they want to know anything else.'

'It's not as simple as that, Seb,' said Carlos. 'The police have reopened the case as a suspicious death, probably murder.'

Seb's eyebrows shot up. 'But Terry and the coroner ruled it an accidental death! Other than the woman having a different identity, nothing's changed.'

'I beg to differ. The senior pathologist discovered that the original pathologist raised serious doubts about the death being accidental. Acting DI Fiona Cook is leading the new investigation.'

'Why isn't DCI Masters in charge?'

Carlos watched Seb carefully. The priest's expression remained neutral.

'He's on holiday at the moment. Acting DI Cook and I pieced together Christina Sand's last days and discovered her real identity.'

Seb sucked in his lips. 'I see. Well, if that's all—'

'There is just one more thing. Do you mind if I ask about another homeless individual who appears to have gone missing at around the same time?' Carlos didn't wait for a reply, instead pulling out the flyer featuring Simeon Vasili. 'Do you recognise this man?'

Seb studied the photo. 'Yes, he stayed at the shelter a few times. But I haven't seen him for a couple of months.'

'Could you be more precise?' Carlos asked.

Seb shifted again. 'Before I met Carrie, now known as Christina, I think. The homeless are transient by nature. They come and they go. We try to help those seeking shelter and nourishment. But they have free will. We cannot force them to stay.'

'Of course,' Carlos replied, his voice smooth and non-confrontational. 'I understand you can't monitor everyone who comes through your shelter. I just thought it was worth mentioning, since Christina Sand seemed quite interested in finding him.'

Seb's eyes darted back to the flyer, and for a moment, Carlos thought he detected a flicker of concern in the priest's gaze. But just as quickly, it vanished behind Seb's outward mask.

'Thank you for bringing this to my attention, Carlos,' he said, handing the flyer back. 'I'll be sure to let you know if Simeon Vasili turns up at the shelter again.'

Carlos detected a hint of impatience in the priest's voice. 'Do you have any theories about why a wealthy woman with a decent job would go on sudden leave, take on a false identity and pretend to be homeless?'

Seb's smile was condescending. 'Understanding the human condition is my life's work, Carlos, but I'm not a psychologist. I wish she had confessed what was on her mind and perhaps we wouldn't be where we are today.' The priest stood, holding out his hand. 'I wish you every success with your investigation.'

'Thank you for your time.'

Carlos was pleased to leave the sterile church with its holier-than-thou priest as he untethered an overjoyed Lady, who barked with happiness.

'We didn't get very far there, Lady, but whether or not I like the man, his answers are plausible. Let's hope Fiona's having better luck than we are.'

Chapter 14

Fiona paced the scuffed lino floor, glaring at the clock on the wall of the GP's waiting room. Twenty minutes had gone since they announced their arrival to the starchy receptionist sitting behind a Perspex screen. Their scheduled appointment time with Dr Andreeva had passed.

The stale air smelled of antiseptic. Fiona and DC Kerry Gray were in the company of a few nervous-looking people sitting in plastic chairs, their eyes fixed on mobile phones. A pile of magazines stacked on a table looked as if it hadn't been touched, and a wall-mounted television screen spouted health advice about weight loss. Fiona was one of those people who didn't mind being overweight and resented endless reminders of the health risks.

She flopped in a chair, but got up immediately and started pacing the waiting room floor again, looking at the noticeboards. There was information about various clinics on offer, including advice on a local counselling service.

Kerry thumbed through the latest copy of *Good Housekeeping*, making notes on her phone. Fiona rejoined the DC, huffing.

'This is ridiculous. We're here on police business, not for a routine flippin' checkup.'

Finally, the inner door opened, and the receptionist gestured for them to go through.

'Last door on the right,' she said.

They walked along a dark and narrow corridor, entering the room with Dr Andreeva's name on the door. As the GP stood, Fiona noted the dark circles beneath his eyes. His shoulders were slumped under his brown suit.

Fiona introduced herself and Kerry, both officers flashing their ID. 'Thank you for seeing us, Dr Andreeva,' Fiona began, taking a seat opposite him as Kerry perched on the edge of an adjacent chair. 'We understand you're a busy man.'

'I'm always happy to assist the police.' His English had the faintest hint of an Eastern European accent. Fiona had done her homework. Dr Andreeva moved from Bulgaria as a teenager and had spent most of his adult life in the UK, including training as a doctor in Liverpool before taking a partnership in this practice.

'I wonder if we might ask you some questions about your work with the homeless.'

'Why? Has something happened?'

Dr Andreeva's face appeared to be set in a permanent frown, no doubt stress related. Fiona noticed the tightness around his eyes and the way he avoided meeting her gaze. She prided herself on her ability to read people, but couldn't work out whether this was a worn-out GP or one with something to hide.

'You could say that, yes.' Fiona tried again to lock eyes, but he looked down at papers on his desk.

In the ensuing silence, Andreeva eventually looked up. 'What is it? And how can I help?'

Fiona leaned back, trying to put the GP at his ease, watching him as she said, 'A young woman named Christina Sand, also known as Carrie Clark, was found dead just over three weeks ago. She was seemingly homeless, and as you work with the homeless, we are hoping you might have known her.'

Andreeva's face paled. He reached for a glass of water, his hand shaking. After taking a long drink, he set the glass down.

'Carrie Clark? Yes, I met a woman by that name, but the other name I don't recognise.' His voice was strained.

Fiona studied him closely. 'Perhaps you could tell us about your dealings with her?'

Andreeva shifted in his seat, wiping his brow with a tissue from the box on his desk, Fiona expected they were usually reserved for upset patients.

'I-I'm not sure I should discuss my patients.'

'This isn't about patient confidentiality, Doctor,' Fiona said sharply. 'This is a murder investigation. What was your connection to the victim?'

Andreeva gasped. 'Murder?'

'That's what we believe.'

'I thought her death was an accident.'

'You already know she's dead? How?'

'Carrie Clark came to the practice to register, as many of the homeless people do, after I met her at Gracious Heart House. It's a shelter where we do outreach. She said she was new to the area, so I gave her a leaflet. A few days later, she registered. That was the last I saw of her until the priest who runs the shelter, Father Crane, called me in the early hours of the thirty-first of October to examine a body. We both knew her as Carrie Clark, but you're saying she was someone else?'

Fiona's eyes narrowed. Why had there been no mention of the GP's attendance in the official police report? Another example of sloppy policing, or something more? She parked those thoughts.

'Why did Father Crane call you?'

'Why he called me when the police and a pathologist were already in attendance, I'm not entirely sure. I assumed it was because he knows I work with the homeless.'

'Did he call you before the pathologist got there to verify death?' Kerry's enthusiasm drew a glare from Fiona.

'Yes, that must have been it.' Kerry mouthed an apology, but she had given Dr Andreeva a lifeline and he sounded more confident when he added, 'That was the extent of my involvement with this woman, Inspector.'

'I see. Did you examine the body?'

'No. The pathologist was already there.'

'What about the bruises on her body?'

'I didn't see any bruises. Thankfully, the woman's clothes were intact. There didn't appear to be any sign of sexual assault. The police chief inspector deemed it an accident.'

'Perhaps you can tell us about the medical research you're conducting with the homeless?' Fiona's gaze was unwavering as she managed to finally lock eyes with the flustered physician.

Andreeva frowned. 'I don't see the relevance, Inspector.'

'It's Acting Detective Inspector but humour me.'

'We're studying the effects of certain gene mutations in cancer development. The hope is to prevent, and also to discover a novel cure.'

'Why homeless subjects?' Kerry asked, incredulous.

'They are ideal candidates for such research, with limited medical histories and frequent exposure to environmental carcinogens. Also, many of them are smokers, heavy drinkers and/or drug users, all of which raise the likelihood of their developing cancer in the future.' Andreeva sounded defensive. 'My involvement is limited to recruitment, an initial screening and some preliminary tests. The research is led by others.'

Fiona's eyes narrowed. 'Who is leading it? The Institute for Evolutionary Genetics or the university, Doctor?'

'The former. It's led by a world-renowned and widely respected physician, Professor Ronald Brooker.'

Fiona stiffened. Brooker was head of the institute where Christina worked and Carlos had also mentioned him leaving a message on Christina's answerphone.

'Where does the funding come from?' Kerry asked. This time, her question impressed Fiona.

Andreeva hesitated before answering. 'From a private company called Genomix Solutions Biotech. They specialise in genomic cancer research.'

Fiona made a mental note to look into Genomix Solutions.

'What exactly does the research entail, Doctor?'

Andreeva shifted again. 'As I said, I merely recruit candidates from my practice and the shelters. I screen them to assess suitability, take some common blood samples and a background history before passing them on. The institute handles any further testing and procedures through ongoing research.'

'You didn't mention consent,' said Kerry.

'What are you implying?'

'I'm assuming you need consent from the people you recruit?'

Andreeva seemed flustered. Beads of sweat formed on his upper lip.

'Naturally.' The answer was casual, but felt forced.

'Can I ask what's in it for you?' Fiona said.

'I receive an upfront and ongoing fee for each subject entered,' he said. 'But it's standard practice and covers the extra time I have to spend on paperwork and other administrative tasks. I assure you, it's quite normal in medical research trials to provide compensation to investigators.'

'Is there any payment involved for the participants themselves?' Kerry pressed, clearly concerned about the ethics of selecting homeless individuals for a potentially risky research study.

'There are incentives,' Dr Andreeva replied evasively, avoiding eye contact once more. 'I'm not sure about the specifics.' He rustled papers on his desk.

Fiona interjected, her voice icy. 'The woman you and Father Crane thought was Carrie Clark – was she part of this research study?'

'No,' Dr Andreeva answered quickly, almost too quickly. 'She wasn't.'

'Why not?' asked Fiona. 'I would have thought she was an ideal candidate.'

Andreeva fiddled with his tie. 'She would have been, and I may have mentioned the study to her, but the next time I saw her, she was dead.'

Fiona slid a photo of Simeon across the desk. 'Did Christina, aka Carrie Clark, ask you about this man, Simeon Vasili?'

Dr Andreeva glanced at the photo. 'Not that I remember.'

'Was Simeon part of your study?' Fiona asked bluntly.

The doctor hesitated. 'I can't divulge confidential patient information.'

Fiona's eyes bored into him. 'I'd advise you to cooperate fully, Doctor.'

Dr Andreeva wilted under her stare. 'Yes, Simeon Vasili was a subject.'

'Where is he now?' Fiona demanded.

'I... I don't know,' Dr Andreeva admitted. 'Once I refer them, I don't have any further involvement with the subjects.'

'Apart from the ongoing payments,' said Kerry.

'Which we've established are all legitimate,' Andreeva snapped, shifting again in his seat, clearly uncomfortable under the detectives' scrutiny.

'I'll ask again, Doctor Andreeva, and I suggest you consider your answer carefully. What exactly happens to the participants once you refer them to the institute? What further tests do the researchers carry out on them?'

'I'm not privy to those details,' Dr Andreeva said. 'I assume there are medical examinations, blood tests, maybe even tissue samples, that sort of thing. Protocols in clinical trials like this are scrupulously adhered to, with full ethics approvals. For further details, I suggest you speak to Professor Brooker.'

Fiona wasn't letting him off that lightly. 'Don't worry, Doctor, we will. But you must have some idea since you're the one recruiting the candidates. How often are they required to go to the institute?'

Andreeva spread his hands helplessly. 'Once I refer them on, the institute takes over. I believe they provide housing for the participants, and I think there's an external site where they have tests.'

'Housing and an external site. Where?'

'I'm just guessing. I reiterate, I never see them again at the shelters after enrolment in the study.'

'You don't find it odd that these people just vanish after you refer them on?' Kerry asked pointedly.

'Not at all. I assume they are well cared for and living a better life than the streets offer. What would you prefer?' Dr Andreeva sounded more confident, but he still wouldn't meet their eyes.

'Dr Andreeva,' Fiona said, her voice like steel, 'tell me about the screening process you mentioned. Is there a subcategory of homeless people chosen for this study?'

'I don't understand.'

'I think you do, Doctor. What specific characteristics make them ideal candidates?'

Andreeva squirmed before giving Fiona a hard stare. 'I'm sure you'll understand, *Acting* Detective Inspector Cook, that research trials are highly confidential and I've already told you more than you need to know. The woman whose death you are investigating was not part of the study. Therefore, I don't believe I should divulge any further information. What I can assure you is that the participants will have access to better healthcare than they have out on the streets.'

Fiona smiled. 'I'm sure you're right, Doctor.'

'But—' Kerry started.

'We've taken up enough of your time, Doctor Andreeva. Thanks again for seeing us,' said Fiona, standing.

'Is that all?' Andreeva asked.

'I'd like a list of study participants.'

'You know I can't give you one. Patient confidentiality is paramount. I've already said too much to try to help you.'

'Right. We'll let you know if we need to speak to you again,' said Fiona, shuffling a confused Kerry out of the surgery.

Once they were back inside Fiona's car, the air was thick with tension. Both women were quiet for a moment, processing the interview. It was Kerry who broke the silence, her voice tinged with anger.

'Why did you stop me in there? Something's off about him, ma'am. This whole thing just feels... wrong,' she said, folding her hands.

'I agree, but we'd got to where he was going to clam up. Besides which, he's right: the woman whose death we're investigating wasn't in the study. And the so-called missing Simeon Vasili case was opened and closed by DCI Masters. Let's see what the others have got from Professor Brooker. Before we dig deeper into this research, I'd like to find out how many homeless people have gone missing since it started.'

'How do we do that?'

'Simple. We send Carlos Jacobi to speak to them.'

'Why the PI?'

Fiona bristled, swinging around to look at Kerry. 'DC Gray, I appreciate your enthusiasm, and you'll make a good detective, but don't let prejudice stop you from getting to the truth. Carlos Jacobi is ex-military. He's not the police, so people who are homeless won't be as reluctant to speak to him as they would be to us. And what else?'

'There are a significant number of veterans living on the streets,' said Kerry.

'Exactly. So trust me on this. I'll drop you back at the station and you can type up what we've got so far. Also, look at Genomix Solutions Biotech while you're about it. I've got an appointment with the super and I'm gonna be late.'

Fiona turned the key in the ignition, her mind racing. It sounded like the world and its brother had attended the dead body that night – all except her. She had wanted to ask the GP if he had any dealings with a Romanian called Nicolae, but that was staying off the record for now.

Chapter 15

Carlos climbed out of his car, pulling his collar up as the cold air threatened to bite through his overcoat. He let Lady out, locked the car and shoved his hands in his pockets, hunching his shoulders against the chill as he hurried into his office building.

The blast of warm air hit him as soon as he opened the door; a welcome relief. He shrugged off his coat and hung it on the hook before making his way through the back corridor to his office. Julie placed a mug of coffee on his desk and filled a bowl with fresh water for Lady.

'I'm just off,' she said. 'I've left notes on your desk.'

'Thanks, Julie. See you tomorrow.' Carlos sipped the hot coffee and watched Lady lapping up her water. The phone buzzed in his pocket.

'Hi, Fiona, how did you get on?'

'Let's just say it was interesting.' She sounded out of breath. Carlos wished she'd take more exercise, but Fiona was seemingly allergic to it. 'Uniform tracked down the homeless guy who made the anonymous phone call to report the body. His name's Henry Cutter. But he won't speak to the police and I don't really want to bring him in. I was wondering if you would try him.'

Carlos's interest was piqued. 'What do we know about him?'

'Not much, apart from he's a stubborn old boy. Uniform are aware of him, say he's ex-military, which should give you an opening. He's been on the streets for years. Keeps to himself mostly. Will you see if you can get him to open up about what he saw that night?'

'Sure. Where can I find him?'

'Apparently he hangs around the High Street. Bench outside the bookshop is his favourite spot, according to uniform.'

Carlos nodded, even though she couldn't see him. 'I'll head over there now. I was planning to visit the shelter and follow up on some things after speaking to that priest, but I'll see if I can track Henry Cutter down before I go there.'

'Great. Let me know how you get on.' Fiona sounded distracted. 'We'll catch up later and you can tell me about your meeting with Father Crane then. I'm not sure about the GP, Dr Andreeva. He enrols homeless people into clinical trials and experiments run by the Institute for

Evolutionary Genetics and Research. Not sure if it's relevant, but he gets paid a tidy sum for each one he recruits. But once they're in, he doesn't see them again.'

Carlos could feel his brow furrowing. 'Did you know the priest called him to see the body that night?'

'Yeah, he told us when he recognised Christina – or rather, Carrie's name. He didn't know her true identity from what we could gather. I don't like this research angle, but it sounds legit. It annoys me that vulnerable people looking for help might be treated like lab rats, but the good doctor said they are well compensated.' Fiona sighed heavily. 'Anyway, I've got to go. I'm meeting with the super and I'm already late. Speak later?'

'Will do. Good luck.'

Carlos ended the call and glanced at his watch. Plenty of time to chat to Henry Cutter before his planned visit to the shelter. He gulped down the last of his coffee, the caffeine kicking in.

'Come on, Lady. We've got work to do.'

The dog jumped up eagerly, tail wagging in anticipation. Carlos clipped on her lead and they headed outside. The autumnal chill clung to the air, and since the clocks had gone back, it got dark so early. He inhaled deeply before setting off.

As they strolled towards the High Street, Carlos felt he and Fiona might be getting somewhere. Christina's interest in the shelter was key. He hoped Henry Cutter could shed more light on events.

Carlos slowed his pace as he and Lady reached the High Street. Some shops were already shutting up for the day. He scanned the faces of three homeless men sitting on the pavement, sharing a cigarette. Lady sniffed the air, as if picking up a scent. Carlos stopped to speak to the trio.

'Excuse me, I'm looking for Henry Cutter. Do you know where I can find him?'

One man looked up sharply, then pointed towards a bench further down.

'Over there, mate. He's not friendly, mind.'

Carlos thanked him and headed in the direction he'd pointed, Lady leading eagerly, as if realising there was a purpose to the walk. As they approached the bench, Carlos could make out a grey-bearded man with strings of long hair. The man had an old army coat wrapped tightly around him and a knitted hat pulled low over his ears. Carlos recognised the thousand-yard stare that haunted the eyes of soldiers, past and present.

'Henry Cutter?' Carlos asked gently.

The man turned, regarding Carlos with bloodshot eyes. He nodded warily. Carlos noticed his big toes poked out from holey shoes below tatty jeans and he caught the strong whiff of stale cigarette smoke mingled with body odour.

'Who wants to know?' Henry responded gruffly, his eyes narrowing with suspicion.

'My name's Carlos. Carlos Jacobi. I'm a private detective. This is Lady. Do you mind if we sit?'

Henry shuffled along the bench, allowing Carlos space. Lady sidled up to the older man and rested her head on his lap. He gave her a toothless grin, stroking her gently.

'I suppose you want to talk to me about that young woman I found. The cops have already asked, and I don't know anything.'

'I see you were in the forces.' Carlos gestured to the coat as he spoke, then acknowledged a couple of uniformed officers. They gave him a nod and walked on.

'Long time ago,' Henry rasped.

'Me too.' Carlos extended his hand. 'Pleased to meet you, Henry.'

Henry shook his hand firmly, showing a hint of pride. 'Twenty years in the army, me,' he said, rubbing his hands together for warmth.

'That's what I call dedication,' said Carlos. 'I served in Afghanistan. You?'

'Bosnia.'

'Difficult times.'

The other man nodded. 'Seeing as you were in the army, I might just know something about that body.' Henry tried a laugh, which ended in a barking cough.

'Let me get you a coffee and some food. There's a café just there.'

Henry nodded. 'All right.' He slowly got to his feet. 'Can't deny I could use a decent meal.'

They headed over to the café with Lady shadowing them. Carlos knew the proprietor was unlikely to want Henry and his odour inside the building, so he gestured to an outside table next to a heater.

'They don't allow dogs inside. Shall we sit over there?'

Henry lowered himself onto the chair with a groan, rubbing his knee.

'Had me kneecap shot to bits,' he explained.

Carlos ordered two coffees, an all-day breakfast for Henry and a bacon sandwich for himself. While they waited for the food, Carlos asked Henry what he did in the army and how he'd ended up living on the streets.

'It's a long story and one I'm sure you ain't got time to listen to.' Henry's eyes saddened, and he gazed into the distance. Carlos took the hint. Whatever had happened, Henry didn't want to talk about it.

Their food and drinks arrived, and after the woman Carlos recognised from his occasional visits had given Henry a disapproving look, she left. Lady stopped leaning against Henry's leg and lay on the floor while they ate.

'Would you mind telling me what happened on the night you found the body?'

Henry paused tucking into his food and looked up at Carlos.

'It was early hours. Some kids woke me up, calling me names and throwing stuff at me.'

Carlos felt a pang of sympathy. As if the homeless didn't have enough on their plates, fighting to survive their own demons while living on the streets, without being tormented for it.

'I moved on and was looking for another place to get some kip. It was bucketing it down and my feet were sodden. I wandered along St Nicholas Walk, the alley between the church and the museum, and climbed into the museum grounds. Them dugouts can be quite cosy and there's a fair bit of tarpaulin about from the renovations they're doing. That's when I found her, like.'

Henry shook his head and took a gulp of coffee. 'My God, she was a beauty.' He shook his head again, his eyes haunted. 'She was just lying there, lifeless eyes staring up at the sky. I knew straight away she was dead. Been around enough death to recognise it.'

Carlos nodded, letting the man take his time. He could see the scene unfolding in his mind's eye.

'What happened next?'

'She had a bag.'

'Did you look inside?'

'The hunger was eating my insides away. I couldn't help it.'

'I understand,' said Carlos. 'What did you find?'

'Nowt much. A bit of money and a photo. Anyway, I felt so guilty, I threw it back, ashamed of what me mam would say.'

'Was there any ID in the bag?' Carlos asked.

'Nope. But I recognised her from the city shelter. I'd seen her twice. Me conscience wouldn't let me leave her there with no-one knowing, so I headed back down the High Street and phoned the police. There's a phone box just around the corner from the clock tower.'

Henry stopped talking to polish off the rest of his meal. Carlos gestured to the woman inside to bring them more coffee, and she came out and refilled their mugs.

'I got waylaid on the way, mind, 'cos I found some food. It was me reward for not robbing the dead,' Henry added, wiping egg off his beard with the back of his hand. 'I made the call anonymous, like; didn't want to get caught up in it, see? And I didn't want them thinking I was involved, you know? But afterwards, I circled back. Hid behind a gravestone in the churchyard and watched them arrive.'

He took a slurp of the fresh coffee.

'The police?'

'Yep. The cops came first; young 'uns, they were. I don't think they knew what to do. Then another car arrived with a pathologist in a white suit. Saw enough of them in the army to know who he was. After that, I had a fright and thought they were going to catch me. A car pulled up outside the church and a priest got out, but he circled round and went over to the body.'

Carlos tensed. Seb had told him he arrived on foot that night during one of his street outreach sessions. Why lie?

'You're sure the priest was in a car?'

'Course I'm sure.'

'What happened next?'

'I don't know. I scarpered before anyone else came along. It was getting a bit too busy for me.'

'Did you ever speak to the dead woman? Christina Sand, her name was, but she used a false name at the shelter, Carrie Clark.'

'Can't say I did. It was the red hair that made her stand out. I keep myself to myself and stay out of trouble that way.'

'What can you tell me about the shelter? I assume you mean Gracious Heart House?'

'That's the one. It's run by a priest and some others.'

'Have you met the priest?'

'Nah. And they don't let the likes of me take up a bed there, but I get meals sometimes.'

'Really?' Carlos asked, surprised. 'Why wouldn't they give you a bed?'

'Can't say for sure,' Henry shrugged. 'But they prefer to help the younger ones. Maybe they think we're too far gone or something. I've tried to get a bed, like, when it's bitter outside. They always say they're full, but then I watch fresh faces coming and going all the time. Young people mostly. I reckon they keep the beds for people like the dead girl.'

Henry took another swig from his mug, wiping his mouth this time with a dirty sleeve. 'I don't ask too many questions, but I've never known them take a person over the age of forty in that place. They're happy enough to give us a meal, though, and a meal's a meal. But it ain't right the way they treat us older folk.'

'Father Crane – he's the priest who runs the place and the one you saw that night – told me they only turn people away when the shelter is full,' Carlos said, his brow creasing as he processed the discrepancy between the priest's and Henry's account. 'But you're saying they show preference to younger people?'

'Yep,' Henry replied, nodding his head.

Carlos cupped his coffee mug. Why did Seb lie about the shelter's policy on who got to stay?

'Have you ever come across a Romanian man there called Nicolae? Dark hair, about my height, early forties, tends to wear beige or cream suits?'

Henry looked up. 'Aye, I've seen him all right. He waltzes in like he owns the place, takes a good look around, but doesn't bother speaking to anyone except the doctor.'

Carlos studied the man as he finished his coffee. Was the shelter a front for something sinister? If Nicolae was involved, it was a high probability. And where did Seb fit into all this?

'Thanks for talking to me, Henry. You've been really helpful.'

'Us ex-forces need to stick together,' said Henry.

'Just one more thing.' Carlos pulled out the flyer of Simeon. 'Did you ever see this man at the shelter?'

'Once. He was talking to the doctor. Here, let me look at that again.' Henry's eyes squinted as he examined the picture. 'That's the guy whose photo she was carrying in her bag. The dead woman, like.'

'Are you sure?' There had been no mention of a photo being among the belongings found on Christina Sand's person.

'It was dark that night, but I think it was him. I thought I recognised him at the time, but I was freaked.'

Carlos went inside and paid extra for the proprietor to fill up Henry's flask with fresh hot coffee.

'If you're sure,' the woman said tersely.

Carlos returned to Henry and shook his hand, thanking him for his time. Then he had a thought.

'Henry, if you hear anything odd relating to the dead woman, or see the Romanian man again, my office is just around the corner.' He handed Henry his business card and a £20 note. 'I'll see you right.'

Henry stuffed the card and money in an inside pocket while the proprietor reluctantly filled his flask, nose wrinkled in disgust.

'Watch your back, Carlos,' Henry said before he left. 'If someone killed a pretty young thing like that woman, they won't hesitate to do away with you.'

'Thanks for the warning, Henry. I'll be careful.'

Chapter 16

Carlos walked the few blocks to Gracious Heart House, his mind churning over the details of what Henry had told him. Incidental things were coming to light, but nothing was clear.

From a few yards away, the shelter looked every bit what it was supposed to be. Men and women lined up outside. Some had canine companions, like he did, and after waiting for a while, they trudged inside. A few drunks were turned away, leaving with sandwiches, which they wolfed down on the way out.

After watching people going in for ten minutes, Carlos approached a small gathering in the queue outside the entrance. The welcome aroma of freshly cooked casserole helped to dispel the unpleasant odours oozing from those waiting to be fed or given a bed for the night.

'Hello, sorry to bother you. My name's Carlos Jacobi. I'm a private investigator.' He flashed his ID. 'I'm looking into the death of a young woman who used to come here. Her name was Christina Sand, but she might have been known to you as Carrie Clark. Do any of you remember seeing her?'

Most of those in the group shuffled their feet ever forward towards the door, averting their eyes, except for one scrawny man leaning against a brick wall.

'Yeah, I seen her around. Real pretty girl, Carrie.'

Carlos moved closer to the man. 'When was the last time you saw her?'

He scratched his stubbled beard. 'Three... four weeks back, maybe. She had an argument with the doctor who comes here, and they threw her out.'

'Dr Andreeva?' Carlos clarified.

'Yeah, that's him. Real nice to the young ones, usually. Not so much to us older fellas, but most of us are registered with his practice.' He spat on the ground.

'Did you hear what they were arguing about?'

'Yeah, the doctor said he was too busy to be answering questions all the time, that he couldn't answer any more, and she should leave him alone.'

'But she didn't?'

The man shrugged. 'Can't have, otherwise Father Crane wouldn't have kicked her out.'

'Father Crane asked her to leave?'

'Yep, although told rather than asked.'

'Is that unusual?'

'Not when people cause trouble, but I wouldn't have put her down as a troublemaker. Still, it was busy that day and there'd been a few fights. Maybe they weren't in the mood. Father Crane got Fran and George to escort her out.'

'Are Fran and George volunteers?'

'Yeah, I think so. Always here when I've been. You wouldn't want to mess with either of 'em. I've been at the wrong end of George's fists when I've turned up drunk.'

'He hit you?'

The man's eyes darted around, nervously. 'I might have imagined it. Like I say, I was drunk. I've got to get some food, mate.' He shuffled away from Carlos.

'Thanks for your help,' Carlos called after him.

His mind raced. The doctor, the one administrating the clinical trials, and the priest, Seb. Most of what Carlos was hearing led back to them. But then, it would, seeing as they were at the shelter a lot of the time. It proved nothing, but why hadn't Seb told him about the disagreement, or about asking Christina to leave?

He turned to others still in the queue. 'If you remember anything about Carrie Clark, please call me or come along to my office.' He handed out his PI business cards to any who would take them.

Carlos followed another row of people inside, surprised at how many there were. He moved from person to person, asking questions and showing the photo of Christina and the flyer about Simeon. A pattern emerged. While most people recognised Christina because of the bright red hair, none seemed to have any information about Simeon Vasili. It was as if he had slipped through unnoticed, leaving no trace behind. And none of them could give him any further information about Christina.

Carlos asked a few if they had ever seen a Romanian man in a smart beige or white suit. Most of them shook their heads, barely paying attention. Then someone pulled at his arm.

'Hey.'

He turned to see a young woman, who couldn't have been more than twenty, with bright green eyes. She had a bruise on her left cheek. When she spoke, her voice was shaky.

'I've seen guys like the ones you're asking about.'

'Which one?' Carlos asked, his heart rate spiking.

'Both.' She pointed at the flyer he'd been showing round. 'I shared a bottle with Simeon once. And I've seen a guy who always wears a white suit as well.'

'Where?'

'Here,' she whispered, leading Carlos away from the crowd of people muttering about wanting to get inside. She glanced around nervously, but these people were used to minding their own business and paid them no attention. 'He comes and goes, always talks to the doctor. He doesn't stay long, but when he leaves, some of the others – including Simeon – leave with him. And as far as I know, they don't come back.'

'Do you know where they go?'

She shook her head. 'No clue, but I don't like the guy in the suit.'

'What about the doctor? Do you like him?'

'Dr Andreeva's all right. Tries to help people like me, I guess, so he can't be bad. Lots of these guys only see him for the methadone he prescribes. He's scared of your suit man, though.'

'What makes you say that?'

'When you live on the streets, you recognise fear when you see it.' She rubbed her cheek. 'It's what keeps you alive.'

'Thank you.' Carlos slipped her a £20 note. 'What's your name?'

She shook her head. 'Need to know only.'

'Fair enough. Do you have a phone?' he asked.

'What do you think?'

'Stupid question. Look, here's my card. My office is not far from here. If you see either of them again, come and tell me. And steer clear of the guy in the suit.'

'Sure,' she said, slipping the card in her jeans pocket before returning to the now shorter queue.

Carlos was panting when he called Lady to heel. Not daring to get his hopes up, he nevertheless wondered whether he was finally getting close to stopping Nicolae. They walked around the queue until a man built like a truck barred their way. Lady growled, but the man sneered.

'Quiet, girl, it's okay,' said Carlos.

'What do you think you're doing? This is private property.'

'I was hoping to speak to the volunteers. I met Seb... Father Crane earlier, and he said I could call by and ask some questions.' Carlos showed his ID.

The man folded his arms. 'Is that so?'

'I can call him if you like,' Carlos offered.

'No need. That way.' He inclined his head behind him.

'Perhaps I could start with you?'

'Maybe later. I'm busy for the next hour. Feeding time at the zoo.' Carlos wondered why a hired heavy was guarding the door of a shelter. He was certainly not a volunteer; at least, Carlos hoped he wasn't.

'Catch you later, then.'

There was no sign of Seb, but he hadn't expected to see him, otherwise the gorilla at the door would have said he was inside. Carlos spoke to a few of the volunteers serving food, but most of them were new. It appeared there was a high turnover at the shelter because of unspecified threats and violence.

Finding little help there, Carlos headed further inside towards a room labelled as a designated sleeping area. A smart woman in her fifties looked up after signing someone in and letting them through the closed door.

'Can I help you?'

'My name is Carlos Jacobi. I'm a private investigator looking into the death of a woman who visited the shelter. Maybe even stayed here.'

A hint of fear came and went before she looked down at her register, and then back at him. 'We have many people come through our doors, Mr Jacobi, with all sorts of problems. As you can imagine, some of them end up dead. It's sad, but a fact of life.'

'This woman died under suspicious circumstances. Her name was Carrie Clark – not her real name – but that's the name she went by.'

He had her, and he knew it from the shocked reaction. 'Suspicious circumstances. What do you mean?'

'The police believe she might have been murdered.'

'Murdered?'

'I take it you knew her?'

'She slept here a few times, yes, but I didn't know her. In fact, the last time I saw her, she was asked to leave.'

'Is your name Fran?' Carlos asked.

'How do you know that?'

'I heard you escorted her off the premises. Why was that?'

'They asked me to. She was upsetting our doctor and other people, asking questions. Most people who live on the streets are hiding something. They don't like people who ask too many questions.'

'What sort of questions was she asking?'

'I wouldn't know anything about that. You'd need to ask Doctor Andreeva.'

'Is he here?'

'No, he comes in most days, but usually in the morning to check on newcomers.'

'Looking for recruits,' said Carlos.

Fran's eyes blazed as she snapped, 'What do you mean by that?'

'I heard he's recruiting homeless people into a clinical trial. Do you know anything about it?'

She relaxed a little. 'Not really. But it's very important from what Father Crane says. We let the surgery know when suitable candidates turn up.'

'What makes a suitable candidate?'

Fran had clearly said more than she meant to because she shook her head. 'I don't remember.'

He tried a different angle. 'What's Father Crane like?'

Fran touched a small crucifix around her neck, looking reverent. 'He's a wonderful man who does so much for the needy. We have him to thank for this facility.'

'So I understand. It must have been hard for him to ask you to eject Carrie from the premises, him being such a kind man.' Carlos tried to conceal the sarcasm in his tone.

'We didn't eject her. Just asked her to leave.' Fran was bristling.

'With a two-person escort. Who helped you put her out?'

'I don't like your tone, Mr Jacobi. We do our best for the people who come through these doors, but some of them don't want to be helped. Carrie Clark was trouble. You yourself have said she lied about her name.'

'Christina Sand.'

'What?'

'In case you were wondering, her real name was Christina Sand. She was looking for this man.' Carlos placed the flyer on the table, watching Fran's reaction. 'You know Simeon Vasili, I take it.'

'He doesn't come here anymore.'

'Do you know where I might find him?'

'No, I don't.'

'Did she ever ask you about him?'

'We don't divulge information about people who stay here, so if she did, I wouldn't have answered.'

'But you knew she was looking for him?' Carlos could see by Fran's reaction she was hiding something.

She folded her arms. 'I have work to do. George was the other person with me when Carrie left.'

'Where can I find him?'

'On the door.'

Just as I suspected, thought Carlos. He knew he wouldn't get anything else out of Fran, and George was unlikely to tell him anything without Fiona's clout behind him.

'Thank you for seeing me. If you do see Simeon Vasili again, please call me.' He retrieved the flyer, replacing it with his card.

'Do you think he had something to do with Carrie's death?'

'*Christina* was looking for him, so he might be able to help with the case.'

Carlos hoped Fiona wasn't going to give him an earful for telling the volunteer about the suspicion of murder. One thing he would not do was mention Nicolae to Fran. If she was part of whatever was going on in this place, he didn't want to warn her he might be onto something.

'Thanks for your time. I may speak to George another day.'

Chapter 17

The Queen of Bradgate was quiet when Carlos arrived and ordered a pint of lager. He'd made a quick dash back to the office with Lady to feed her before they came out again. Now, Lady was happy to settle at his feet.

Carlos watched the door, waiting for Bethany. Her eyes scanned the room when she came in and she smiled when Lady jumped up. Carlos gave her a wave, and she joined him at the table.

'Sorry I didn't get back to you last night. I was late finishing. I got your message, though.' Carlos had texted her after he'd met with Seb, asking her to meet him at the pub, which wasn't far from the museum. She had texted back to say okay.

'How were the photo shoots and the film scouting?' he asked.

'Both great.' Bethany's eyes sparkled with happiness. Carlos felt the knot forming in his stomach. He hated what he was about to do.

'Can I get you a drink?'

'Soda and lime, please. I'm driving.'

Carlos walked to the bar, his feet feeling like lead. He could have left this to the police, but had opted to do it himself. He watched Bethany making a fuss of Lady while he waited to be served.

When he arrived back at the table with her drink and dropped himself heavily into the chair, Bethany looked up from stroking Lady to thank him. Her eyes changed from bright to concerned.

'What is it? What's happened?'

'Bethany, I've got bad news to tell you.'

She shook her head. 'Has something happened to Christina? Where is she?'

Carlos looked down at his hands cupping the pint glass before meeting her eyes. 'There's no easy way to tell you this, but Christina's dead.'

Stunned silence followed as the shock settled in. He'd seen this reaction more times than he cared to remember. Disbelief crossed Bethany's face, then confusion, followed by determination. Carlos suspected the tears would come later.

'What happened?'

Carlos explained how he believed Christina had gone undercover, pretending to be homeless while looking for Simeon.

'But Simeon wasn't homeless! He comes from money. They were so well suited.' Bethany took a large gulp of her drink.

'I thought you said last night you didn't know whether they'd been together,' Carlos said.

'Sorry about that, but Christina would have been livid if she thought I'd mentioned it. The thing is, they split up, and she hated him for years, but recently, she'd become obsessed with finding him again. Before you ask, I don't know why. But I know he wouldn't be homeless. Unless—'

'Unless what?' Carlos asked.

Bethany frowned. 'Christina never said, but I think he might have been working as a freelance reporter or something.'

'If that was the case, why would Christina be looking for him?'

Bethany shrugged. 'Who knows? It was a sudden thing, though. For years, he was persona non grata, a man not to be mentioned, then came this desire to find him. She only told me because she wanted me to move in and look after Jemmy while she was away, and knew she'd have to have a good reason. I knew nothing about her going undercover, though. Truth is, I hoped they'd get back together, so I was pleased to help. He was good for her.'

'Her parents mentioned there might have been a boyfriend a few months back. Do you know anything about that?'

'No. She had a lot of admirers, though.'

Carlos stared at Bethany. 'Is there anything else you know you're not telling me?'

'No. Cross my heart.' She motioned the sign of the cross with her right hand. 'I hated lying, if I'm honest.' Bethany stared at the table. 'But I thought she would be home last night. Christina hated being talked about.'

'Did she give you any clue about where she thought Simeon was?'

'None. I got the feeling she'd seen him recently, though. Call it a best friend's intuition. Maybe he had gone off the rails, like you say. You haven't told me how she died.'

'Christina used a false name to get into the shelter, which is why I believe she was doing some covert investigating.'

'Into what?'

'I think it had something to do with Simeon. Anyway, the body of a young homeless woman was found on Halloween—'

Bethany's hand flew to her mouth as she gasped. Tears filled her eyes.

'I read about that in the paper. A short paragraph was all it got.'

It will get a lot more than that once I've had my next meeting, thought Carlos.

'The body has now been identified from photos and dental records, confirming it as that of Christina. Even more sad news: she'd already been cremated by the time we discovered her real identity.' Carlos put a hand across the table and squeezed Bethany's. 'I'm so sorry.'

Taking his hand away, Carlos gave her a few minutes to recover before going on, quietly.

'Her parents have been informed.'

'The newspaper said the woman fell into one of the dugout trenches at the museum. To think, I was there last night and all day today. I didn't give that poor girl a second thought. But now she means something to me—'

'You can't blame yourself for that. We've learned to push things to the back of our minds, otherwise we wouldn't survive.'

'You're right. But now it's personal. Why was she cremated already?'

'Because the authorities were under the impression she had no living relatives. It's what happens when the homeless or people without relatives to pay for a funeral die.'

'That's awful.'

'Her parents will be given her ashes. I expect they'll arrange for a proper funeral once they get over the shock.' Carlos thought back to how businesslike Rose had pretended to be and how crumpled her husband looked after he and Fiona broke the news.

Bethany nodded. 'What about Jemmy?'

'The police have arranged with the RSPCA for her to stay in a foster home. I didn't ask Christina's parents—'

'They don't like animals. I'll take her. It's the least I can do. Christina would have wanted that.'

Carlos watched the bottom lip tremble. Bethany was unable to go on.

'I was hoping you'd say that, which is why I asked for her not to be rehomed until I'd seen you. Perhaps you could clear it with her parents. By rights, they're the next of kin, but I didn't feel it appropriate to bring it up this morning.'

'Christina loved that cat and she's no trouble with me, but she can be a right pain with people she doesn't know. They say animals are like their owners, don't they? Jemmy can be prickly with strangers. I hope whoever's got her will survive the night. If I take her, it might help us both, being with each other. And don't worry, Rose won't want a cat in her life.'

Lady whined, nudging up to Bethany and putting her head on her lap, as if sensing her sorrow.

'I believe you're right.'

'It's been a long day. I'm going to go home. I'll call her parents later, and I'll call the RSPCA and collect Jemmy from wherever she is tomorrow.'

'There's just one other thing, Bethany. I apologise, but the story is likely to make the headlines tomorrow. I'm working with the police and we don't believe Christina's death was an accident.'

Bethany's mouth dropped open and her eyes widened. 'You think she was murdered?'

Carlos nodded slowly.

'Why?'

'That's what I intend to find out,' he said.

'You think Simeon did it?'

'It's one possibility.'

Bethany stood, and he did the same. She grabbed his hand and looked at him through tear-filled eyes.

'If my friend was murdered, make sure you get the person responsible, Carlos. But I don't believe for one minute it will turn out to be Simeon.'

He pulled her into a hug before releasing her. Nobody in the pub appeared to notice the distressed woman exiting – too wrapped up in their own conversations, their own worries or joys.

Carlos returned to his seat and sipped his drink, waiting for the next person to arrive.

Chapter 18

Tony Hadden walked with a limp since his brush with death and he was a shadow of the man he had been before the accident. Still, Carlos admired him for getting back on his feet after months of rehab, and for the determination it must have taken from him to return to work. The accident and what he had discovered about Nicolae remained a taboo subject, but if Tony was going to follow this story through, he might have to face his demons.

Lady jumped up and demanded his attention before her old friend sat down. Tony willingly obliged.

'Still a beauty, eh, Lady?' He ruffled her silky coat.

'What can I get you?' Carlos asked.

'A pint of bitter would go down nicely. Have you eaten?'

'Not really.' Carlos thought back to the half-eaten greasy bacon butty he'd left a few hours before, pretty certain Henry Cutter would have finished it after he departed the café.

'In which case, I'll have a steak, well done. Can't stand any visible blood. The landlord knows how I like it.'

'Pleased to see you haven't lost your appetite.'

Tony parked himself down at the table while Carlos ordered meals for them both, a bitter for the reporter and another pint of lager for himself. He would sleep in the flat above the office tonight, where he kept spare clothes.

The two men exchanged small talk until they had eaten, after which Tony pushed his plate away and wiped his mouth.

'Let me get you another before we get down to business.' He took Carlos's empty glass to the bar. Three pints were on the cusp of Carlos's limit, so he would sip the one Tony placed down.

'What have you got for me?' Tony's eyes met Carlos's, not the first Carlos had seen today with dark lines underneath them. Despite the enthusiasm, Tony seemed older and more worldly worn.

'It's about Christina Sand.'

'Did she find her boyfriend?'

'He was her boyfriend when they were at university.'

'Was? Is he dead?' Tony took a notepad from his pocket. He was old school and liked to use shorthand when gathering news stories.

'I don't know, but I'm afraid Christina is.'

Tony's brow furrowed. 'We haven't heard of any new bodies, especially a young woman. Did she die out of the area?' Despite the hangovers from the trauma he'd suffered, Tony was still sharp, Carlos was pleased to note.

He shook his head. 'Did you cover the story of the homeless woman found dead at the end of October? Apparently, it only got a paragraph in the paper.' Carlos reiterated what Bethany had told him about the lack of coverage.

Tony whistled. 'Carrie Clark? Yes, we covered it, but what's that got to do with Christina? Are the deaths linked?'

'You could say that. Carrie Clark was Christina Sand. And obviously she wasn't homeless.'

Tony glugged a mouthful of bitter. 'Well, I'll be blown. I didn't see that one coming.'

'Was it you who covered the original story?' Carlos was looking for a fair exchange of information, and Tony was usually a reliable source.

'No, I was writing a piece about a historical Halloween murder. One that was never solved. We were aiming to bring any potential witnesses out of the woodwork.'

'Did it work?'

'Let's just say I've got a few leads. If I get anywhere with them, I'll contact the boys and girls in blue. It was one of my colleagues, Doreen, who covered the homeless woman story. I'll ask to see her notes.'

'So this historical crime was the reason a young woman's death got just one paragraph?' Carlos almost spat the words out, disgusted that the most vulnerable in society were dismissed so readily.

Tony held his hands up. 'Hey. Don't blame me. I don't decide what gets top spot, and like it or not, Carlos, our readership isn't that interested in the latest homeless death. Not compared to the ruthless killing of a teenager, even if it did date back forty years.'

Carlos shook his head.

'Besides that, the woman's death was an accident. We report on them more often than I care to remember.' Tony rubbed his left thigh while taking another drink. 'Even if we'd known the girl was Christina Sand, the story might still only have got a small portion of the front page. But if you're telling me this was police incompetence, I'll make sure we give it the full treatment.'

'And if I tell you it wasn't an accident?'

Tony grabbed his pen again. 'Then we have a much bigger story. Tell me what you know about it.'

Carlos related the same story to Tony as he had to Bethany, but with a few more details. 'I'm working with Fiona Cook – you remember her? We believe Christina Sand pretended to be homeless in order to track down Simeon Vasili. They were an item at university, but it turns out his parents sent him over from the US to befriend the daughter of a competitor.'

'I looked her family up after she tried to get me to write about this Simeon fella, so I know they're bigwigs when it comes to horse racing stock. Why didn't she tell me about this? I could have run with it.'

'Because she was a private person. She only ever shared snippets about herself.'

'Right. Shame, though. She might still be alive if she'd come clean.'

'We don't know if it has anything to do with Simeon yet, but as she used a false name to get into the homeless shelter, and one of your witnesses informs me she saw Simeon in that shelter, we have to assume he's the reason she was there. He's still missing.'

'A person who responded to the ad. I'm slacking.'

Carlos grinned. He knew Tony would break the story now.

'When she died, Christina had bruises to her body consistent with taking a beating a few days beforehand. The senior pathologist has examined the case and believes another bruise to her chest shows someone pushed her to her death.'

Tony stopped scribbling and looked up. 'Is that Tabitha Swinson? I'm guessing she's done a second post-mortem?'

'She would have, but sadly, she can't. The body was released following the coroner's report of accidental death, and as per council policy, she has already been cremated.'

Returning to his pad, Tony chuckled. 'This just gets better and better.'

'Good to see someone's happy about it,' Carlos said cynically.

'I told you last night, I liked this woman, and if my writing the story leads to justice being served, we'll have both done our jobs, and done them well.'

'Just don't embellish it too much, and I don't want to see my name anywhere near your story.'

'You don't want to take credit for finding her true identity? You're a strange one, Carlos.'

'And please, Tony, I'm asking you as a friend: leave the parents alone.'

'What if they don't want to be left alone? This sounds more and more like a complete police shambles. Did your mate Fiona lead the initial inquiry?'

Carlos grinned. 'Now that I don't mind you mentioning. DCI Terry Masters headed up the investigation into the homeless woman's death. I'm sure you'll find more information from your contacts within the police force and at the morgue. The case was opened and closed within twenty-four hours.'

'Now who's embellishing?' Tony laughed, taking another slurp of beer.

'I'll leave you to establish the facts.'

'Is that everything?' Tony asked.

'For now,' said Carlos.

'So there's more? Is Simeon Vasili a suspect?'

'I'm not going to tell you anything about an active inquiry any more than the police will. You've got enough to run with for now. Simeon is a person of interest and we need to find him. Remember, this goes two ways. If you hear anything about Simeon's whereabouts or find out anything else, run it by me before it hits the printed page.'

'I'll get the lowdown on the original story, and if there's anything to add to that, I'll email it over, but I don't think there will be anything earth-shattering in there. That said, Doreen's got a good nose for these things. She might have some thoughts and ideas that didn't get past the editor. If she has, you'll be the first to know.'

Tony bit the tip of his pen. 'So, the ex-boyfriend is still missing? I wonder if she found him and he turned on her—'

Tony was thinking out loud. Carlos could almost see the cogs turning as he mulled over which angle to follow. Carlos didn't want to mention the botched missing-person inquiry just yet, nor his suspicions about something being amiss at the shelter. He also held back on the recruitment of homeless subjects into a research study, not knowing yet how relevant it was. It wouldn't take Tony long to find out about the shelter and Sebastian Crane's involvement with it, but he might also find other leads that would be useful to Carlos and Fiona.

Tony polished off the remains of his beer. 'Thanks, Carlos. I owe you.'

'Just remember that. Keep in touch,' said Carlos.

Watching Tony leave with a slight spring in his step gave Carlos hope that the man's mental recovery would follow that of his body. He still blamed himself for Tony's being run off the road; he'd pointed him in the direction that led to him becoming a target in the first place. For that, he owed the man. Plus, when Tony got the whiff of a good story, his dogged determination knew no bounds, and he had connections everywhere. If anyone could help with this case, should corruption be involved, it would be Tony.

Carlos just hoped he hadn't put the man in danger again.

Chapter 19

Fiona arrived at the fourth floor gasping for breath. Stopping on the stairwell, she leaned against the wall, doubling over. Late or not, she couldn't go into the super's office panting and sweating.

After gathering herself for a few minutes, she moved her hands from her knees and stood upright. The moment she took her first step towards the door, it flew open, almost hitting her in the face. Stunned, she watched a priest descending the steps two at a time, whistling a tune as he went. Fiona scowled after him, tempted to give him a piece of her mind, but held back. He hadn't even noticed the door almost flattening her.

Composing herself, not wanting to waste any more time, Fiona entered the corridor, marching along the carpeted floor until she arrived at the sealed-off bulletproof glass door. She rang the bell, waving at

Superintendent Henley's personal assistant. The door buzzed, and she moved through.

'You're late. They're expecting you.' Clara Fielding wasn't one for small talk at the best of times. The woman presumed that working on the senior floor meant she was above everyone else, especially an *acting* detective inspector. The title always made Fiona feel a fraud.

'Who's they?' Fiona asked. 'I thought I was meeting with Superintendent Henley.'

'You know where it is.' Clara wafted her away with one sweep of the hand.

There wasn't time to argue with the condescending PA. Fiona made her way to the superintendent's office and knocked.

'Come in.'

Fiona entered, and Superintendent Henley gave her a tight-lipped smile.

'At last,' she said.

'I'm sorry I'm late, I was interviewing a—'

Fiona gasped, noticing the man sitting on a chair opposite the super. Confusion filled her head and her heart beat faster.

'Sir? I thought you were on holiday.'

DCI Masters forced a smile. 'I felt, under the circumstances, I should be here, Fiona.'

'What circumstances?' Fiona was trying to work out the time difference between the UK and the Maldives. They were ahead of the UK, so he'd travelled back in time. The flight must have been over ten hours. Who'd had enough time to contact him? It had to be Gary.

Fiona pushed down her anger.

'Take a seat, Fiona,' Henley commanded. 'I'm sure you'll be pleased to have a little help from someone familiar with the homeless case.'

'Except it isn't a homeless case.' Fiona could never hold her tongue. It had been a problem throughout her school and work life, and was why she wasn't sure her position would ever become permanent. She just wasn't a yes-woman.

'Quite,' said Henley, 'but nobody could have known that when the victim was carrying false identification and pretending to be someone else. We all want to sort this case out as soon as possible.'

'Don't worry, Fiona. I won't step on your toes, but it's best if you have someone to bounce ideas off.' Masters sounded relaxed, but he was faking it. Fiona sensed the tension, despite his crisp suit and shiny shoes. He'd clearly had time to get a tan, considering his bronzed face and hands.

'DCI Masters and I have agreed you will continue to be the lead investigator, but I expect you to report to him. It's important we don't let this matter get out of hand. If the press gets wind of it, they'll make it look like police incompetence. I don't need to tell you what sells papers.'

'I think it's too late for that, ma'am. Mr and Mrs Sand were... are... very upset. Their daughter was misidentified and cremated before they returned from their cruise.

Incompetence is exactly what Mrs Sand accused me of when I broke the news this morning.'

Fiona felt petulant. She didn't know whether the Sands would speak to the press or not, but if it became necessary, she would make sure they caused as much of a stir as possible. She would not allow Terry Masters to sweep in on her case and bring it to another poorly investigated conclusion. No doubt that would be his aim.

Henley frowned. 'Perhaps you should speak to the family, Terry. See if you can calm things down a little. If necessary, tell them about the new lead.'

DCI Masters smiled. 'Of course, ma'am.'

'What new lead?' Fiona was being blindsided, and she didn't like it.

Henley turned her gaze on Fiona. 'We'll come to that. First, tell us where you've got to.'

Fiona was reluctant to share too much information with Masters present, but the super left her with no choice.

'As you know, ma'am, Tabitha Swinson suspects that Christina Sand's death was not an accident and doesn't understand why that was the initial conclusion.' Fiona felt the DCI's eyes boring into the side of her head, but continued looking at Superintendent Henley. 'Dr Swinson's convinced of foul play because of a faint bruise on the deceased's chest. This was clear to her from the photos taken at the initial *crime* scene and subsequent post-mortem.'

Fiona's emphasis on the word crime was deliberately aimed at the DCI.

'Dr Swinson believes someone pushed Miss Sand into the foundation dugout. I couldn't dissuade her from making a formal complaint. She's angry that the initial pathologist's findings and concerns didn't appear to have been addressed.'

Fiona paused, noting Masters and the super exchanging eye rolls, but they said nothing. Henley was never going to give the DCI a dressing down in front of her, but any hope that he'd had or would get one melted when she witnessed their shared disdain for the senior pathologist.

'Having confirmed the identity of the victim as Christina Sand, we suspect she went undercover as a homeless person to trace a man.'

'It's always a man, isn't it?' Masters quipped. But he didn't get the response from the superintendent he had been hoping for. She gave him a hard stare.

'And who is this man?' Henley asked.

'His name is Simeon Vasili.' Was that a confident smirk on Masters's face? 'Christina's parents have confirmed he is an ex-boyfriend, but the relationship ended acrimoniously and they haven't seen each other for seven years. Why she chose now to search for him is uncertain. But we have discovered he was seen in the Gracious Heart homeless shelter. It appears a GP enrolled him into a research study, which is headed up by Christina Sand's boss. I've interviewed the GP, Dr Mishka Andreeva. The doctor tells us that once enrolled, these people disappear.'

'Disappear?' Masters scoffed. 'Fiona, I think you're letting your imagination get the better of you. One of the most eminent professors of the modern age leads the research. A man who is striving to find a cure for cancer. Tread carefully with your insinuations.'

'Did the GP use that term specifically?' Henley asked.

'Erm… not specifically, but he doesn't see them at the shelter again after they have enrolled in the study.' Fiona realised from the super and Masters's expressions that she was sounding like a conspiracy theorist. 'I'd like to look into it in more detail.'

'DCI Masters has filled me in on the research study conducted by the Institute for Evolutionary Genetics and Research. Professor Brooker is not to be disturbed, Fiona. Do you understand?'

Fiona's brow furrowed. What did Masters know about the research? She would make it her business to find out.

'I'm sorry I didn't realise that earlier, ma'am. Sergeant Barber and DC Munro have already been to interview the professor this afternoon. I haven't had the chance to speak to them yet to find out what they discovered.'

Masters smirked. 'They went to the university, Fiona, before going on to the institute. I spoke to DC Munro and told him to speak to the deceased's work colleagues, but informed him Professor Brooker was a no-go.'

Blimey! How did he do that so quickly? Fiona's temper was rising. She clenched her fists in her lap.

'He left a message on the dead woman's answering machine, ma'am. Surely we need to speak to him about that. I'll do it myself if you'd rather it be a senior officer.'

'No need,' said Henley. 'I'll be seeing him at a function this evening, along with the chief constable. If there's anything to report, I'll let you know.'

'But ma'am—'

'That's final, Fiona. What else have you found out?'

Fiona forced her emotions into submission. She wouldn't let Masters see how much he had riled her and was determined not to be taken off the case, no matter how much he undermined her.

'Uniform tracked down the anonymous caller. The one who found the body. He's long-term homeless and wouldn't talk to uniform, but Carlos Jacobi was going to speak to him.'

Masters's head shot in Fiona's direction, face puce. Now it was her turn to smirk, albeit inwardly.

'Jacobi? What's he got to do with anything?'

Obviously his spy or spies hadn't told him everything. Fiona ignored Masters and looked at the super.

'He's the private investigator I mentioned. The one the Sands hired to find their missing daughter. If it hadn't been for him, we wouldn't be where we are.' Fiona relaxed for the first time since entering the room. Watching Masters squirm was giving her far more pleasure than it should. She usually tried to work with him in a way that kept them both happy, but she feared this case would put an end to that.

'I take it you're bringing him in on the case?'

'We have no choice, ma'am. The parents insisted he continue to investigate. They don't trust us after what happened.'

Masters stiffened. She was walking on thin ice.

'Besides, better to have him in the fold than working against us from the outside.'

'Yes. You're quite right. Will he be trouble?'

'Not if we play him right,' said Fiona. Masters still didn't know she and Carlos were friends. There were few things she had managed to keep from the DCI, but that was one of them.

'Terry?' Henley said.

'Fiona's right. She can handle him. She's done it before. He might be useful.'

'I can't guarantee he won't speak to the professor, though,' said Fiona.

Henley shuffled papers on her desk. 'I'd appreciate you trying to keep him on a short leash, but without letting him know what you're doing.'

Masters looked smug again. 'We don't think it will be too long before we solve this case anyway.'

'What makes you say that?' Fiona had a feeling she would not like what came next.

'As I mentioned earlier,' the super smiled at Fiona, 'there is a new line of inquiry, and one I'm certain you would have come to yourself. It involves Simeon Vasili, who I'm sure is on your suspect list.'

'The one Miss Sand was obsessed with.' Masters couldn't stop his misogynistic opinions coming to the fore, but he was forgetting himself.

'It's more often men that do the stalking, Chief Inspector.' Henley's tone was terse.

Masters cleared his throat. 'Of course, ma'am. I apologise if I sounded flippant. My enthusiasm for justice gets the better of me sometimes.'

Your enthusiasm for the golf course and your fancy women more like, thought Fiona.

'It turns out a man, who we believe to be Simeon Vasili, was tiring of being pursued by a clingy ex-girlfriend. He threatened to do her harm.' DCI Masters was now in his usual arrogant mode.

Fiona's hands gripped the chair arms. This didn't fit with the conversation she and Carlos had had with Harry Sand that morning.

'We haven't got that impression at all from our initial enquiries. We know she was looking for him and he's a person of interest... where has this information come from?'

'Our source wishes their identity to remain confidential,' said Masters.

'Even from the SIO?' Fiona snapped.

'It's better it remains that way for now.' Henley looked uncomfortable.

'Does this have anything to do with the priest who almost knocked me out on my way up here? I'm guessing he's Father Crane.' Fiona blurted it out, exasperated. She knew she was right even before the exchanged looks between her seniors.

Henley sighed. 'As you know, priests are bound by strict rules of confidentiality, and what's revealed in the confessional is sacrosanct. Father Crane came to us in order to help. He can't be certain the man who shared murderous thoughts was in fact Simeon Vasili.'

'But he as good as told us it was,' said Masters as his phone rang. He checked the screen. 'I'd better take this, ma'am.'

Henley looked at Fiona as if expecting her to leave the room with the DCI, but she stayed put.

'What's on your mind, Fiona?'

'It just seems odd that a priest who was at the crime scene shortly after a body was discovered and who knows DCI Masters well enough to call him there in the early hours of the morning...' Fiona hesitated, '...is now pointing us away from the homeless shelter, which he runs, towards Christina's ex-boyfriend. We've confirmed Simeon was homeless, or pretending to be—'

Fiona hesitated again, not sure how far she could push this.

'Whatever it is, spit it out. I might not like it, but I'll be far less happy if I find something out later which I should know now.'

Fiona looked at the door, which was ajar. She got up and checked the corridor. Masters was having an intense conversation with someone a few feet away, so she closed the door.

Remaining on her feet, she said, 'Christina Sand reported Simeon missing a few weeks before she herself went missing.'

'And?' Henley's stare was intense.

'There's no record of it.'

'What are you implying?'

'Ma'am, there's something strange going on. If I hadn't forced the information out of DC Munro, we wouldn't know there had been a report at all.'

'Was it investigated?'

'According to DC Munro, yes.'

'Who led the investigation?'

'DCI Masters, ma'am. Munro told me they found Simeon safe and well, but there's no evidence to support the claim. The file is missing, and as we've now discovered, he was homeless... well—'

'There's more, isn't there?'

'As I said earlier, the GP we interviewed says he enrolled Simeon into this research study, which I don't yet know much about, and he hasn't been seen since. I believe he went missing around the time we supposedly found him alive and well.'

'There could be an innocent explanation for it. Perhaps he was found, and then went missing again.'

'Yes, ma'am. There could be an innocent explanation, and I'd like to find out if there is.'

Henley's lips were tight as she nodded. 'Go ahead, Fiona, but tread carefully. I don't want us chasing shadows to prove a point. There's nothing yet suggesting any kind of conspiracy. And if you find evidence to support one, you report it to me directly. Do you understand?'

'I do, ma'am.' Fiona wondered whether to mention Simeon's background, but the superintendent had clearly heard enough.

'I'll let you get on with it, then.'

Fiona left the room, determined to find out if there was anything sinister going on at the shelter and what the heck Masters was playing at.

Chapter 20

Masters was still on the phone in the corridor when Fiona stormed past. They gave each other a cursory nod. This would not be easy. Masters had been made to look incompetent, but was it worse than that? Was he somehow involved in a cover up?

Fiona shook the thought from her head. She knew he bent the rules and even broke them to get a result, but lawbreaking and corruption were on different levels. Surely he wouldn't go that far?

The few officers still in the open-plan office-cum-incident-room stopped talking when Fiona entered. She checked the board. Nothing had been added. They were waiting for her.

Munro, Gray, Barber, and PC Barry King turned their chairs around to look at her. Fiona avoided eye contact with Gary Munro lest she say something she might regret. Instead, she looked at Barber.

'What have you got, Hugh?'

'Not a lot. We spoke to a few of Christina's colleagues at the university but they didn't know her at all. She was well respected but only taught one module and didn't hang around. Her colleagues at the institute said the same thing: she was conscientious, dedicated and lived for her work. None of them knew her well, despite her being there for over six years. No boyfriends that they knew about, and no close friends.'

'Except for Bethany, the one who was cat sitting. Did we sort out somewhere for the cat?'

'Yes, ma'am,' Barry chipped in. 'The RSPCA have arranged for it to be looked after in a foster home for the next day or two.'

'Carlos Jacobi thinks her friend Bethany might take it on,' said Fiona. 'So what about enemies, Hugh?'

The sergeant shook his head, holding his hands out. 'None that we could make out. Gary spoke to one of her students.'

Fiona forced herself to eye Gary Munro. 'Well?' she snapped.

'Paul Brand. He's not a student, Sarge. He was her research assistant at the institute. Says she was standoffish, but had a brilliant mind. She wasn't popular, but they admired her.'

'What about professional jealousies? Surely there's some of that in such a competitive environment?'

'That's just it, ma'am,' Hugh interrupted, clearly sensing the tension between Munro and Fiona. 'They all have one purpose, and that is to find a cure for cancer. It's a cohesive team.'

Fiona sighed. *If only that could be said of this one.*

'Ma'am, now that DCI Masters is back, will he be heading up the investigation?'

Fiona glared at Gary. He was audacious, but had played his hand too early. He was well and truly in the DCI's camp.

She ignored him momentarily, taking a few deep breaths while looking at the board. Fiona moved things around, and then turned back to the team.

'As DC Munro has pointed out, the DCI is back from the Maldives. I've just come from a meeting with him and Superintendent Henley. Whilst DCI Masters has cut short his holiday, I'm still the senior investigating officer in this case.

'Hugh, I gather neither you nor Gary could speak to the institute's head today, but the superintendent will talk to Professor Brooker herself this evening. She's attending a function he will be at. As he was Christina's boss and supervisor, we need to establish their relationship.'

'There was no relationship.' Gary muttered this under his breath, but Fiona had acute hearing.

'If you've got something to say, speak up, DC Munro.'

Hugh glared at Munro, who looked at his feet, shaking his head. Fiona was in no doubt it had been Gary who called Terry Masters back from his holiday and the earlier telephone call with the DCI had clearly emboldened him into verging on the subordinate.

Fiona let it go, for now. 'Tell me what you found out about their research study, Hugh.'

'Christina was the senior researcher. Apparently it's part of a doctorate and she was working under Professor Brooker's supervision,' Hugh explained. Fiona added the information to the board.

'Was it her idea to recruit the homeless?' Fiona asked.

Hugh looked at Gary, who shrugged. 'Erm… we didn't ask. The homeless are just one arm of the study, though. There are others.' Hugh checked his notebook. 'They were quite secretive about the research itself, but I spoke to a lab assistant who told me they also recruit refugees and victims of domestic abuse.'

'Good work, Hugh! What I want to know is why the focus is on the most vulnerable in society. Go back there tomorrow and dig deeper. Find out whatever you can about this research. We need to know exactly what it entails and what happens to the participants once they're recruited. Check whether the ones enrolled have family.'

'Are you suggesting there might be something illegal going on?' Hugh asked. Fiona suspected just that, but wasn't ready to share it.

'That's unlikely. They seem like people dedicated to helping humanity, not the opposite.' Munro was almost scoffing.

'However unlikely, DC Munro, we need to investigate. It's what we do. I don't suppose anybody could tell you why their lead researcher took sudden leave?'

'Paul thought it was family trouble,' said Munro.

'The only family she had, her parents, were on a cruise and she phoned them after she disappeared. Did she tell him that, or was he just assuming?'

'Not sure,' said Munro.

'Interview him again tomorrow. Dig a little deeper into his working relationship with Christina.'

'Yes, ma'am.' Munro was grating on Fiona's last nerve, but she would not let him or Masters undermine this investigation.

'Have we found the file on Simeon Vasili?'

'No, ma'am.' This time Barry King answered. 'There is no file.' He gave Munro a quick sideways glance. Barry was a good copper, and she hoped to get him over to CID as soon as there was a vacancy. Which might be sooner than anyone had expected, at the rate Gary Munro was going.

'And I don't suppose we've traced his whereabouts?'

'No, ma'am,' said Kerry. 'Barry's been on it since I got back from our meeting with the GP. Sergeant Barber and I searched Miss Sand's flat like you asked, but found nothing of use. Only the flyers PI Jacobi found. We've sent her phone for analysis and the CSI team will go over the flat again tomorrow. They've agreed to check the initial crime scene too, but don't hold out much hope they'll find anything.'

'They're right there,' Fiona muttered. 'Okay, I've changed my mind. Kerry, you go with Hugh to the institute tomorrow. Gary, you can stay here and write a backdated report on the missing file. Add everything you remember about the case, including where Mr Vasili was purported to be found and what he said when you interviewed him—'

'But the DCI—'

'Let me stop you there, Gary. I hope you're not implying that a senior officer, DCI Masters, failed to write or submit a report. Because if you are, I can ask him to come in here.'

'No, ma'am. That won't be necessary.'

'Make sure you include EVERYTHING about the case, and if there are omissions, detail them so that we can learn from them and discuss them at your next review.'

Fiona hoped she hadn't gone too far in front of the team, but she had to nip any rebellion in the bud before it became more widespread. In a softer voice, she added, 'And I'd like you to find out where Simeon Vasili is now. He was last seen at the homeless shelter and Dr Andreeva informed us he enrolled him in the trial.'

Gary's jaw dropped open. 'Yes, ma'am.'

Fiona spent the next fifteen minutes filling the team in on what she and Kerry had found out from the GP. 'He's hiding something. Before you go out tomorrow, Kerry, check our systems and see if he's ever popped up on our radar. Also, do a background check, including where he got his qualifications and work record. I did a quick check, but contact the University of Liverpool and confirm details. Let's find out everything we can about Dr Mishka Andreeva.'

'Understood,' said Kerry.

'Did you discover anything about the company funding the research? Genomix whatever it was?'

'Genomix Solutions Biotech,' said Kerry. 'I've looked them up, ma'am. They appear to be a legitimate company. They are privately listed, and it's difficult to tell where their funding comes from, but they're not skint.'

Fiona chuckled. 'I'm meeting PI Jacobi after we've finished here. He and I will pay them a visit tomorrow. Where's their head office?'

'Edinburgh. Here's what I printed from their website.' Kerry handed Fiona a thin file.

'Not very thick, is it? Right, team, let's finish up for the day and come at this fresh again in the morning.'

Gary got up immediately, pulled his jacket from the back of his chair, and stomped from the room. Fiona would have a quiet word with him as soon as she got the chance. Whether it was possible to pull him back from the *dark side* or not, she didn't know, but she'd like to try. He'd shown promise before he got in with Terry Masters.

Hugh hung back after the others left. 'What is it, Hugh?'

'I was just wondering why DCI Masters came back from his holiday. Is there anything I should know?'

Fiona studied her sergeant. She'd love to be able to share her concerns, but it wouldn't be right at the moment.

'I think he felt responsible for the case closing, and as he was involved in both the homeless body and the Simeon Vasili missing person, he thought he could be helpful.'

'Right.' Hugh didn't look at all convinced, but he let it drop. She wondered if she should tell him about Father

Crane's visit to the super and what he'd said, but she was sure if she did that, the team wouldn't stay as focused as she wanted them to be. It was important some convenient misdirection did not steer them away from a thorough investigation after what had already happened.

'I'd better get out of here. Jacobi will wonder where I've got to.'

'Are you really going up to Edinburgh tomorrow?' Hugh asked.

Fiona shook her head. 'Thinking about it, I will have to make do with a phone call for now, unless I can find a good reason to go up there. See you tomorrow, Hugh.'

'Ma'am?'

'Yes, Hugh.'

'Cut Gary some slack. Something's going on with him. Maybe he's got relationship problems.'

'See you in the morning.'

Fiona left her sulking sergeant in the office. She knew he would stay for at least another hour, putting the work in. He was desperate for a DI job and it had been hard for her to get him to work with her when she was promoted to act up. Underneath it all, Fiona suspected he was one of the good guys, even if he was bitter and might choose to undermine her at the first opportunity. Problems for another day, she suspected.

Chapter 21

The Corn Exchange was busy, as it always was at this time of night. Carlos bought a bottle of zero per cent lager and found a vacated table to wait for Fiona to arrive. The manager had given him special permission to bring Lady inside ever since Fiona invented a story about her being an assistance dog. She'd told the manager Carlos was diabetic and his dog alerted him to changes in blood sugar. Carlos didn't like lying, but nobody had questioned the story since, so that was an irrelevance. This was one of his preferred places for meeting Fiona, away from prying eyes. The only time the police visited the pub was to arrest people.

Carlos watched Fiona stomp inside and head straight to the bar without even looking at him. She arrived at the table a couple of minutes later, armed with two pints of lager. Lady was put out when Fiona didn't respond to her exuberant welcome.

'Bad day?'

'You could say that.' Fiona gulped a couple of mouthfuls of lager before finally acknowledging Lady. 'Sorry, girl. Good to see you too,' she said, stroking her.

'Perhaps you should start, seeing as you've got more to get off your chest than I have.'

Fiona shook her head as the manager arrived with a well-cooked steak and a plateful of chips. 'I phoned ahead. You go on while I eat. I would have ordered you a meal, but he told me he'd already offered and you said you'd eaten.' She gestured towards the manager. He returned to their table armed with all the condiments he knew Fiona liked, including English mustard.

Carlos watched Fiona squeeze the mustard on her steak, followed by ketchup, salt and pepper. She cut into the steak and stuffed the first chunk into her mouth before looking up with a *don't you dare say anything about my diet* glare.

'Right. Let's start with Father Crane, or Seb, as he likes to be called. I went there after leaving your interesting briefing.'

Fiona scowled into her pint, then continued shovelling down her food.

'From that look, I take it you don't like him. I didn't know you'd met.'

'We haven't. Well, not properly. I'll tell you about that soon. Sorry,' she said, moving her chips around in the ketchup, 'I haven't eaten since breakfast. What did you get from him?'

'Seb is quite the entrepreneur. For a priest, that is. You should see the church.'

'I've passed it when I've driven up that way, but never been inside. It's a bit of an eyesore for where it is, but you can't argue it's not modern.'

'My opinion, for what it's worth, is the man is as sterile as his church.'

'Well, he would be, wouldn't he, being a Catholic priest?'

'Hilarious, except strictly speaking, he would be celibate rather than sterile.'

'Don't get technical. I'm not in the mood.'

'He wasn't much help, to be honest. Said he'd met Christina and believed her to be Carrie Clark. He paid lip service to being sorry about the misidentification, then in the next breath, defended himself. When I asked why he was out at that time in the morning, he said he'd been doing outreach with others from his congregation. The interesting thing is, he either lied or got muddled about a couple of things.'

Fiona wiped her mouth with a napkin and leaned forward. 'What things?'

'For a start, the bit about doing outreach with members of his congregation because they were worried about the homeless. Apparently the weather was dire that night—'

'It was. Trust me.'

'But Henry Cutter told me a priest had pulled up in a car and went straight to the scene. Seb told me he was on foot.'

'Mm. Okay. Although Henry Cutter is homeless, and a drinker from what uniform told me, whereas this priest is a pillar of the community. Why would he lie?'

'I've no idea. He also told me the dead woman carried ID, but according to Henry, she didn't. Both of those things might be explained away, but the most significant thing I got from a different person. Seb didn't mention that Christina argued with the doctor at the shelter, and he – Seb – had her removed.'

Fiona's eyes widened. 'Neither did the doctor. We need to talk to both of them again.'

'I was hoping you'd say that. Guaranteed, Seb knows more about Simeon Vasili than he lets on as well. I showed him the flyer and initially he was vague, but he was twitched.'

Fiona's frown deepened. 'I might as well tell you something that could explain that, although I've been sworn to secrecy. Father Crane has broken his vow of confidentiality and has made allegations that a man, he thinks was Simeon, confessed to wanting to kill a stalking ex.'

'You don't believe him, do you? Not after what Harry Sand said this morning.'

'I'm not inclined to, but it wasn't me he told. You're going to hate this as much as I do. DCI Masters has flown back from his holiday in the Maldives.'

Now it was Carlos's turn to scowl. 'Did your super call him back?'

'No. She wouldn't do that. It has to be DC Munro. I reckon he called him last night after I gave him an ear bashing about Vasili. Something's up there.'

'Worried about being found to be incompetent or something more?' Carlos quizzed.

'It's hard to say. Anyway, no sooner is he back than the priest shows up to tell him and Superintendent Henley this valuable information,' Fiona leaned back in her chair and held her fingers up in air quotes, 'although Father Crane can't swear to knowing it was Simeon in his confessional.'

A mixture of emotions shot through Carlos's body and mind. Past and present turmoil made him feel like he was going to pass out. He shook his head, trying to focus. Fiona's lips were moving, but he couldn't hear what she was saying.

'...So we've been warned off.' Fiona was looking at him.

'Warned off what?'

'Professor Brooker.'

'Sorry, I think my mind must have been elsewhere. Would you mind repeating what you've just said?'

Fiona looked concerned, but did as he asked. 'The super is taking what Father Crane said seriously because of him breaking the sanctity of the confessional. But I argued the case for continuing to investigate the research angle. However, Professor Brooker, who is the leading light of that institute, is off-limits. I'm not allowed to go anywhere near him, and I'm supposed to persuade you to leave him alone as well.'

Carlos grinned. 'But I'm not going to. Right?'

'Right,' said Fiona. 'Christina was the lead researcher, though, and worked under the professor's supervision. The guys spoke to her research assistant, a guy called Paul Brand.'

'Hold it, I've heard that name… just a sec…' Carlos checked his notes from the answerphone in Christina's apartment. 'I expect you know this, but he left a message on her answering machine. Why would he do that if he knew she was on leave?'

'Interesting. No-one's mentioned the answerphone, but they knew you'd checked it, so probably assumed you'd tell me what was on there. I think we can forget the university but I've got Hugh and Kerry revisiting the institute tomorrow. I'll ask Hugh to press Paul Brand. Apparently, they're a strong and cohesive team with no rivalries. I want my officers to push some buttons and see how true that is.'

Carlos grinned again. 'Spoken like a true cynic.'

'I'll tell you what we got from the GP, and then you can give me what else Henry Cutter told you.' Fiona looked brighter after eating, but he could sense she was worried about her team. Or, more likely, Masters.

'Remind me to tell you about the girl I met at the shelter, and about Bethany.'

Fiona nodded. 'Okay. Now this GP, Dr Mishka Andreeva, was definitely rattled by the time we left. We started slowly by telling him about the dead woman from the shelter being misidentified.'

'You said he admitted attending the scene that night?'

'Yes, he did. Sounds like the whole of Leicester attended that scene apart from me. Masters made sure of that.' Fiona scowled once more, swigging back a mouthful of lager. 'Anyway, Dr Andreeva is paid to enrol people in the research study into... guess what?'

'Something to do with genetics?'

'Clever clogs. Spot on. They're looking for a treatment that will prevent cancer from developing in the future. He says the homeless are a population at high risk of developing cancer because of their lifestyle.'

'I would have thought cancer would be the least of their worries,' said Carlos.

'How do you mean?'

'They're more likely to die from starvation, hypothermia, tuberculosis, heart attacks, liver disease, violence—'

'Okay, I get the message. How do you know all this stuff?'

'Julie did a bit of background research on the topic of homelessness. I picked up her notes when I popped back to the office to feed Lady. They made interesting reading while I was waiting for you to arrive. Do you want to see?'

'Ask Julie to send me a copy, will you? What you say makes sense. So, why the interest in the homeless?'

Carlos took a sip of his zero lager and pushed the glass Fiona had bought away. He looked at her across the table. She had bags under her eyes from sleepless nights, and looked worn out.

'I don't know. It's odd,' he said. 'But it's not just the homeless they recruit. It's the young homeless with no living relatives, or none who care about them.'

'Just what I suspected. I knew there was something iffy about that research. Hugh discovered they also recruit refugees and battered women into the study. The GP neglected to mention them, unless he doesn't know. He told us that once the subjects are enrolled, he doesn't see them again. They get referred to the institute and disappear.'

'Where to?'

'When pressed, he said they are offered compensation for their participation, food and a place to stay, but he wouldn't reveal where the subjects go to. He said he didn't know. What worries me is Christina's involvement in the research.'

Carlos slapped his head. 'She must have known they enrolled Simeon. Why go looking for him?'

'That's the confusing part. My working theory is maybe he left the trial and went back on the streets. That's if he was homeless at all. I tell you what, Carlos, my head's spinning with it all.'

'Something about Simeon's homelessness doesn't sit right. What if he's not in the study at all, but part of something illegal?'

'In which case, the good Father might be right about his malicious intent.' Fiona looked deflated.

'What did Christina's colleagues say about her?'

'Nothing we don't know already. Those at the university hardly knew her at all and, according to those at the institute who she worked with most, she kept her personal life to herself. As we know, both Christina and Simeon came from wealthy backgrounds. I'm going to phone his parents in the US when I get back to the boat tonight. It's afternoon over there. They might know where their son is. Did I mention this research was for Christina's PhD?'

'What have you discovered about her past? Would she get involved in anything dodgy?'

'Not on the face of it. No criminal record, that's for sure. It's hard to dig deeper when Professor Brooker is her supervisor and I'm not allowed to go anywhere near him.'

'Leave that to me. He's gone to the top of my list. Is it the institute that's funding the research?'

'No. It's a company called Genomix Solutions Biotech. Kerry thinks they're legit. I'm going to call them up in the morning and see what they can tell me about it.'

'Why not visit?'

'Because the head office is in Edinburgh and I can't take the time out to travel up there without justification. Besides, I don't know what Masters would get up to in my absence.'

'Fair enough. I'd better warn you the case will hit the local paper tomorrow. If it gets any murkier, or if Christina's parents get a nod from us, it might even hit the nationals.'

Fiona smirked. 'That's exactly what Superintendent Henley and Masters didn't want to happen. I'm glad. It should shake a few branches. We'll see what falls. Is this because you spoke to your mate Tony Hadden? Personally, I avoid him like an infectious disease, but he's got people in the force who tip him off.'

'Not any of those in Masters's circle, though, or Tony would have known about the Simeon cover up.'

'How much did you tell him?'

'Just about the mix-up with Christina's identity and it being a murder inquiry. I didn't mention the research or the shelter, but it won't be long before he finds out. He also knows Vasili is still missing and is a person of interest. He'd already looked her family up when Christina first contacted him. It won't take him long to find Simeon's, but he might also track him down before we do. I've asked him to keep me in the loop.'

'I'll make that call as soon as I get home. One more thing. I got the super's ear for five minutes without Masters, which is why she's given me the go ahead to keep looking into the GP and the shelter. We've also got a bit of latitude with Father Crane, but I'm to inform her if I find any signs of corruption.'

'Makes sense,' said Carlos. He took a sip of lager before leaning forward to drop his bombshell. 'I mentioned a young woman I spoke to at the shelter. We have to be careful moving forward, Fiona. Your sergeant mentioned someone from vice telling him about a new player... he's right. Nicolae has got links to that shelter and the doctor.

My witness has seen him there, talking to Andreeva. It wouldn't surprise me if he's not in bed – figuratively speaking – with Seb as well, seeing as he runs the place. She's seen a man answering Nicolae's description leaving with people from the shelter... including Simeon.'

Fiona exhaled, closing her eyes. Carlos knew just how she felt. Was Simeon a victim or a player?

Chapter 22

Henry felt as if his life was worth something for the first time in years. That Carlos fella had treated him as an equal, worthy of respect. It had been a long time since anyone saw him as an actual man and paid attention to what he said, and it filled him with a longing for more.

Sharing stories with an ex-army man reminded him of his better self. Maybe, if he tried real hard, he might be able to reclaim his life and get off these filthy streets, hold his head high again. Might even see his son one day if he got it together enough.

Where to start? The question haunted him now like a cynic, waiting to drag him down. It was all right feeling like he could start over while his stomach was full and he had money in his pocket, but experience had taught him it wouldn't last long without a job or a purpose. He'd soon be sucked back to the same place he had been in before he met Carlos and his beautiful Lady. That dog knew how to treat people, just like her owner.

Mourning the loss of his wife, Lori, had driven him to bury trauma in alcohol. He'd been running away for so long, hiding his grief, but all it did was numb the pain for a little while.

As he shuffled along the High Street, people gave him a wide berth. He didn't blame them. At one time, he would have done the same thing, and he certainly wouldn't have let Lori and Ben anywhere near the likes of him as he was now.

Henry stopped in the middle of the street, his chest tight, heart aching for the love he once had. His parents would say his beloved Lori was in heaven. Was she? Henry's hand moved over his eyes and all the pain returned. His other hand felt the money Carlos had given him inside his pocket, and he looked across the road to the off-licence. It was icy cold again as he clutched his threadbare coat closer like a comfort blanket. Maybe a bottle of whisky would help.

Henry's feet moved on autopilot towards the shop, but then he stopped suddenly, allowing himself to recall his wife's dying words. He had been sitting at her bedside, sobbing inwardly, but his eyes were filled with anger at God who was about to take the love of his life away. The doctor had given her morphine and told him she wouldn't last the night.

Henry was holding her hand when she stirred. She had opened her eyes and looked directly at him with a clarity that shocked him.

'Henry, please don't die with me,' she pleaded. 'Promise me you'll find happiness again.'

His eyes had locked onto hers. 'I promise,' he'd lied.

Henry's heart ached with the pain of his grief, no matter how much time passed since that dreadful night. Every time he thought of Lori, he felt an overwhelming guilt for not keeping his promise to her. But tonight, something in him stirred differently as he stood outside the off-licence door.

His memory switched to the night he found the body of that young woman. He'd suspected at the time someone had done her in, and he was pretty convinced Carlos thought the same. Henry exerted all his willpower and turned his back on the off-licence. He looked up into the dark sky, his thoughts turning heavenwards.

'I promise, Lori. I'll try.' It was empowering, speaking to his wife after all these years.

Henry headed towards the shelter with a new determination. He was going to help Carlos find out who killed Christina Sand, the angel with the beautiful red hair. Henry hoped she was in heaven now too. If she was, he was sure Lori would welcome her with open arms.

He was lost in happy memories as he approached St Nicholas Circle. A van screeched to a halt, forcing him to stop. He was about to give the driver a mouthful when the side door opened and two men wearing balaclavas pulled him inside. Someone closed the door, and the van sped off. He tried to fight, but even with a full stomach, he was weak and easily overpowered.

One of the brawny men forced a hood over his head. Memories of a similar abduction in Bosnia came flooding back, but instead of cowering in fear like he normally would, he remembered he had survived then. Whatever was going on here, he would survive again.

'What are you doing?' he yelled through the hood while the van kept moving.

'Shut up.' The voice was deep and menacing. He could hear two more men speaking in the front and listened.

'We've got him,' one said.

'You know what to do.'

The idiot was talking on a car phone with the speaker on. It gave Henry hope; he was dealing with muscle rather than brains.

The van drew to a halt, and the side door opened again. The occupants dragged Henry out into the freezing cold night, and he heard bigger doors being slid open. He was pushed forward, and the doors slid closed behind him.

Someone pulled the hood from his head. He blinked a few times, trying to work out where he was. It was a warehouse.

'Get the lights,' one man barked. Big and threatening, he was clearly in charge. There were five of them. Too many to even attempt to fight. Henry's heart raced in his chest. 'Take him in there.'

Someone shoved him again, propelling Henry into a room at the far end of the warehouse. The men pulled his coat and shirt off before forcing him into a chair. They then prowled around like hyenas checking their prey. If they were trying to be intimidating, they were succeeding.

'What do you want with me?' he asked, searching for the confidence he'd had in the van.

'We'll ask the questions. You'll give the answers. That's how this works.' The man in charge stood near the door.

'Ask about what?'

Henry doubled over as a fist hit him full in the stomach. He was winded.

'Have you got trouble wiv yer hearing? He told you we ask the questions.' It was a short, stocky man who had thrown the first punch. Henry was in no doubt more would follow.

'What did you tell the PI?'

'Who?' Henry felt another punch, this time to his ribs. He and the chair fell backwards.

'Carlos Jacobi. What did he want with yer?' another of the thugs asked. Henry was trying to think, to remember his army training, but his thoughts were jumbled from years of alcohol abuse. A kick came while he considered his response. Then the men dragged him up from the floor.

'He was looking for yer. Bought yer a meal even. Why would he do that?' An elbow slammed down on his back.

'Okay, okay,' Henry groaned in pain. 'He was asking about a girl I found dead at the Jewry Wall.'

'What did you tell him?' the leader asked.

'Just that I found her in the grounds and phoned the police.'

'What else?'

'There was nothing else. I don't know anything about it.'

Henry took a few more blows before the leader spoke again.

'Did he ask about anyone in particular?'

'Like who?' Henry dodged one punch, but the second and third got him.

'Don't get clever with us. We can do this all night. If you answer our questions, we might just let you go back to your miserable life.'

Henry figured that if someone had seen him with Carlos, they would have seen the PI show him the flyer.

'He asked if I recognised a guy,' Henry said.

'Name?'

'Simeon, I think. It's hard to remember.'

'Perhaps we can help you,' the stocky guy said, throwing a few more punches at him. Henry gasped, falling backwards. He closed his eyes. The man shook him, but he remained floppy.

'Passed out, boss.'

'Let's get some coffee, and then we'll throw a bucket of cold water over him. It stinks in here.'

Henry heard the door slam shut and the click of a lock as the men left. He waited a minute or two, his heart pulsating in his ears as he forced his battered body off the floor.

There was no time to waste. He had surveyed the room when they brought him in. There was a window high up, near the ceiling. Henry used every ounce of strength he had to move an old computer table. It was on wheels, but one of them squeaked so he had to lift that side off the floor. His ribs screamed in pain every time he did so, but adrenaline came to his rescue.

Henry grabbed his coat and used a chair to climb onto the table, thanking God when it took his weight. The windowsill was chest height. Taking a deep breath, and knowing he would only get one shot at this, he hauled his body up, pushing the hinged window upwards to open it. He clambered over the sill and looked down. It was a sheer drop and would hurt, but it was doable.

Anchoring himself to the sill with one hand, Henry was beginning to lower himself down when his grip slipped and he fell. He hit the pavement with an agonising crack, pain shooting through his right ankle.

There was no time to think about the agony he was in. Henry had to get away. Gritting his teeth, he hobbled and hopped from the building, but he would not get far like this, not with the men likely to return to the room at any minute.

Henry spied a red rubbish skip and scrambled inside. He buried himself beneath a musty, wet old mattress and waited.

Loud shouting and running footsteps echoed on the surrounding street. His heart pounded wildly in his chest. When one of the men leaned against the skip while lighting up a cigarette, he stopped breathing.

'Have you checked that?' Henry heard another ask. He was convinced the smoking man was going to hear his heartbeat and lift the mattress.

'Just gonna do it now,' the smoker answered gruffly. Henry saw the shadow of a hand reach into the skip and in an instant withdraw again as the man cursed under his breath.

'Nothing in there,' he said. 'But I'm gonna need stitches now.'

'Come on. Let's go.'

The footsteps retreated into the distance and Henry allowed himself to breathe, though he still didn't dare move from his hideaway. He closed his eyes, waiting.

Then everything went black.

Chapter 23

It seemed like minutes since Carlos closed his eyes. He had mulled over everything Fiona had told him before going to sleep, but woke in the middle of the night, worried about the Edinburgh link. Was it coincidence that a firm that might be funding dodgy research was based in Edinburgh?

That on its own wouldn't have concerned him. It was the fact that Nicolae was also in the mix. From what Fiona had told him about Seb's revelation and his contact with Masters, he couldn't rule the DCI out of being a part of the ugly position Christina Sand had found herself in. Did she uncover something that wasn't meant to be found? Is that why she took leave and pretended to be homeless? But had the GP not met her before? It was possible he hadn't visited the institute where she worked. Did he tell someone about her and her questions? Did Seb?

Fiona was convinced the doctor wasn't the killer, and Carlos trusted her instinct, but the GP was mixed up in something. Why else would he have been angry when Christina asked questions? If this was a conspiracy of some sort, it would take some unpicking.

Those were the thoughts that had consumed Carlos during the night, but in the chill of the morning, he wondered if he was letting his imagination run away with him. Perhaps he wanted Masters to be involved so he could finally put his own demons to rest. He couldn't get the man for the death of his friend; he would be glad of an excuse to get him for something else.

'That might be it, Lady.'

Lady was already looking at him, eyes boring deep into his soul. It was as if she felt his pain. He pulled himself together and went downstairs to let her out while filling her bowl with fresh water. A jog would help clear his mind.

It was 6am when Carlos and Lady headed onto the Leicester streets, but they didn't get far. Police sirens raced past him and Fiona's car pulled up.

'Get in.'

Carlos and Lady climbed in. Minutes later, they were at the Jewry Wall Museum.

'Stay in the background,' Fiona commanded. She walked over to where her sergeant, DS Hugh Barber, was standing, illuminated by floodlights. A woman Carlos assumed to be the pathologist was kneeling over a corpse. They looked in Carlos's direction, but Fiona said something and they carried on with their work.

Carlos saw Henry Cutter hiding in the shadows of St Nicholas Walk. The veteran motioned for him to join him. Carlos and Lady strolled over.

'Found another one,' the older man said. 'It could have been me.'

'Who is it?' Carlos asked.

'Don't know his name. Someone who goes to the shelter.'

Carlos handed Henry his bottle of water. 'It's clean,' he said.

Henry glugged the fluid down in seconds and wiped his mouth with the back of his hand. 'Thanks.'

'You stuck around this time.'

'Yeah. I ain't got nothing to hide. Besides, I'm not feeling so good.'

Henry burst into a coughing fit, clutching his ribs. His face looked paler than when they'd spoken the day before. Once he stopped coughing, he staggered back against the church fence.

'Let me get you to a doctor,' Carlos said.

'No. I don't want no doctor. Don't trust 'em, not after the wife died.'

Carlos gripped his shoulder, and Henry winced. Under the moonlight, he noticed the older man's bruised eyes.

'My office is just up the road. Let's go and have a chat while I make you some breakfast.'

'Now you're talking,' said Henry.

'I'll just let my friend know where we're going. She'll want to talk to you.'

Henry buckled under the weight of his emaciated body, sinking down into a crouch. Fiona was in deep conversation with the woman who had been examining the body.

'Are you sure?' she was asking when Carlos joined them.

'I won't be sure until I've run some tests and done a post-mortem, but that's what it looks like.'

The woman looked up and Fiona turned around.

'Tabitha, this is Carlos Jacobi. He's the PI I told you about.'

'I'd shake hands,' said Tabitha, 'but as you can see—'

Carlos smiled, acknowledging the white suit and gloved hands. 'I'm taking Henry to my office for some breakfast. He's not in a good way. Been in a fight, I think.'

'I'll come with you,' said Fiona. 'Thanks, Tabitha. See you later. Hugh, make sure we seal this place off, will you?'

'Yes, ma'am. What then?'

'Leave an officer in charge here, and you and Kerry get to the institute as soon as it opens. We need details of that research.'

'What's with all the lights?' Carlos asked.

'Floodlights left by a film crew. I think they were planning to pack up today, but they won't get in here for a while.'

'I know it's not far, but I don't think he's going to be able to walk.' Carlos inclined his head to where Henry was still crouching.

'Shouldn't we get him to the hospital or something?' Fiona asked.

'He doesn't trust doctors.'

'After the one I met yesterday, I'm not surprised. Let's get him to my car and see how he goes.'

Carlos and Fiona supported Henry into the passenger seat of Fiona's Mini. 'We'll run,' said Carlos. 'I'll get there around the same time as you take to drive.'

'Okay.' Carlos saw Fiona wrinkle her nose up at the odour when she got in the car, but she was kind enough not to open the window. Henry was cold enough.

'Come on, Lady. We're on foot.' Carlos began the jog back to the office. He had been right. Fiona was just pulling into the carpark at the back when they got there. He unlocked the building and headed straight for the kitchen to put the kettle on before returning to help Fiona bring Henry in. Putting aside his desire for cleanliness and order, Carlos settled Henry into one of the easy chairs where he had met the Sands only a couple of days before.

He returned to the kitchen and found eggs and bread in the fridge. Carlos took a plateful of fried egg on toast and handed it to the veteran. As the man's odour hit him, he told himself he'd had to put up with a lot worse than this in the field, so it wouldn't kill him to treat it as one of those situations.

Fiona grinned. 'That smells good. Have you got any more? I didn't get time for breakfast.'

Carlos raised an eyebrow, but realised Henry wouldn't be able to talk for a bit while wolfing his breakfast down.

'Coming right up.'

'I'll give you a hand.' Fiona followed him out to the kitchen while Lady snuggled up to Henry, sensing he needed comfort.

'Henry told me the body was someone from the shelter,' Carlos said, pouring coffee and preparing Fiona breakfast at the same time.

'Makes sense. Does he know him?'

'I don't think so, said he didn't know the guy's name.'

'Ray Sylvester. First he finds Christina, now this.' Fiona appeared momentarily sceptical.

'How did he die?'

'It looks like suicide. There was a note.'

'What did it say?'

'Sorry about the girl,' Fiona said as she took the plate of food from him. Carlos grabbed three mugs of coffee and they joined Henry.

'Are you saying this guy was supposed to have killed Christina, and then, filled with remorse, killed himself?'

'That's what it looks like, but—' Fiona looked at Henry before saying anything else. He had finished his breakfast and was leaning back in the chair with his eyes closed. 'Tabitha thinks someone staged it to look that way.'

'Another murder?'

Fiona nodded. 'She's not certain yet, but she believes he was held down shortly before death.'

'That he was,' said Henry.

They both stared at him, Fiona's eyes wide. 'What makes you say that?'

Henry leaned forward and drank his coffee in two glugs. 'Carlos, help me get this coat off, will yer?'

Carlos did as requested and was horrified to see the bruises on Henry's torso underneath the coat. 'Where's your shirt?' He had been wearing one yesterday.

'Dunno. When the lowlifes weren't looking, I grabbed my coat and got away.'

'Let me get some soap and water,' said Carlos. 'We'll get you cleaned up and into some fresh clothes while you tell us about it.'

Carlos bathed Henry's torso while the older man explained what had happened.

'A few hours, maybe later, after I spoke to you yesterday, these guys grabbed me off the street and put me in the back of a van. They drove me to a warehouse and gave me a beating.'

'Why?' Fiona asked.

'They wanted to know what Carlos asked me and what I told him.'

'What did you tell them?' Carlos had finished bathing Henry, with the older man wincing every so often. He couldn't get him clean without pressing too hard, but did the best he could. Henry took the towel from him and patted himself dry.

'I told 'em I couldn't remember, but they started punching me. Played ignorant for a bit, but they weren't having it. All I told them was that you were asking about the dead woman. I figured from what they said that someone had seen us at the café, so I told them about the flyer. Anyway, they laid into me for a bit longer, and I pretended to pass out. Army training kicking in.'

He winked at Carlos, who understood it was an excellent tactic when being interrogated.

'They locked me in a room and went to get a cuppa. I grabbed my coat and got outta there through a window. Thanks to my full belly from the food you gave me, I had just about enough energy to get away. I hid in a red skip because I couldn't walk very well.' Henry laughed.

'Then what?'

'They almost found me, except one of them cut his hand on some broken glass in the skip. Soon after, they left. Must have fell asleep in there for a bit. When I woke, I climbed out and hobbled to me secret spot. It's where any of us go when there's trouble or police around.'

He looked at Fiona.

'So, how did you end up finding the body?' Fiona asked while Carlos rubbed arnica cream into Henry's bruises. It might be too late, but it was better than nothing.

'What time is it?'

Carlos checked his watch. 'Coming up to 8am, why?'

'I had to give her time to get away. Persuaded her to go home.'

'Who?'

'The girl who found him. She spotted him with a fella who she recognised, says you were asking about him.'

Carlos felt sick. 'The girl at the shelter. Was it Simeon?'

'She didn't say. Told me she followed them to see where they was going, like, and she was going to tell you, Carlos.

Said you paid well, but once they got to the museum, things turned bad.'

'What happened?' Carlos asked, helping Henry into a clean t-shirt and jumper.

'Five goons turned up in a van. I reckon it was the same ones who got me. The first fella left them to it, and then it was as she said.' Henry nodded his head at Fiona. 'They did him in. Real quiet like, not a bit like the roughing up they gave me. Once they left, she went over to see if she could help the guy, but it was too late. They must have given him something. She came to the safe spot and found me. A right state she was in too. I told her she had to get out of Leicester and go back to her parents. That as soon as she was gone, I'd call you lot.' He looked at Fiona again.

'I'm going to need to speak to this girl,' said Fiona.

'Yeah. She knows that, but it needs to be in secret or you won't get anything out of her. She'll trust Carlos.'

'And you're staying here until we find out who attacked you,' said Carlos. 'There's a flat upstairs.'

'I'd argue the toss, but I think me ankle's broke.' Carlos had been so busy dealing with the bruises he hadn't examined the rest of Henry's body. He looked down and noticed Henry wasn't wearing a shoe on his right foot. The ankle was inverted.

'We need to get that X-rayed and set. I'll deal with this, Fiona. You do what you've got to do. Once he's sorted, we'll meet up again.'

Carlos walked Fiona to the back door. 'I can't keep this to myself for long,' she said, 'but I'll buy us some time while you get him to safety.' She reached into her mac and pulled out her phone, showing him a photo. 'This is the dead guy. Did you meet him?'

Carlos swallowed a hard lump in his throat. 'I spoke to him. Fiona, people are getting killed and attacked because of me.'

'You can't blame yourself. We need to stay focused. Sort Henry out. You know he can't stay here. They'll find him.'

'I've got an idea about that.'

'Which is?'

'The less you know, the better. Then you won't be compromised.'

Carlos watched Fiona get into her car and leave. He needed to hurry if he was going to get Henry out before Julie arrived. He picked up the phone and dialled.

Chapter 24

Masters and Gary Munro were huddled together in a corner of the incident room when Fiona arrived. The DCI looked up when he saw her, his face red with anger.

'My office,' he commanded, walking out.

If he expected her to follow like an obedient dog, he was mistaken. Fiona would have loved to wipe the smirk off Gary's face as he waltzed back to his desk with confidence, but instead, she moved to the board and made a few changes, writing up the name of the latest victim. Satisfied she had taken enough time to regain her composure, she headed out.

Terry Masters barely acknowledged her when she knocked and entered his office. It was minimalistic. *Like his work*, thought Fiona, grinning inwardly.

'Take a seat,' he said.

Fiona sighed, but did as requested.

'What's going on, Fiona? Why have we got two detectives wasting their time at the institute again when it's obvious this homeless man, Ray Sylvester, killed Christina Sand and then took his own life? She was obviously a nuisance to men, just as—'

'Father Crane predicted,' Fiona finished. 'Perhaps we should employ him for his divination skills, then we could get all our crimes solved within a week. Except it wasn't Simeon Vasili whose body we found.' Her voice dripped with sarcasm, even though she knew she should hold her tongue.

'Look, Fiona. Swallow your pride. I know you like to do things your way, but it's time to accept the case is solved. The guy left a note. You've got your killer. Case solved; you should be pleased. I'll even credit your work with the super.'

Fiona swallowed down her anger, but stared him in the eye. 'Thank you, but I'm sorry, sir, that two young people are dead. I find nothing pleasing about that.'

'Don't take things so literally; you know what I mean. We can tick another case off. We've got enough unsolved cases on the books. Call DS Barber and DC Gray back, Fiona, and let's move on.'

'I can't do that, sir.'

The friendly smile disappeared from Masters's face as he glared at her. 'Be careful. You're treading a thin line here.'

'I'm not trying to be difficult, sir, but it appears Mr Sylvester was murdered. Tabitha believes he was held down prior to death, and most likely injected with opiates to make it look like a suicidal overdose.'

'But the note?'

'I'm assuming the killer, or killers, wanted us to stop investigating and fabricated it. Printed words on a page are all we have. I'll find out more when I've been to the post-mortem.'

Masters swallowed hard. His Adam's apple bobbed above his starched collar and tie. The snake's head of his neck tattoo peeped out above the collar threateningly.

'Munro said the man's death was suicide.'

'I don't know how DC Munro could know anything about it. He wasn't at the scene. DS Barber and a few uniformed officers were with me.'

'Hugh must have filled him in.'

I doubt that, thought Fiona, because Hugh was well aware of Tabitha's findings. There was a leak coming from somewhere, maybe one of the uniformed officers who had attended before she arrived.

'Anyway, I'd better get on with the briefing. I can update the others when they get back from the institute. The case has just become even more complicated. Is there anything else, sir?'

'Yes, there is. I expect you've considered this Cutter bloke as a suspect. It hasn't escaped my notice he found both bodies.'

Fiona wanted to laugh in his face, having seen the state of Henry this morning. 'An eyewitness saw the victim with a man, and a short time later, five more men appeared who killed him.' She knew she'd have to come clean about her witness later or suffer the consequences, but she didn't want to mention the young woman yet. She crossed her fingers behind her back. Normally, Fiona would enjoy the confusion which was causing her DCI to falter, but she was well aware of how dangerous he could be when riled. A wounded wild animal was far more lethal than a healthy one.

'Cutter?'

That's exactly what she'd wanted him to think right now. 'He told me and Jacobi what happened.'

'How come Jacobi knows about this before I do?'

'He was jogging past the scene, sir, and offered to take Mr Cutter back to his office. It's just around the corner from the museum. I couldn't refuse. The man could barely stand. It's freezing out there.'

'Right. But Cutter could be lying to cover his tracks. Where is he now?'

Fiona again wanted to laugh at the idea of the frail Henry Cutter being involved in either murder, but she was worried about him and the real eyewitness. Heavies had already beaten Henry half to death. What would they do to the young woman who had actually witnessed the murder if they found out about her?

'He gave us the slip, sir.'

Masters looked incredulous. 'Seriously? How?'

'Jacobi and I were discussing what to do next when he slipped out of the back door. I'm sorry, that's on me.'

'Well, he can't have gone far. Who's looking for him? And don't tell me it's Carlos Jacobi.' The DCI's voice had risen several decibels.

'No, sir. When I get back to the incident room, I'll get uniform onto it.'

'Fine. Keep me informed.'

Fiona got up and headed for the door.

'And Fiona?'

'Yes, sir.'

'Focus your resources on the homeless community, or consider the fact some yobs might have got it in for them, rather than upsetting important people. Maybe Father Crane's right about Simeon Vasili, and he killed them both.'

'I can just about see a motive for the first murder, but not the second,' said Fiona.

'Misdirection, Fiona. Misdirection.'

On that, we agree, she thought. 'I'd better get on, sir.' Fiona knew exactly where she would focus the team's resources.

Munro was lolling over a female officer's desk with a mug in his hand when Fiona got back to the incident room. He hadn't seen her enter, despite the PC trying to warn him with her eyes.

Fiona tapped him on the shoulder. He jumped, spilling hot liquid down his shirt.

'Ma'am?'

'Oh, I'm sorry, Gary. Did I startle you? I was just wondering if you've got that report for me.'

The DC was still trying to wipe coffee stains from his clean shirt with tissues taken from the PC's desk. 'I didn't think it was important now we solved the case, ma'am.'

'It's more important than ever since we're treating the body we found this morning as another murder.'

Fiona noticed a slight smirk on the PC's face as Gary squirmed.

'Murdered? I thought it was suicide.'

'Why would you think that? Did I miss you at the crime scene this morning?'

'Erm... No, I heard—'

Fiona leaned in. 'Whatever you heard, Gary, you heard wrong. We don't deal in hearsay here, we deal in facts, and good old-fashioned evidence. Now, I'll leave you to get on with that report.' She raised her voice. 'Can I have your attention, please?'

The other officers stopped what they were doing and moved their chairs, following her towards the incident board.

'This morning, we found the body of another homeless man called Ray Sylvester in the grounds of the Jewry Wall Museum.' Fiona hesitated, watching Masters enter and lean against the wall. He nodded for her to continue.

'CSIs are on the scene now, and Tabitha Swinson, our senior pathologist, attended first thing. She believes this second death is also suspicious. When I've finished here, I'll head over to the infirmary for the post-mortem. We have a witness who saw the attack and reported it, but that witness has gone missing.'

Fiona crossed her fingers behind her back again, hoping that Carlos had found an exceptionally safe place to conceal Henry.

'I need uniform to track down a homeless man called Henry Cutter. Barry, I think it was you who found him before?' She hated wasting a good PC's time, but there was no choice.

'I'll find him, ma'am.'

'Let me know when you do.' Fiona looked at Masters before adding, 'Prior to giving us the slip, Henry said he took a beating yesterday evening after speaking to the private investigator, Carlos Jacobi. He reported being bundled into a white van with a side-opening door and taken to an abandoned warehouse somewhere near Charles Street. Cutter said five men wearing black balaclavas beat him up. They wanted to know what he had told Jacobi.'

Fiona paused to let the new information register and looked at Masters again. 'Of course, he could be making it up and sending us off on a wild goose chase, but for now, I'm taking his allegations seriously because he was badly bruised when Jacobi and I spoke to him. Please find the warehouse where he says they held him. Mr Cutter hid in a red skip containing broken glass with an old mattress on top. Does anyone know which firm uses red skips?'

The officer Munro had been trying to impress raised her hand. 'That'll most likely be Glenfield Ltd. Their skips are red.'

'Good. Get on to them, will you, and find out locations of their skips in that area? That should help narrow it down a bit.

'Once you find the warehouse, seal it off, don't disturb anything, and call me. If what Mr Cutter says is true, the same five men who beat him up killed Ray Sylvester. We need to find them, and the other man Mr Sylvester was seen talking to before they arrived.'

Nods around the room. Masters gave her a brief nod and left. She continued the briefing, explaining that they should follow all leads.

'Barry, I need you to find out more about Gracious Heart House, its visitors, and occupants. The rest of you interview as many people who visit the place as possible. I want to know everything about that shelter. And Barry, also get me a list of the volunteers who work there with full names and addresses. DS Barber and DC Gray will continue with the institute angle, where Miss Sand led research involving homeless and other vulnerable recruits. DC Munro is following up on Simeon Vasili and his last known whereabouts. I spoke to Vasili's father last night, and he said the family haven't heard from him in six months.'

Fiona had been suspicious when Simeon's father hadn't seemed in the slightest bit concerned about his son being seen in a homeless shelter, something she wanted to discuss with Carlos when she got the chance.

'We'll meet again at 4pm, but if you find anything in the meantime, call me.'

A flurry of activity followed with officers leaving to get on with their tasks. Fiona headed out, satisfied she had got the team following all angles. Now it was up to her to contact the biotech company before attending the post-mortem. She and Carlos would speak to the actual witness once Henry told Carlos where she was, and he himself was safe.

Chapter 25

'Where to?' Carlos had picked Fiona up from outside the main entrance of the Leicester Royal Infirmary.

'I've got the address of a warehouse where we think they took Henry after his abduction. Here's the postcode.'

Carlos took the piece of paper from Fiona and tapped the postcode on to his Sat Nav. They drove in silence while Fiona fired off a few text messages to members of her team. Eventually, she spoke.

'Tabitha confirms the second death is also murder. It was a clumsy attempt at staging it to look like a suicide. She's sent blood and saliva away for toxicology, but from the needle mark on his arm, she's pretty sure they gave him a heroin overdose. These guys are idiots. Ray Sylvester wasn't a user, so how would he get hold of that amount of heroin, or know what to do with it if he could?'

'That's what Henry told me after you left us this morning. It's good because they're so clumsy, they can't control themselves, hence the bruising to both victims. And even better – if Nicolae is the guy who gave the order, he's starting to make mistakes.'

'Or he's so arrogant because he's got Alastair *The Crooked* McTavish behind him and thinks he's untouchable.'

Carlos considered what Fiona had said and hoped she was right. If so, Nicolae was making himself catchable.

'I wonder if one or all of those five guys roughed up Christina before she died, to warn her off. Both murders seem to be hurried last-minute decisions, rather than well thought-out.'

'I was wondering the same thing. It's funny how a guy turns up dead the day after Father Sebastian Crane comes into the station with his crisis of conscience.'

'If Simeon didn't kill Christina, who did? I guess it would have looked more suspicious if Simeon had turned up dead,' said Carlos. 'Someone put Seb up to it. Masters, do you think?'

Fiona rubbed her temples. 'It's looking that way. He gets called back from his luxury holiday on the same day his priest friend comes in to see the super. Then I nearly get pulled off the case, and finally, Masters calls me into his office first thing this morning, trying to get me to bring the team back from the institute. Although it might be Vasili taking us all for fools, with him still being missing.'

'Maybe.' Carlos wasn't convinced. 'Masters should know by now that telling you not to do something is going to make you do the opposite. Did your guys find anything new at the institute?'

'Not really. They've all clammed up and are hiding behind the confidentiality of research subjects and all that. It's time you spoke to Professor Brooker because I can't. By the way, I had to tell the team, and Masters, about the eyewitness to the second death, but I've let them assume it's Henry for now. We've got uniform looking for him. Please tell me you've hidden him somewhere no-one will find him, because you can bet the word's out and whoever's doing this will have no qualms about killing him.'

'He's out of the area and somewhere no-one will think of looking for him.'

'Don't tell me where, but how did you move him so quickly?'

'I called in a favour for a story.'

'Tony Hadden's got him.'

'No. But he's offered to be a taxi service for today. He called an hour ago to tell me the ankle's been plastered and they're almost at their destination.' Carlos noted a concerned look on Fiona's face. 'Don't worry, they used a busy hospital in a different city, and a false name. It wasn't hard for the doctors to believe Henry was of no fixed abode.'

Fiona chuckled. 'Even wearing your clothes? Did the doctors say anything about the bruises?'

'He kept them hidden. They were only interested in getting the ankle X-rayed, diagnosed and treated. Hey, looks like this is the place.' Carlos parked the car outside a large, rundown warehouse. A police car was waiting for them. Fiona got out and spoke to a uniformed officer while he waited.

'That's Barry King,' she said, leading Carlos inside. 'Before you ask, totally trustworthy and someone I want on my team if my DC turns out to be crooked. The warehouse belongs to an investment company and the padlock on the outside has been broken. We've told them about the break in, but also informed them it's a potential crime scene. Here, put these on.' Fiona handed him overshoes from her pocket and put some on herself.

'Have they found anything?'

'I told them not to go in. We're the first. Come on.'

'Hang on, I'll get my assistant.' Carlos returned to the car and let Lady out. PC King gave him a nod as he passed him to go inside. Carlos told his dog to prepare. 'Here you go, Lady.' He took a wet and smelly sock from a plastic bag. He'd kept it from Henry's old clothes; the rest he'd put in a black bin liner and shoved in a cupboard in case Fiona needed them. Lady sniffed and snuffled at the sock, put her nose in the air and started her search. The dog ran around the warehouse while Carlos and Fiona watched on.

'It'll be quicker this way. This place is enormous. Look, she's found the scent.' Carlos pointed to where Lady was walking with her nose to the ground. They followed her to the back of the building, where she stopped, snuffling at the floor in front of a door. There was a key in the lock.

'You'd think the owners would have removed these,' he said.

'They might have stashed them away somewhere and our goons found them,' Fiona suggested, opening the door.

Lady hurried inside, still on the scent. She stopped in the centre of the room.

'Good girl, Lady,' said Fiona.

'Very good girl,' said Carlos, giving her a handful of treats and releasing her from the command.

Carlos and Fiona looked around carefully. Boot prints lined the floor, most likely from the men who had carried out the beating. Carlos picked up a discarded shirt from the side of the room, handing it to Fiona, who bagged it.

'Henry's. That must have been his escape route.' He pointed to a wobbly table below a window.

'Good. We're getting somewhere. Let's get out of here. I'll call the CSI team and wait for them. Meanwhile, Barry and I will check the warehouse and surrounding area for any CCTV. You never know, we might be lucky enough to get a number plate for the van.'

Carlos was pleased they were making progress, although he suspected the goons were just fists for hire. Still, if they were the same men who had killed Ray Sylvester and Christina Sand, at least one of them knew the person giving the orders.

Fiona removed her overshoes once they got outside, and Carlos followed suit. She had a brief conversation with Barry King before getting onto her phone.

Barry sealed off the entrance to the warehouse with police tape before heading up the road to what looked like a waste tyre disposal firm. Carlos put Lady into the car and strapped her in at the back, leaving the door open so she got some air. Even in the cold, he liked to keep the car well ventilated. Once Fiona finished on the phone, she joined him.

'Do you want me to help scout the businesses for CCTV?' he asked.

'Thanks, but no. Just in case DCI Masters comes along. I can get a lift back with Barry. You get to the institute and rattle Professor Brooker's cage. I'll deal with any fallout later.'

Carlos grinned. 'Gladly. What say we inform the good priest about the death after I'm done?'

'He'll already know about it, but I'd like to see his face and meet him for myself, so if we've got time, you're on. Text me when you're done with the professor.'

'He might refuse to see me,' said Carlos.

'Use your charm.' Fiona grinned.

'Righto.'

'Remind me to fill you in on the conversation I had with Vasili's father last night and the biotech company this morning. With so much going on, I haven't had the chance.'

'We can talk about it on the way to see the priest.' Carlos climbed back inside his Capri and called Julie.

'Hello, I was thinking you'd left me,' she said.

He laughed. 'Never. Do me a favour, will you? Call the Institute for Evolutionary Genetics and Research and get me an appointment to see Professor Brooker this afternoon. And get me some background on him. I'm on my way back to the office now.'

'No problem. I'll put the coffee machine on. I've also got a last known address for Simeon Vasili, but there's no reply from the landline.'

'Great work, Julie. I'll see you in a few minutes.'

A text came through on his phone from Tony.

'Package delivered. On my way back. Story goes out today.'

Carlos felt enormous relief knowing Henry would be safe where he had placed him, as long as he did nothing silly. He started the engine and reversed away from the police car before swinging around and heading back to his office. It was easy enough to walk to the institute from there.

Chapter 26

Carlos sat at an imposing mahogany desk, assessing the fifty-three-year-old man wearing a navy blue and yellow checked suit seated opposite. Julie had carried out some preparatory research on his behalf. The professor was married with two daughters who went to private school; he lived in the suburbs and subscribed to several exclusive membership organisations, including a prestigious tennis club. Both his daughters took private tennis lessons and showed promise, already winning some junior tournaments.

Professor Ronald Brooker's office – like Seb's – was full of pictures of him standing alongside important people, including the Prime Minister and one where he was shaking hands with Prince William. There was a stack of medical journals and what looked like clinical trial protocols on another desk. The roomy office was flooded with natural light from two generously sized windows, affording it a view of Leicester's skyscape.

'Thank you for seeing me, Professor. Please accept my condolences for the loss of your researcher, Christina Sand. My assistant may have told you over the phone, her parents have hired me to work alongside the police. We're looking into the circumstances of her death.'

Brooker nodded, his face impassive. 'My team tells me she may have been pushed to her death, or mugged. Such a terrible tragedy. Christina was a gifted scientist and lecturer. We miss her.'

We, or I? Carlos studied the professor's inscrutable expression. Was that a glimmer of sadness hidden behind his dark blue eyes?

'How well did you know Christina, Professor?'

The professor fiddled with the knot in his tie. 'I'm sorry, I didn't offer you a drink. Would you like coffee?'

'No, thank you.'

'If you don't mind.' Professor Brooker stood up and switched on a kettle on a counter next to a table. It came immediately to the boil, but he took an eternity to prepare himself a cup of coffee, adding full-fat milk. 'Are you sure you won't have one?'

'Okay. Milk, no sugar, thanks.'

With cups and saucers in front of them, the professor looked up. 'Where were we? Ah, yes... Christina. We worked together for around six years, perhaps longer. I was overseeing her doctorate. So sad she won't ever complete it. Such potential—'

'Did you know her outside of work?' Carlos asked.

'No, I can't say I did. Paul Brand may have seen her socially from time to time. He's her research associate. Christina liked to keep her work and social life separate, and when I'm not working, I'm home with my wife and children.'

Or at one of your many clubs, thought Carlos. 'You left a message on her home answerphone. Why was that?'

Surprise flickered across the professor's face. 'Did I? Erm... I can't remember... I expect we were busy. Sometimes I forget when people are off.'

'Why use her landline?'

The professor shook his head, palms up. 'Perhaps she wasn't answering her mobile.'

'I understand Christina was working on a research project that recruits homeless people and other vulnerable adults,' Carlos probed.

'Yes, the study is examining cancer risk in marginalised populations,' Brooker replied. 'It could have important implications for cancer prevention in the future. Our Human Resources department has advertised for a replacement. Paul's good, but not capable enough to take over the reins, as it were.'

Carlos wasn't interested in the professor's recruitment headaches. 'And what happens to these vulnerable people once they are recruited into the trial?'

'We take blood and tissue samples, study the blood results and, more importantly, genetic samples for markers. The samples are then stored and will be compared, at intervals, for as long as possible. The main crux of the research is to compare these subgroups' genetic makeup to that of other populations already studied. It will show us whether they have a predisposition for developing cancer and we might pick up some new genetic traits in the process.' Whilst the professor was sounding enthusiastic, his body language and eyes weren't convincing.

'I wouldn't have thought the homeless an ideal subset for long-term research. Surely they won't attend follow-ups?'

The professor shrugged. 'We have to try.'

'Do they get to know if they are predisposed to developing cancer?'

'I see you've done your homework, Mr Jacobi. Alas, no, they don't. It's a blind study.'

'What does that mean?'

'Only Christina could match the samples to the test subjects for follow-up purposes. She was a diligent record keeper – we all are. Otherwise, the samples are labelled with study numbers, rather than names. The research is more about benefitting tomorrow's generation. For the greater good. We inform the participants of all of this when they consent.'

'Who has access to the matching now that Christina's no longer with you?'

Professor Brooker frowned. 'The police have removed her computer, but when it's returned, I can speak to our IT department about accessing it.'

'Surely there must be something in it for your recruits?'

'As well as contributing to science, you mean?' Professor Brooker's tone was condescending and judgemental, but Carlos wasn't biting.

'Yes.'

Brooker sighed, bored almost. 'As far as I'm aware, they receive housing for as long as they stay in the study and remuneration for travel expenses and any inconvenience, that sort of thing.'

'What do you mean by, as far as you're aware?'

Brooker hesitated briefly before answering. 'Genomix Solutions Biotech funds the research and deals with the incidentals. They take a great interest in our work.'

Carlos's eyes narrowed. 'Yes, I heard they fund the study. That's very generous of them. I presume they would get exclusive rights to develop any lucrative new treatments?'

Brooker looked away, focusing intently on straightening a stack of papers. 'They are one of many companies eager to... collaborate with someone of my reputation.'

The professor's arrogance was masking something. Carlos leaned back in his chair, steepling his fingers as he continued to study the older man.

'Such collaborations must require contracts and legal agreements,' he remarked. 'Especially with a major corporation funding research involving vulnerable human subjects.'

Brooker waved a hand dismissively, though his eyes betrayed a hint of wariness. 'Everything is legitimate, Mr Jacobi, I assure you. Our research could be of significant benefit to future generations. And, as it stands now, it benefits everyone: the homeless get compensation, the institute gets funding, the research moves forward and one day – if I have my way – cancer will be a thing of the past. Genomix understands the value of investing in work that could lead to monumental breakthroughs.'

Carlos nodded thoughtfully. Brooker still appeared animated about his research, but uncertain for the first time since Carlos had entered the room.

'I'm afraid I don't know the details of the legal arrangements. Administrators and lawyers handled that side of things. I'm a man of science, not business,' Brooker said, an edge creeping into his voice.

'How does the funding work? Does Genomix pay the institute, and you pay the staff?'

'That's how it works from our side, yes. They have funded a PhD student – that was Christina – to head up the research, and they pay the staff salaries via secondment arrangements.'

'Apart from the blood tests and tissue sampling, what else happens to the study recruits?'

'They are looked after.'

'How?'

'I'm not entirely sure. Genomix has hired their own team of nurses and a medical director to deal with the nitty gritty. They fund a GP who recruits subjects and passes all suitable ones on to the private team.'

Carlos raised his eyes in disbelief. 'Do you mean Christina might never have met any of the people enrolled in the study?'

'She or Paul would have one meeting with them to discuss their understanding of what they are consenting to, explaining the study details and checking eligibility prior to referring them on.'

'Is it unusual for a company to employ a private team?'

'Not particularly. Pharmaceutical companies often provide independent staff to deal with the day-to-day, both in the community and within hospital environments. It's a quid pro quo, as it were.'

'Surely that has ethical implications?'

'The staff Genomix recruits must remain independent. Research protocols take all these things into account, Mr Jacobi. Every study goes through our research ethics committee, of which I'm the chair.'

Of course you are, thought Carlos.

'It's the first time we've dealt with an outside arrangement and, if I'm honest, the study Christina was leading was a favour.'

'What sort of favour?'

'Genomix Solutions Biotech is funding a far more expensive, but invaluable, top-priority study I've been wanting to carry out for years. After they offered to fund it, they asked if I would be happy to take on the homeless one on their behalf. They offered to pay for everything and fund a PhD. We don't get opportunities like this every day. How could I refuse?'

'Why are they so interested?'

'It's their speciality, genome research.'

'And your involvement would give it credibility?' Carlos asked.

'Precisely.'

'I'm surprised no-one in your team thought to mention any of this to the police,' said Carlos. 'I take it you didn't tell Superintendent Henley when you spoke to her?'

'My, my. You are well informed, Mr Jacobi. It didn't come up. I saw the superintendent at a do and she offered her condolences for the loss of our researcher. She asked a few questions about the study Christina was involved in and that was it; a friendly chat during a busy evening, hardly an in-depth interview.'

Pushing down his annoyance, Carlos asked, 'Do you know the name of the medical director you mentioned earlier?'

'I can look it up for you.' Professor Brooker walked over to the table containing the protocols and picked one up. 'Here it is, Dr June Meacher. But why all the questions about our research? Surely you can't think any of this is linked to Christina's death?'

'At the moment, we're considering every aspect of Christina's life, and her work was very important to her. It might be nothing, but then again—' Carlos let his words sink in.

Brooker looked far less self-assured than he had, but Carlos suspected it was selfish concern, rather than because he was involved in murder. Genomix Solutions Biotech, however; they were definitely of interest right now.

'I've taken up enough of your time. I'll let you get on.'

Professor Brooker walked Carlos to the door. 'Let me know if I can be of any further help. We were all fond of Christina.'

Carlos stopped in his tracks, scrutinising the man. 'Thanks again for seeing me, Professor.'

He strode through the pristine corridors, feeling much happier. They were inching closer and closer to a solution.

Chapter 27

When Carlos checked his phone, there was a voicemail from Fiona.

'I'm chasing up a few leads regarding Genomix Solutions Biotech, so let's leave the priest for now, unless you can come up with a good reason to see him again. If you've got the time, feel free to check out our GP friend. I've moved our briefing to four-thirty. See you there.'

Carlos texted her the information he'd got from the professor about Genomix hiring its own research team. His phone rang almost immediately.

'That explains why nobody knows where these people go once they're referred to the institute. Do you think the company's legit?'

'Thinking about it, I'm not sure. The professor told me it wasn't unusual for companies to fund extra staff and pay for secondments, and to be honest, if Nicolae wasn't involved, I'd say there was nothing out of the ordinary, but—'

'Yeah, I know. He's muddying the waters.'

'That, along with two bodies linked to the homeless shelter, and possibly the research,' said Carlos.

'What else did you get from the professor?'

'He had a thing for Christina, but I don't believe he killed her.'

'Did he tell you this?'

'No, but I got that impression. When I asked about their relationship, he was defensive and cagey, went on about being married and all that. Either way, I don't believe she reciprocated his feelings. He's full of himself, so it might have been all about getting what he couldn't have – he's that type, you know?'

'Yeah, Tabitha more or less said the same thing. Her words included misogynist and narcissist if I remember correctly. She has occasional dealings with him in her line of work. Anything else?'

'Here's the interesting thing. The homeless research is a favour.'

'In what way?'

'Genomix has funded a trial that's really important to Brooker, and in return, he's allowing his name and his people to be attached to the homeless research. The protocol more or less came from Genomix, with the funding for Christina's PhD and salaries for any others involved in the research.'

'That sounds fishy to me.'

'Me too, except the company specialises in genome research, so it could just be in their interests to get a high-profile name to agree that they get first crack and exclusive rights to develop and licence whatever comes out of it. A quid pro quo, the professor called it.'

'I'd have a different name for it myself. Like money talks. I'm starting to feel we're back at square one, but as you say, the Nicolae factor means there's definitely something shady going on.'

'Plus... this might sound like I'm being neurotic... but with Genomix being in Edinburgh—' Carlos finally aired what had been bugging him.

'There are hundreds, if not thousands of companies in Edinburgh, Carlos. I want to get Alastair McTavish as much as you do, but don't get sidetracked.'

'Okay, good point,' Carlos conceded. 'The professor gave me the name of the medical director Genomix employs to oversee the research. I'm on my way to have a word with Paul Brand, Christina's associate, and get a phone number. He might also know where the recruits go to once they're enrolled. Christina or Paul meet – or met, in her case – every recruit once.'

'Don't waste your time on Brand. He's called in sick today. Hugh and Kerry have been to his home address, but he's not there. We're trying to trace him. They spoke to a few people who help with the trial, but didn't get very far. They input data, that's all.'

'Do you think Paul Brand's done a runner?'

'Not sure. He could just be having a skive off work day. Or maybe the stress has got to him. Hugh thought he might also have had a thing for Christina.'

'Mm. She was a beauty, even Henry said that. Although I suspect this thing goes a lot deeper than we realise.'

'The Nicolae factor?'

'Yes.'

'Look, let's focus on what we've got. The team will keep looking for Brand and probably find him at the gym or something – Hugh said it was obvious he works out. I'll speak to Genomix again, hopefully without alerting them to any suspicions from our side in case they close things down,' said Fiona. 'What's the name of the medical director?'

'June Meacher.'

'On second thoughts, I'll get an address and speak to her first. Why don't you have another word with our GP, Dr Mishka Andreeva, then I'll see you at the briefing and we can compare notes? Be prepared, Masters might be there.'

'Thanks for the warning.'

'Another warning, Carlos.'

'What?'

'Remember Henry and our victim from this morning? These guys are on to you. Watch your back.'

'Sure.'

'Is something else on your mind?'

'Yes. Christina Sand. She was a brilliant scientist and a meticulous record keeper, according to Professor Brooker.

If she suspected something shady was going on regarding the research, or the homeless shelter, she would have recorded it somewhere. Did CSI find anything in the details that came from her apartment?'

'Nothing on paper. We've got a specialist accessing her laptop and work computer. There's quite a lot of security to get behind because she took work home, but they'll get through it. If there's anything there, they'll find it.'

'Good. I should just about have time to visit the GP before the briefing. I'm on foot. See you later.'

'You and your fitness,' Fiona teased.

Carlos ended the call and tapped the surgery's postcode into his phone before inserting an EarPod and starting a jog back towards town. After running for a while, he picked up on a white van driving slowly behind him. Unlike most vans on the busy road, it didn't seem in any hurry to overtake cars in front. Was it tailing him? He jogged across the road and noticed the van getting beeped at when it tried to switch lanes. It was hidden by traffic, so he couldn't make out a number plate.

Carlos about-turned and ran back across the road towards the vehicle, but it sped up and turned left before he got anywhere near it.

'Could have been someone not sure where they were going,' he muttered. According to the navigation system on his phone, he was a few minutes away from the doctor's surgery.

He stopped jogging when his phone rang. The number was withheld.

'Hello?'

'Hiya, Carlos, I'm ringing from the office. Just to confirm the package was delivered safely and tell you to buy a copy of this evening's paper.' Tony sounded happy. In exchange for his jaunt down the motorway, Carlos had given him the story on the latest body, and that, coupled with the information from the night before, had been enough to persuade Carlos's unconventional Good Samaritan to help him out. He had been expecting the breaking story to cover the front page of the *Leicester Mercury*.

'I got your text. Thanks, Tony. I owe you.' Carlos continued his walk, strolling towards the doctor's surgery.

'Not at all. We'll run this story until its conclusion. I expect the nationals will want a piece of it, so I'm holding you to your end of the bargain – me first. My police sources tell me they think Simeon Vasili killed Christina.'

'Not sure on that one, Tony, but we need to find him.'

'I'll put feelers out.'

'Let me know if you track him down before I do, though.'

'Will do. If you don't think it was him, who do you think it was?'

Carlos inhaled a deep breath, pausing on the pavement. 'Nicolae Romanescu might be involved.'

The phone went quiet at the other end. Carlos grimaced. He'd not mentioned it before because he knew one of Nicolae's men had gone to the hospital after Tony's brush with death and warned him from talking about what he'd found out on that fateful day. Tony hadn't mentioned the man since.

He finally spoke. 'How long have you known?'

'Too long. Sorry, I should have mentioned it before. You don't have to get involved if you don't want to, but I thought it was time to warn you.'

'Thanks. I'll be in touch.' Tony hung up.

Carlos approached the dingy surgery, conflicted. Perhaps he shouldn't have mentioned Nicolae, but he didn't want to be responsible for Tony stumbling across something else that would put him in danger. It was the right thing to do.

Bedlam greeted Carlos when he entered the surgery. The waiting room was full to standing room only, and the phones were ringing out endlessly with no-one answering. Could this be one of those old-fashioned non-appointment surgeries?

After a quick glance around, he headed to the reception desk and waited for the woman behind the glass to deal with the couple in front. He expected to be told the doctor was too busy to see him.

'Good afternoon. I'm sorry to arrive without an appointment, but is Doctor Andreeva in?' Carlos flashed a smile along with his ID.

The receptionist huffed in frustration, gesturing to the room behind him. 'If he was, I wouldn't have a waiting room full of people with appointments now being transferred to the other doctors' lists.'

'Oh dear. Sorry to hear that. Could you tell me where I can find him?'

'Who knows?' The receptionist huffed again.

'Is he unwell?' Carlos persisted.

'If he is, he's too sick to pick up the phone and let us know. Now if you'll excuse me.' She inclined her head to the people waiting behind him.

Carlos decided he'd have more luck getting the GP's address from Fiona at the briefing. 'Thank you for your help. I hope things get better for you.'

'Me too,' she said, before lowering her voice. 'Try the homeless shelter. Dr Andreeva seems to spend more time there these days than here. And if you find him, tell him he's in big trouble when the practice manager gets hold of him. He's had enough warnings.'

'Thanks again,' said Carlos.

Once outside, he checked his watch. Time was getting on and he wanted to be at the briefing with Fiona. Dr Andreeva could wait. He decided to nip back to the office and collect Lady and his car.

Carlos's phone rang as he was about to exit his office. 'Hey, Fiona, I was just leaving to come to the briefing.'

'Don't. Have you seen the paper?'

Carlos grinned. 'No, but Tony told me to buy one.'

'The super's going mad. Your friend has not only mentioned police incompetence, he's named Masters as being responsible for the mess ups. You can imagine his reaction.'

'It's no more than he deserves.' Carlos wondered if he should have held back last night, but he hadn't realised then there would be another body.

'And they have chucked me off the case.'

'You're kidding?'

Fiona cackled. 'That's the official line. DCI Masters has been told to clear up his mess. Unofficially, I'm on the boat, packing before leaving on the overnight train to Edinburgh. I'll be visiting that medical director you mentioned, Doctor June Meacher, first thing in the morning. She's based at Genomix's head office. Masters hasn't been told about this. I think the super's got enough to be suspicious that he's trying to cover up his incompetence now. She's told me to liaise with an old colleague of hers who's a DCI up there.

'In the meantime, she's got uniform looking for Paul Brand. Masters has been put in charge, but she's gonna be watching his every move.'

'Do you really think he might be mixed up in all this?' Carlos asked.

'From the way he and DC Gary Munro are behaving, let's just say I wouldn't be surprised. Although at the same time, I would, if you know what I mean.'

'Yes, I think I do. Have they cancelled the briefing?'

'No, but I won't be there and you're not invited.'

'Fair enough. You need to know something else before you leave.'

'Why do I get the feeling I'm not going to like it?'

He chuckled. 'Because you're not going to like it. Not only are Simeon Vasili and Paul Brand missing, but Dr Andreeva didn't turn up to work today, and he didn't report in sick.'

'That doesn't sound good. Any ideas?'

'From what the receptionist said, I don't think it's the first time he's done this. She suggested I try the shelter, so I could do that now I have the time. No-one's reported him missing, but should I let your team know?'

'Hold fire for now. See if you can find him and let me know in the morning.'

'Righto. Have a pleasant trip. Something tells me it's going to be eventful.'

Chapter 28

After wasting a large part of the evening trudging around the shelter and asking more questions, Carlos hadn't located Dr Andreeva or found anyone else who remembered Christina or Simeon. The GP had been there first thing according to a person lining up for food, which provided some reassurance that he was AWOL rather than missing. None of the volunteers would speak to Carlos. It was as if they had been advised not to.

Carlos climbed up the stairs to the flat above his office with an aching head. The image of Bethany's anguished face and the guilt he felt over Ray Sylvester's death lingered in his mind; it was as if every door that opened had closed again. He worried for Fiona with Masters back in charge of the murder investigations. If the superintendent suspected the DCI was corrupt, why send Fiona to Scotland and give him the opportunity to fabricate... or lose... evidence? Could Superintendent Henley herself be involved? Fiona didn't think so, and had sounded hopeful she was going to get somewhere on the Edinburgh trip.

A feeling of helplessness tightened around his chest like a band, along with fury at the thought of Terry Masters being anywhere near this case. All the information they had gathered so far was circumstantial; there was no concrete evidence suggesting the research was corrupt, just hints and a suspicion it might be. Carlos's biggest fear was that Nicolae would get away with whatever it was he was doing... again. He rubbed his temples, trying to ease the tension building in his skull.

He scooped coffee granules into a mug, his movements slow and automatic. The aroma, usually therapeutic, did nothing to soothe him as he carried the steaming drink to one of the easy chairs he had furnished the flat with. He scrolled through his phone. Should he call Fiona and tell her the GP had been seen earlier in the day? It wasn't important, and he didn't want to wake her if she was catching a nap.

Carlos's legs were restless. He had to do something. It was obvious he wasn't going to get to sleep anytime soon. The confines of the flat seemed to close in on him. It was stuffy and suffocating. Perhaps he should go home.

Grabbing his keys, he walked back downstairs and opened the back door. Lady followed automatically. He attached her lead.

'Let's go for a walk, girl.' They started down the road, and he found himself heading towards the museum where it had all begun.

The Roman Wall loomed like a forbidding centurion in the darkness. It appeared more sinister than Carlos recalled. He turned into St Nicholas Walk and strolled between the museum grounds and the church graveyard. Carlos tried retracing the steps Henry might have taken on the night he discovered Christina's body.

The temporary fencing that closed off the ruins was stacked to one side. Renovation and excavation works had been paused for the film crew, and now it was a crime scene. The film crew's floodlights were still there, powered by a generator that hadn't been switched off. Its faint hum came from the far side of the ruins.

It was midnight, according to the huge clock on the tower of St Nicholas Church. The powerful beams from the floodlights cast eerie shadows across the dugouts of the ancient baths, illuminating the historic ruins with a sinister glow. Carlos entered the grounds and wandered around the excavations, avoiding the police cordon.

Headlights from a few passing cars moved across the ruins, casting more weird shadows. The museum itself was in darkness. Carlos shivered in the chilly night air. The cold penetrated his fleece. In his hurry to get out, he hadn't put his overcoat on. Lady trotted alongside him, her eyes perky and her tail wagging, until he stopped, realising they were wasting their time.

'What are we doing here, Lady? Let's go.'

Carlos's dog wasn't playing ball; she wouldn't move. He bent down to cup her head in his hands.

'You're a good girl. I don't know what I'd do without you.'

She licked his nose.

'Yuck. That wasn't code for slobber all over me.'

He stood again and tugged at the lead. Lady still wasn't budging. Instead, she had her nose in the air.

'Okay, have it your way.' He removed the lead and walked away, expecting her to follow. She didn't. Lady moved with determination, nose to the ground, zigzagging backwards and forwards. Carlos watched her carefully, looking for any change in behaviour. She was focussed, concentrated, her training kicking in. Was this one of her games, or was she onto something?

Suddenly, Lady's head shot up. The change in her demeanour was instant – she was tense, her hind legs coiled like springs and her nose locked onto something in the distance, something only she could smell. With a sudden burst of speed, she darted away from the ruins and leapt the low iron gate into the graveyard of St Nicholas Church.

'Lady, wait!' Carlos called, but she ignored him, focused on whatever scent she had picked up. He hurried to catch up, but his shoes were sticking in the mud. She could be a real pain when she got something in her head. 'Lady, stop this now! I know there are dead bodies in here. It's a graveyard, now come here.'

Carlos didn't need to climb over the gate. It was unlocked, but it creaked as he opened it. Unlike the ruins, the graveyard was shrouded in darkness. The shadows of the ancient gravestones seemed to loom over him. He shuddered, wondering what secrets lay beneath their cold, silent vigil. No wonder Henry had been frightened to sleep in here.

By the time he caught up with his dog, she was sniffing intently near an old oak tree, tail wagging excitedly. Carlos looked around, wary before speaking.

'Chasing foxes, eh, girl?' He shook his head, dismissing the idea that she had picked up anything significant. 'Come on, Lady, let's get back to the flat. I've already told you this is a graveyard.'

Lady glanced up at him, her head cocked to one side, eyes alert, but she didn't respond to his command. Avoiding his hand as he reached for her collar, and with a determined snort, she turned and raced back to the ruins.

'Stubborn mutt, you're taking advantage now,' Carlos grumbled. He followed her back to the museum grounds, but despite his scepticism, he could no longer deny his precious pooch might be onto something. She had proven herself repeatedly. The sixth sense that complemented her olfactory perceptions was impressive.

'What is it, girl? What do you smell?'

Lady leapt a knee-high picket fence he hadn't noticed before and gave a low bark before she began digging frantically at a mound of freshly turned earth. It looked like new excavations had been taking place. She continued pawing at the soil, her movements urgent.

Lady's whine pierced the night as she turned to look at Carlos, seeming to plead with him to understand the importance of her discovery. He hesitated, then climbed over the barrier, panicking that she was going to disturb some valuable ancient artefact uncovered by archaeologists. He reached for her when she finally stopped digging and took a hold of her collar, but she still wouldn't budge.

'This is what they mean by digging your heels in, I suppose.' He crouched down, looking into his dog's eyes. 'Lady, listen to me. We have to go before you get me in big trouble. Come.' He attached the lead and stood again. Lady ignored his command, sitting rooted to the ground with her big brown eyes fixed on his.

Carlos's instinct was to get out of there, but looking at his dog, he couldn't. Her quirky behaviour hadn't let him down before. Stepping closer to her, he dropped the lead and began inspecting the mound. It was freshly dug, but that could explain the picket fence. Was it shielding whatever archaeological treasures were still to be unearthed?

Doubt crept over him. Lady's behaviour suggested there could be human remains buried here.

'But if there are bones under there, Lady, they'll be Roman.'

An inner voice questioned why the archaeologists would have filled the hole again, unless they had finished their work. He wasn't sure how deep Lady's cadaver training went. Carlos knew she could detect human bones, she'd proven that, but from as far back as Roman times?

Carlos looked at his dog once more, inhaling a deep breath. 'This had better be something, or you're in trouble,' he warned as he grabbed a nearby piece of wood. He used it as a makeshift shovel to move the earth away from where Lady had directed her interest. After a while, he continued with his hands.

He had shifted around a bucketful of soil and piled it to one side, but the hole revealed nothing. Lady continued to whine, pawing at the ground, urging him on. He froze when his hand felt something. Groping around it, he moved the earth until he could see a man's shoe, and what was unmistakably a human leg.

'This is no Roman, this body's fresh. Well done, Lady.' Carlos's pulse raced. Whoever was buried here couldn't have been there long, not with all the activity that had gone on this morning.

Lady whined again, watching Carlos intently. He gave her a nod.

'Good girl. You found something big here.' He reached into his pocket with muddy, wet hands and gave her a handful of treats before stepping back over the fence. This time, Lady followed.

Carlos moved away from the mound towards the Roman wall and wiped his hands with one of the wipes he always carried for cleaning when he picked up after his dog. Once his hands were cleaner, he pulled out his phone, tapping a familiar number.

'Pick up, Fiona,' he pleaded, his eyes not moving from the grisly sight a short distance away.

Chapter 29

The cold air burned Carlos's ears as he leaned on the wall. Eerie shadows from the graveyard across the way created an unsettling atmosphere that amplified the gravity of his and Lady's discovery. His jaw clenched when he reached Fiona's voicemail.

'Fiona, I'm at the Jewry Wall. There's another body. Ring me.'

His eyes darted back to the mound of earth. He should dial 999 and be done with it, irrespective of who was in charge.

A low growl interrupted Carlos's conflicted thoughts. He glanced down at Lady and saw her staring at the main road, hackles raised. Moments later, a van mounted the kerb before screeching to a stop. A car swerved to avoid hitting it and the driver honked their horn in annoyance.

A man jumped out of the passenger seat of the van and slid the side door open. Even at a distance, it was obvious he was burly, with broad shoulders and a thick waist. Three other men and the driver poured out of the vehicle, dressed in black from head to toe. These had to be the guys who had abducted and beaten Henry. The largest, who was built like a rugby prop, barked orders at the others. Three tall, muscular men, exuding an air of menace, and one shorter, but no less menacing, scrambled to obey.

Lady's growl deepened, her muscles taut. Carlos's heart hammered in his chest. Were they here for him? He glanced back at the mound of earth. The body. They must know about the body.

'Come on, girl. We have to leave.'

They slipped around the stone wall, taking advantage of the deep shadows before darting across and back to the graveyard. This time, Carlos lifted Lady over the gate before scrambling over himself, not wanting to set off the creak.

They were just in time. The stomping of the men's boots along the alley marked their arrival. They walked with purpose, every step heavy and determined, but not quiet.

Carlos dived behind a tombstone, pulling Lady with him. He held the lead and murmured, 'Shush, girl.' She stopped growling.

'All right, let's get this done quickly,' the goon leader barked at his companions. 'We don't have much time.'

The men paused at the gap in the fencing as an elderly couple walked along the path, most likely taking a shortcut. Carlos braced himself for a fight, concerned for them.

'Good evening, gentlemen,' the old man said. 'Bit late to be working out here, isn't it?'

'Evening,' the leader replied gruffly. 'Yeah, tell me about it. We're just closing up the area. There's been a film crew scoping it out.'

'Is that so?' the old man said. Carlos noticed him looking up at the leader's balaclava through thick spectacles, and hoped he wasn't about to challenge him. 'What kind of film is it?'

'Uh, some sort of historical drama.' The leader's voice wavered. Carlos could feel the tension from the men with him, who were probably debating with themselves what to do about the couple.

'How interesting,' the old woman chimed in. 'We'd better let you get on, then.' She pulled her husband away, whispering something to him as they went, after which they quickened their pace.

'Come on, men, be quick,' the leader ordered.

Thoughts raced through Carlos's mind. He felt a surge of relief when the couple disappeared into the darkness. At least they were out of harm's way. He wondered if the old lady might call the police when they got home.

Carlos peeped around the tombstone, watching four of the men walk straight towards the mound of earth concealing the body. He could make out their spades and heard them dig. Carlos swallowed hard as he watched them work from his hiding place.

One man stood next to the wall, keeping watch while the others undertook the gruesome deed, digging rapidly. Carlos debated whether to escape through the main road exit, but with the watchman glancing in every direction, he couldn't risk it.

Lady was on full alert, her eyes fixed on the man keeping watch. Every so often, Carlos could feel the growling in her throat as he held his arm around her, but she didn't let it become audible.

His phone vibrated inside his pocket. He ducked back behind the headstone and pulled it out to see Fiona's number illuminated on the screen.

Now she calls!

He didn't dare take the call. Any conversation would easily transfer to the watchman, who was only a few feet away. He pressed the cancel button and switched the phone off. Barely able to breathe, he waited.

The men talked in hushed whispers as their shovels dug into the ground. Some of the louder parts of the murmured conversation reached Carlos's ears.

'Can't believe they're making us dig this up,' one man grumbled, brandishing his spade like a weapon. 'Why put the damn thing here in the first place?'

Another one joined in with the griping. 'I don't like this. What are we supposed to do with it when we get it out of here? We ain't gonna stay out here all night.'

'Shut it,' the leader snapped. 'You're getting paid good money. Just do as you're told.'

'I'm still not sure why we have to dig it up.'

The leader growled, 'Because I said so. Now keep digging or you'll be joining 'im.'

With a nervous laugh and a disgruntled sigh, the men went back to work.

Abruptly, the shovels stopped. Carlos peered around the tombstone. One of the men gathered some of the tools and moved towards the end of the alley, putting them back in the van. There was rapid movement as the three next to the newly dug soil spoke in urgent tones.

The man in charge motioned for the watchman to move to the other end of the walk. 'Make sure no-one gets through,' he commanded. The man near the van stood blocking the entrance to the walk from that end. Next, the other two lackeys emerged from the shadows, carrying the body between them. Carlos craned his neck, trying to get a glimpse, but he could barely make anything out in the alley's darkness.

They worked fast, hurrying towards the van, then paused at the entrance to the alley, waiting for a bus to pass. Once the road was quiet, without hesitation, they threw the body into the van like a sack of rubbish. The door slammed shut.

Carlos slumped behind the tombstone, his pulse hammering. It was done. Now, he just had to wait for them to leave. Beside him, Lady whined softly, nudging his hand in reassurance.

The first watchman and one of his accomplices returned to the grounds, picked up the remaining shovels, and refilled the hole. After they had finished, they raked it over. Carlos watched them scrubbing stones, erasing all traces of what had transpired. Methodical. Efficient. Whoever these men were, they were more experienced at this sort of thing than he had given them credit for.

At last, with their task complete, the men tossed the tools into the back of the van and piled inside. The vehicle's engine roared to life, its headlights slicing through the dark as it pulled away.

Carlos remained crouched behind the tombstone, every muscle tensed, until the red glow of the taillights disappeared. Only then did he rise, joints creaking in protest. He blew out a long breath, scanning the now empty grounds. His back felt stiff and cold from crouching for so long.

As he took a deep breath, Carlos wondered if this had been the same tombstone Henry Cutter had hidden behind on the night he'd discovered Christina. Lady nudged against his leg, reminding him it was time to move.

Carlos made his way towards the mound of freshly dug earth once more, his mind racing. Whose was the body they had just taken away? Who had given the order they had talked about, and what was the motive? He knelt down beside the disturbed earth, his fingers brushing against the soil, feeling the anger and frustration building up inside him.

Lady nudged him again with her nose, as if sensing his thoughts. He stroked her head and took the lead. As Carlos and his dog left the scene and headed back towards his office, he switched his phone on and called Fiona.

Chapter 30

Fiona answered right away. 'I've been trying to get you. What's happening? What body?'

'You're not going believe this,' said Carlos, still pacing towards his office.

'Try me.'

'Lady found a body, but now it's gone.'

'What do you mean, gone? You're not making any sense, Carlos.' Fiona sounded tired.

'Five guys – most likely the ones who beat up Henry – turned up and dug it up again. Then they took it away in their van.'

'You didn't tell me it was buried in the first place.'

'Sorry. Well, it was.' Carlos turned to walk along the side of his building, heading towards the back door. 'It was—'

Lady snarled next to him.

'I'll call you back.' He ended the call. Lady's hackles were up again as she continued growling. When he got closer, he too sensed something was wrong. Then he saw the smashed window.

Carlos tried the handle, finding the door unlocked. Inside, the place was in darkness. He listened. Nothing.

'Lady, stay.' Carlos tethered his dog to a hook on the wall and slowly opened the door, stepping over broken glass as he went inside. After checking the back room and kitchen, he switched the light on in the office. Papers and files were strewn across the floor, drawers were wide open, and the computer monitors were smashed. The place had been ransacked.

Fiona had been nagging him to get an alarm fitted ever since he was attacked by a bunch of heavies a few months before. Perhaps now he would take her advice. He returned to the back door and swept the glass out of the way before bringing Lady inside.

His phone buzzed again.

'What's happening?' Fiona sounded frantic.

'My guess is the goons came here before collecting the body. Someone's broken into the office. The hard drives have gone, everything else has been trashed.' He collapsed into a chair.

'Call the police, Carlos.'

'No. You can deal with it when you get back. I'm not having Masters making excuses to attend a burglary. I'm reporting it to you.'

'I'll give Sheila Sanderson from CSI a call first thing and get her over to you. She can ask one of her team to check your place, and you can take her to the site where you saw the body. Could you tell if it was new or old?'

'New. Male is all I could get. I didn't want to disturb a crime scene after uncovering a foot. That's when I rang you. We had to hide behind a tombstone while the goons dug it up again. I heard them complaining to the guy who seemed to be the leader and mentioning they were under orders. I can guess who from.'

'Nicolae?'

'That's my first thought.'

Carlos heard a creaking stair. The concealed door to the flat was closed, but he was sure he'd left it open when he went out.

'Someone's here. I'll put you on speaker,' he said.

'Right. I'm calling it in,' she said.

'Hold on.'

A man opened the door, bruised, dishevelled and shaking. He looked as if he hadn't slept in days.

Carlos glared at him. 'What are you doing here? You've got some explaining to do.'

'I can tell you what happened. At least they didn't get upstairs.' Simeon Vasili had an infectious smile, despite whatever it was he'd been through.

'How do I know you didn't do this?'

'You don't.'

'Okay, Mr Vasili, how did you get in? This place was locked.'

'Sorry, I forced the front door.'

Carlos saw the broken wood.

'Brilliant. Back window smashed and front door bust. Who did this?' Carlos swept an arm towards the mess.

'Men hired by a guy called Nicolae.'

Carlos leaned back in his chair. 'You'd better start from the beginning.'

'It's a long story.'

'In that case, hang on a minute.' Carlos picked up the phone and took it off speaker. 'Did you get all that?' he said to Fiona. 'I'm with Simeon Vasili.'

'Yeah, I heard. Ask him about Dr Meacher and ring me back.'

'He's not on your suspect list, then?'

'Nope. My call to his dad got him worried, made him have second thoughts about his son's whereabouts. He phoned me earlier. I'll let Simeon fill you in on his story.'

'Fine, I'll talk to you later. Be careful up there, Fiona.'

'Sounds like you need to take your own advice. But don't worry, I will.'

Carlos hung up and looked at the man, who was still shaking.

'Take a seat. I'll make us some coffee.'

Simeon obeyed, and Lady moved over to him, asking for fuss. She was an excellent judge of character and hadn't given Carlos any sign that Simeon was dangerous.

Carlos shifted papers from the table next to where Simeon was sitting, moving them onto Julie's desk. He then went to the kitchen and made coffee. Returning with two mugs, he placed them down, along with a sugar bowl, figuring Simeon could do with the energy.

'It appears your dad has finally cooperated with the police and called my friend.'

'He can't have. These people have contacts everywhere.'

'Don't worry. Acting DI Fiona Cook, who I was speaking to when you turned up, is the only one who knows. She is totally trustworthy. We know who Nicolae is. We've been investigating him off the books for some time. Now it's your turn.'

'Okay. I'll be as brief as I can, but it's a long story.'

'I'm not going anywhere.'

'You probably know already that my family breeds racehorses in Arizona for the international market.'

Carlos nodded. 'I knew it was in the States.'

'What you might not realise is that we also have a racing stables in the UK under a different name. It's to keep the racing and breeding side of things separate. I'm the CEO of our stables based in Herefordshire. A year ago, we got worried when some of our outside odds horses started winning races, more often than they would by chance.'

'Most people would be happy.'

'No. Because if you get too many unexpected wins, the regulators want to know why. Sometimes it's okay, as long as it doesn't go on for too long. My dad asked me to check it out before that happened. When I started looking into it, I noticed a lot of people were betting on our outsiders and winning.'

'Insider betting?' Carlos quizzed.

'That's what it looked like, but the bets weren't coming from one source; rather from hundreds. I suspected there was some sort of syndicate set up to make it look more legitimate. At the same time, my stable manager noticed some odd behaviour in the horses that were winning.'

'Why didn't you go to the police?'

'Because I wasn't sure enough about it. Drug tests were coming back normal. Vet checks were okay; it was only a suspicion. Then one of the horses died. Secretly, I had an expert vet examine the body, testing for anything out of the ordinary.'

'And?'

'He discovered an odd genetic sequence. Things were starting to make sense, but there had to be an insider working in the stables to do this because we bought the horses from all over the place. We believed this person must have been falsifying the blood results somewhere within our supply chain because it's something we always check.'

'And you made the link to Leicester?' Carlos asked.

'Not straight away. I called Christina, knowing she was an expert in genetics.' Simeon put his head in his hands. 'I wish to God I'd never made that call. It's my fault she's dead.'

'I'm truly sorry about Christina. But what happened next?'

'She pointed me to the homeless shelter.'

'We were told you were persona non grata with Christina.'

Simeon lifted his head, adding a few spoonfuls of sugar to his coffee before gulping it back. 'I was for years, but we met by chance at Uttoxeter Racecourse a couple of years back, and made up enough to become friends. I told her how sorry I was about what had happened – I'm sure you've been told about it. She accepted I was young and stupid to have ever tried to use her, and she forgave me.'

'She didn't tell her parents.'

'Christina liked her privacy, especially from her mum, who was always overprotective because of her wealth.'

'She had good reason to be in your case,' said Carlos pointedly.

'Fair comment. Anyway, Christina was well over me and had a steady boyfriend.'

'Who?'

'She never said.'

Carlos wondered if she made the boyfriend up to prevent any further approaches from Simeon. No-one, other than admirers, had shown up on his or the police's radar.

'What made you pretend to be homeless?'

'Christina called me around four months back to say she was about to lead a study for a biotech company and it involved recruiting vulnerable sectors of society. She was excited because it came with PhD funding – not that she needed the money, but it was prestigious. A few weeks later she called again. She had gotten suspicious.'

'Why?'

'Considering the groups they would recruit, she had doubts the proposal would ever get through the ethics committee without major changes, some of which she suggested. Her suggestions weren't taken up, but the study proposal passed with flying colours and… unusually… with no protocol changes. That's when she dug a little deeper. She told me ethics committees always insisted on alterations. It's what they did and why they were there.'

'I met with Professor Brooker today… well, yesterday now… and he told me he chairs the ethics committee. Is that why it passed?' Carlos quizzed.

'As chair, he could call an extraordinary meeting when a lot of the members weren't available, and pass the research by himself with just the secretary in attendance.'

'All very interesting,' said Carlos, 'but what has this to do with horses?'

'After the study got ethics approval, Christina researched the funding company, Genomix Solutions Biotech. She was brilliant at that sort of thing.'

'My friend – the detective I spoke to – is on her way to Genomix now. She's on the train to Edinburgh and wants to know about Dr Meacher?'

'I've only heard the name. She's an independent in charge of staff taking the study samples.'

'Okay. I still don't understand why you got involved. Are you suggesting the biotech company is involved in animal genetics as well as human?'

'You got it,' said Simeon. 'Christina became more concerned when the study was set up with an outside base.

Professor Brooker accepted Genomix's reasoning that they would help the homeless, which, on the face of it, sounded reasonable.'

'And it still does. But you went undercover anyway?'

Simeon nodded, putting his head in his hands again. 'If I'd realised how dangerous it was, I'd never have gotten either of us involved… now Christina's dead.'

Carlos didn't have the heart to tell him at this point that she had gone undercover herself to look for him when he went missing.

'Tell me what you found out about the research.'

'Not much. They were onto me almost as soon as I arrived at the farm.'

'The farm?'

'It's what they call the place they take the research candidates to. This sort of thing isn't my bag. I was stupid and asked too many questions right from the get-go. A few days after arriving there, I found out they had stables and did a bit of investigating. I know how to take blood samples from horses and had gone well equipped. Turns out I'm not a good spy. They caught me and they kept me locked up away from the others.'

'Let's just take a step back. What about the recruitment process?' Carlos asked.

'Rumours go around the shelter that some rich guy comes to the place offering people a decent roof over their heads, and money, if they join a research study. Like healthy guinea pigs. It doesn't take much persuading. Some of these guys are barely surviving. Not everyone gets in, though. A GP vets volunteers, and actively recruits others. Those enrolled have no living relatives and nobody who would come looking for them if they go missing.'

'We know about the GP, Dr Andreeva. Do you think he knows why he's recruiting people?'

'No. He's low down the pecking order, but he might have been willing to turn a blind eye and not ask too many questions for a tidy sum of money. Except now, he's all shook up and threatening to expose the farm if they don't tell him what's going on.'

'How do you know that?'

'Because he helped me escape. While they kept me locked up away from all the other recruits, they still took samples every day. The others are well fed and the people overseeing the trial don't mind them doing drugs or alcohol as long as they stay at the farm and don't cause trouble.

'This afternoon, the GP turned up asking to see Nicolae just as one of the so-called nurses was taking my blood. The nurse told Dr Andreeva that Nicolae wasn't there. This is the only nurse I ever saw after being caught at the stables, so he's definitely in on whatever's going on. The nurse locked me back up, and I listened at the door. I heard the doctor kicking off. A bit later, he came back, unlocked the room and told me to follow him. He brought me back to Leicester, gave me your name and told me to find you.'

'Why my name? It was Fiona Cook who interviewed him.'

'He said not to go to the police, that some of them are involved. Someone at the shelter mentioned to him you were looking for me. I said I needed to contact Christina first. That's when I found out…' Tears filled Simeon's eyes, he couldn't finish the sentence.

Carlos paused before asking. 'Where is this farm?'

'I don't know this area well enough to tell you. But they run it like it's a legitimate enterprise and the other recruits are happy. It's what they do with the samples I'm concerned about, and that will only be answered by visiting Genomix Solutions Biotech. Your friend will get nowhere without proof.'

Simeon took a gulp of coffee, looking up at Carlos.

'I'm worried about Dr Andreeva. He told me he was having a meeting with Nicolae after dropping me off. I tried to warn him not to trust that man, but he wanted him to explain what's been happening and why two people have died. To be honest, he wasn't making a lot of sense, I think he had taken some pills or something. He was extremely volatile.'

Carlos feared they were already past being able to help the GP. 'It's vital we get proof of what's going on. Did Christina give you any?'

'No. But knowing her, she would have kept evidence. Didn't you find anything?'

'Nothing. She must have hidden it.'

Simeon shook his head. 'Or the police took it. Who do you think killed her?'

'I'm guessing one of the men who came here tonight. She was asking a lot of questions. I hate to break this to you, Simeon, but she was searching for you.'

Simeon rubbed his eyes with his right hand. 'We have to do something.'

'Do you know where Dr Andreeva was meeting Nicolae?'

'St Nicholas Church. I think he said Father Crane sorted it.'

'Come on. Let's go.'

'What about this place?'

'I'll deal with it later.' Carlos put Lady's lead on again, shut the concealed door to the flat in case anyone else came inside, collected a big torch and headed to the front door. 'We might as well use this one, seeing as it's open.'

Chapter 31

On the way to St Nicholas Church, Carlos told Simeon about the body he and Lady had discovered and witnessed being moved. He explained it was likely to have been that of Dr Andreeva.

Once inside the graveyard, Lady headed straight for the oak tree, as she had done earlier. Carlos shone his torch around and spotted a piece of torn material caught on a jagged branch. He took a photo, but told Simeon to leave it in place for evidence.

'Fiona's sending her CSI team along in the morning.'

'There, look,' said Simeon, pointing to recent footprints, different to his and Lady's, leading to the gate.

'Why didn't I see these earlier?' Carlos moaned. 'Sorry, Lady, I should have trusted you.'

They walked beside the prints and Carlos led the way to the picket fence around the freshly dug mound. 'Don't go in there,' he warned Simeon. 'We'll leave it to CSI, but have a look around, see if you can see any blood staining or anything. You use this and I'll use my phone torch.' Carlos gave the handheld torch to Simeon.

His heart missed a couple of beats when he saw something glowing in the dark. Carlos moved away... waited... then back. There it was again.

'We're leaving,' he said, hurrying away from the scene.

Simeon looked confused as he trotted after him. 'Did you find something?'

'I'm not sure yet. Keep up.' Carlos slowed. Feeling sorry for the weak Simeon who was struggling to keep pace, he stopped. 'I tell you what. Take this.' He handed over a £20 note. 'Go and get yourself some food from the all-night place across the road from my office, and then go back there.'

'I want to come with you.'

'It makes more sense for you to keep an eye on my place. You can bolt the front door from the inside, shove something under the back door handle and hide upstairs. You should call your parents and let them know you're safe. They'll be worried. I'll let you know what I find out. Take Lady with you. She'll warn you if anyone comes near the place, and if they do, stay quiet. Nobody's ever found that flat who doesn't know it's there. You only found it because I left the door open.'

'Okay, you're right, I should call Dad. My mom will be worried sick.' Carlos could see Simeon's heart was in the chase, but at present, he was nothing like the healthy man whose picture was on the flyers Christina had used to search for him.

'Good. Keep the doors locked. I don't think the heavies will be back again, so the back door should be fine overnight. Don't go downstairs or answer the door to anyone except for me. Understand? I'll phone you on the landline when I'm coming back. You can use it to ring home.'

'Thanks. And I'll pay you back.' Simeon held up the £20 note.

'It's fine. I'll call you later, or in the morning.'

'Where are you going?'

'Best if you don't know,' Carlos called over his shoulder. 'Look after him, Lady.' As he broke into a jog, Lady gave an affirmative bark.

Carlos was soon driving to the south of the city. He stopped outside a house on a road bordering Evington and Stoneygate. The house was in darkness, but he saw a flicker of light between the upstairs curtains. Not wanting to startle its occupant, he texted to say he was outside in the car.

He watched as the downstairs lights came on, taking it as a signal for him to get out. As he approached the front door, Bethany came out in her dressing gown. Light from the hallway revealed red and swollen eyes.

'Have you found out who killed her?'

Carlos grimaced. He hadn't realised she'd jump to that conclusion.

'Almost. I wouldn't have bothered you at this time of night, Bethany, but it's important.'

'Come in,' she said, shoulders sagging. 'I couldn't sleep anyway.'

'Thanks,' he said.

'Come through to the lounge and take a seat. Can I get you a soft drink or something stronger?' Although Bethany still spoke quickly, there was a dullness to the tone.

'If you have a can of zero alcohol lager, I wouldn't say no. I'm driving.'

'I've got low alcohol ones if that will do.'

'Perfect.'

Bethany left him in a cosy sitting room, returning a few minutes later with a can and a glass for Carlos and a hot chocolate for herself.

'What can I help you with? I'm sure I told you everything I know.'

'Did you put an infra-red camera in the Jewry Wall Museum grounds?'

Bethany's hand went to her mouth. 'It's not illegal, is it? I was going to collect them, but after hearing Christina died in that place, I haven't been able to face going back.'

'I don't know whether it's illegal... did you say them?'

'Yes, I left three of them to record from different angles.'

'Even better. How do they work?'

'They're wildlife cameras. Capturing images of wildlife is a secondary hobby of mine. I placed them after the night-time photo shoot ended, hoping to catch images of badgers or foxes – anything really.'

'So what you're saying is movement activates them?' Carlos could feel the excitement growing.

'Yes, but why are you interested?'

'Have you checked what's been filmed?'

Bethany's eyes filled up. 'I can't bring myself to. I was meaning to collect them and delete anything they captured. It wouldn't feel right to keep it after what happened.'

'Did you hear the police found another person dead in the museum grounds this morning? Well, yesterday morning now.'

Bethany's eyes widened. 'No! I've not watched any news. To be honest, I've taken a few days off to get myself together, and to give me and Jemmy time to get used to life without Christina.' Her eyes threatened to spill over again.

'I'm pleased you kept her. Where is she?'

'Fast asleep on my bed.'

Carlos nodded. 'Would you mind if I accessed the footage your cameras have captured?'

'Okay, as long as I don't have to look at it.'

'If they contain what I'm hoping they do, I'd rather you didn't look anyway. Just show me how to operate the system and how to save the footage to a USB stick and I'll do the rest.'

'No problem. Follow me.' Carlos followed Bethany to a room she had turned into an office where she gave him a crash course in wildlife photography videoing and told him how to pull the footage. After that, she left him to watch it.

Carlos heard a cat meowing and Bethany speaking fondly to her in the background, but he was too engrossed to pay too much attention. After a few false starts, where people wandering too close to the grounds set the cameras off, plus a shot of a cat taking a shortcut, he eventually arrived at what he was searching for.

In the early hours of Thursday morning, two men appeared in shot. Carlos tried all camera angles, but could only get them below waist height. One wore pale trousers than the other, the black and white recording revealed. Just like Henry's friend had told him, more men arrived. At least, Carlos assumed they were men from the shoes and waists. The pale trousers disappeared from shot, which must have been that man leaving.

Carlos watched in horror as the man who'd arrived wearing darker coloured trousers – he assumed it must be Ray – was forced to the ground. One of the new arrivals injected the deadly opiates into his arm while the others held him down. Finally, Carlos got a glimpse of two of the men's faces as they bent to the ground. He zoomed in and took still photos. As he continued watching, he got a shot of a third man.

It was a struggle to detach his emotions while saving the footage. How could they be so ruthless? Carlos was pleased he'd got enough footage and stills of three of Ray's killers. He was sure there would be CCTV of the van once the police had the times shown on camera to help narrow it down. However, if Pale Trousers was Nicolae, he still had deniability because Ray Sylvester was alive when he left.

'Found anything?' Bethany poked her head around the door. Jemmy was purring around her legs.

'Yes. But I'm hoping to get more.'

'I'll be in the other room.'

Carlos continued his search, his heart racing as he fast-forwarded and watched. He felt the tension in his neck, praying the cameras wouldn't die on him. Was he going to get the breakthrough he was hoping for?

Finally!

Three pairs of men's legs appeared in shot. He watched the inconclusive waist-height video, barely breathing, until he grimaced at what came next. One of the men fell to the ground, clutching his chest. Carlos zoomed in and snapped a couple of still images. It was obvious the man had been stabbed. A quick search of the internet revealed him to be Dr Mishka Andreeva.

Once he was on the ground, the other two men lifted him over the picket fence. Carlos watched as they dropped him in a pre-dug hole. They must have known about it before they killed him. Carlos checked the video from every angle, hoping they weren't wearing balaclavas.

He leaned forward, jaw dropping open. His hands shook as he recorded every bit of footage. Carlos didn't need to watch the rest because he knew it would show Lady and him finding the body and everything that happened afterwards. Someone could assess all of that later. He powered down the computer, pocketed the memory stick and dropped his head on the desk.

'Are you okay?'

Carlos jumped, turning to see Bethany at the door. 'Whatever you do, don't delete any of that footage, although I've got most of what I need on this.' He took the memory stick from his pocket and held it up.

'You look like you need to finish your beer, even if it is only the pretend sort.'

Carlos grinned. He wanted to get out and shout the news from the hilltops, but that wouldn't be fair on Bethany.

'Sure,' he said, getting up and following her back to the lounge. Sitting on the sofa, he felt himself relax for the first time in days.

'Have you found out who killed Christina?'

'I think so. I forgot to tell you, Simeon's okay. It wasn't him.'

'I never believed it would be. Who was it?'

'Best if I don't say anything just now. There are still a few missing pieces. You don't know where Christina would hide a memory stick or memory card, do you?'

'Sorry, no.'

Jemmy climbed onto Carlos's lap and started pawing at his legs with her claws, trying to make herself comfortable. He picked her up and held her up to his face.

'Hey, that hurts.' Carlos put her down next to him. Stroking her was soothing. 'That's a chunky collar you've got there,' he said to the cat.

'I've bought her a new one. That one's too thick for her neck. I don't know why Christina bought it. It's nothing like her old one.'

Suddenly, Carlos had a thought. From what he'd learned of Christina, she was as OCD as he was. There's no way she'd put the wrong sized collar around her precious cat's neck... unless...

'Do you mind if I take a look at this, girl?' He gently removed the collar from Jemmy's neck, running his fingers over every part while he scrutinised it. He felt something hard on the inside, near the catch.

'There's something in here.' He picked around until he could get a nail beneath a secret flap. 'Do you have a pair of tweezers?'

Bethany returned with the tweezers and Carlos prised them inside the pouch. After a few attempts, he pulled out a micro SD card.

Bethany stared at him, wide-eyed. 'I'll get an adapter.'

Carlos followed Bethany back to her office. There, they both examined the contents of the card.

'Bethany, you've been amazing,' said Carlos eventually, 'but I have to go.'

'Let me know how things turn out.'

'I will.' Carlos hurried to his car, tapping Fiona's number as he went.

Chapter 32

DCI Bryony Shah wasn't what Fiona had imagined. She was tiny compared to Superintendent Henley, and was someone who exuded energy. Shah had a sharp, angular face with fierce, intelligent eyes. Her silky black hair was pulled back into a ponytail. There was a faint smell of tobacco on her clothes, not quite disguised by the mints she constantly sucked. Fiona soon discovered she wasn't one to mince her words, and from the way her team responded to her, she commanded respect.

Bryony had greeted Fiona with a curt friendliness, laced with suspicion. But once Fiona explained her change of mission, accompanied by the new knowledge Carlos had given her, it was clear they shared a common desire to put away bad guys.

An hour later, while one team raided the offices of Genomix Solutions Biotech, Fiona, Bryony, and another team of officers burst into the offices of McTavish and Partners. They had timed the raids to perfection to avoid one organisation warning the other.

Fiona and Bryony headed to one particular office. Bypassing the man's secretary, they headed straight inside.

A tall man with dark grey eyes, sandy brown hair and a paunch looked up from his desk in surprise. When he stood, it was clear he only wore the best: a neatly tailored suit fitted perfectly.

'What's going on here? Do you have an appointment?'

He was playing it cool, but Fiona could see their rapid entrance was having the desired effect. 'I'm Acting Detective Inspector Cook, and this is DCI Bryony Shah. Are you Mr Alastair McTavish?'

'The name's on the door.' He smirked, staring at Fiona with his cold eyes.

'We meet at last, Mr McTavish. We're here to speak to you about the testing of experimental drugs and therapies without proper safety checks, and about your involvement with a company specialising in illegal genetic manipulation.'

'Don't be so ridiculous.'

DCI Bryony Shah intervened. 'Try this for ridiculous,' she said. 'Mr Alastair McTavish, I'm arresting you for the illegal testing…' she repeated what Fiona had said, at the same time adding the required caution. 'Do you understand?' she finished.

'Of course I understand. But do *you* understand I'm the best defence lawyer in the United Kingdom and your superiors will hear about this? I'll be free within a couple of hours when it's shown that you have no evidence regarding any of these charges.'

Bryony's phone rang. 'Wait there.'

McTavish returned to his seat while Fiona remained standing. He eyed her with smug contempt.

'Do you really think you can take me down?'

Fiona stood her ground. 'I don't think it, Mr McTavish. I know it.'

McTavish erupted into sarcastic laughter. 'From this day forward, Acting DI Cook, there will be nowhere to hide for you or your brother.'

Fiona rushed over to his desk, placing her hands on top. She bore down on him.

'Leave my brother out of this. You are in no position to make threats.'

Moving his chair back, he smirked. 'I know your weakness, Fiona Cook.'

'And I know yours, McTavish. Greed and stupidity.'

Bryony re-entered the office and Fiona moved back. 'That was my sergeant. Your fellow director of Genomix Solutions Biotech has been very forthcoming since we raided his office. It appears he's kept video diaries and records of all of your meetings, including those where you insisted he expand the company's research to target the homeless. How did you put it?'

Bryony took her time, looking at her phone. She read from the screen. 'I have a transcript of one such meeting here. These are your words, Mr McTavish, and I quote,

"The homeless are ideal test subjects because they are invisible, plus they lack advocacy. Their marginalised status makes them perfect for our studies." This is the best bit.' Bryony continued reading. '"They" – the homeless – "will go unnoticed and have no access to legal resources. We can use that in our favour. They can be manipulated or coerced if need be to do what we want."

'When your partner raises concerns, you raise your voice. That's what it says here.'

Fiona enjoyed seeing the lawyer, who had tried to threaten her, squirm.

Bryony continued, '"The company should take advantage of their vulnerability and recruit participants under the cover of a legitimate research trial. Look, Peter," you shout again, "these people are expendable. Using them will shortcut the system and be cheaper in the long run." I think that about sums it up, Mr McTavish.'

McTavish grunted. 'We'll see about this. And don't think you've heard the last of me,' he snarled in Fiona's direction.

'I hope that's not a threat,' said Fiona. 'Did you hear him threaten me, DCI Shah?'

'I did. It will be entered in my report.' Superintendent Henley had been right. Shah was the perfect partner for a case like this. Fiona would love to hear more about her super's days as a street cop. It was a shame there wouldn't be time.

'You'll be hearing from my lawyers,' said McTavish.

'Good luck with finding one. From what I've heard, Edinburgh will be glad to see the back of its most crooked lawyer,' Fiona retorted. She would be sorry to leave Edinburgh; she would have enjoyed sitting in on the police interview, suspecting McTavish would indeed find it difficult to obtain legal representation, but she had more work to do back in Leicester, and a plane to catch.

'It's been a pleasure witnessing your arrest, Mr McTavish. I'll see you in court.'

McTavish glared at Fiona. 'How's your brother keeping?'

Fiona had been expecting another swipe at her heart, but it was surprising to hear it spoken in front of Bryony and the officers that were now waiting to take him away.

'Sadly, he got in with a bad lot and the Edinburgh force has arrested him. He will be returned to England to stand trial for crimes committed in London.'

Having wracked her brains after Carlos's phone call over how she could save her brother from being found dead in a gutter while the police closed in on McTavish's contacts, Fiona had concluded that having him arrested for past crimes was the solution. It had been the hardest decision she had ever made, but it was the only way to keep her brother safe and get him away from anyone on McTavish's payroll who would remain loyal. In the meantime, she hoped most of them would be arrested.

Panic filled McTavish's eyes as he registered his leverage going up in smoke. He struggled with the handcuffs.

'You can't do this to me.'

'I'm sorry, sir,' said Bryony. 'The law says we can. Furthermore, I have a warrant to search these offices and your home. I'm sure we'll be bringing more charges in the not too distant future.'

Fiona watched with intense satisfaction as Bryony's officers assisted McTavish into the police car. The nightmare was almost over.

Bryony came over and whispered in her ear. 'You did the right thing. Shame we didn't get to spend more time together.'

They shook hands and Fiona climbed into a waiting taxi.

'Edinburgh airport, please.'

Chapter 33

DS Hugh Barber strode into Carlos's office along with PC Barry King. The CSI team arrived a few minutes later. Instead of escorting the team leader, Sheila Sanderson, to where he'd discovered the body the night before, Carlos explained where it had been and told her there was video evidence from the scene as well. Sheila listened intently, taking notes before leaving with a few of her team. Two stayed behind with Julie, who would try to restore order once they'd finished.

'We'll leave you to it, then,' Hugh said to Barry. 'Coming, Jacobi?'

Carlos followed the surly detective out to Barber's waiting Ford Focus. 'If we're going to be working together, please call me Carlos.'

'Hugh,' the detective said with an almost smile.

It's a start, thought Carlos.

Once they were in the car, Hugh became more chatty. 'Acting DI Cook told me to pick you up and drive you to the destination, but she didn't tell me what it was all about. She said she'd leave that up to you.'

Carlos told Hugh what the DS needed to know about the evidence he'd uncovered on Christina's memory card.

'Wow! I've gotta say, I didn't see that one coming,' Hugh remarked.

'Me neither, to be frank.'

Hugh parked his car in the carpark, ensuring it was neatly between the lines of the bays marked out, even though there were only two other cars there. It was just what Carlos would have done. He smiled to himself, wondering how the DS coped with Fiona's mess when they were at work.

The two of them got out of the car and rang the bell outside the Gracious Heart Church. A cleaner answered the door and Hugh showed his identification. Carlos led the way to the priest's office. He knocked, and they walked in.

Seb looked up in surprise. 'Carlos! Good to see you again,' but his pretence of warmth didn't meet his eyes.

'This is Detective Sergeant Hugh Barber. We have a few more questions for you in relation to the death of Christina Sand.'

'Of course. As I said before, I'll do anything I can to help, but I told you everything at our last meeting. Is it about my report to Superintendent Henley? I understand the police are concluding their investigation.'

Ignoring the last remark, Carlos said, 'You didn't tell me everything, Father Crane.'

'I don't understand.'

'You omitted to tell me that Christina Sand visited you in this church on the night she died. And you didn't tell me she trusted you enough to tell you what she'd uncovered. Things like the illegal aspects of the homeless research.'

'I'm not sure where you're getting this information from, but I can assure you the young woman I knew as Carrie Clark didn't come anywhere near this church.'

'You're lying, Father Crane,' said Carlos.

Seb's eyes narrowed with annoyance, but he said nothing.

'Christina Sand kept meticulous records, returning to her flat, probably on the day she died, to record her discoveries and save them onto a memory card.'

'There was no evidence of that on her computers.'

'You're remarkably well informed,' Hugh piped in, 'about a police investigation.'

Seb shifted in his seat and intertwined the fingers of both hands. 'I felt bad after misidentifying that poor young woman and asked your DCI to keep me up to date on any fresh developments. He's a friend of mine, as is the mayor.' Seb shot Hugh a challenging look.

'What Christina didn't realise was that you were uninterested in what was happening to the homeless, as long as the generous donations to your church and the shelter kept coming in.'

'Churches operate on generous donations from benefactors, Carlos. I don't like what you're insinuating.'

'It appears your bank balance has also benefited from personal donations, but let's get back to the night Christina came to see you.'

'I've told you, she didn't come to see me.'

'Once I learned of Christina's arranged meeting with you – the last thing she recorded – I called a friend who checked the church diary for the day in question. You married a couple that day, didn't you?'

'I don't remember. What date was it again?'

'It was the thirtieth of October. I'm sure the date is etched in your memory.'

'I don't know what it has to do with your mistaken allegation that Christina Sand came here.'

'Are you suggesting the flower arranger I phoned this morning was imagining things when she told me she had been clearing the church after the wedding and saw Christina arrive?'

Seb steepled his hands on his desk. 'Okay. The woman came here with some ludicrous story about the illegal use of samples and genetic manipulation, something like that.'

'And I'm sure she would have told you her real name,' Carlos pressed.

'She can't have, otherwise I would have known it when I was asked to identify her.'

'When you were out walking the streets, doing outreach in the early hours of a Sunday morning?'

'Yes.'

'Except you weren't, were you? After you killed Christina Sand, you calmly attended the wedding reception for the couple you had married, where you stayed until 1am. I expect it was your friend, Nicolae Romanescu, who disposed of Miss Sand's body.'

'That's preposterous. Miss Sand was alive and well when she left. The only reason I didn't mention it before was that I know how you people work. I didn't want the name of this church embroiled in a scandal.'

'Really?' Carlos challenged. 'I find it hard to imagine your good friend, DCI Masters, would accuse you of being involved. Isn't it time to tell the truth?'

'You just said *Miss Sand* left alive and well, so you did know her name,' Hugh added. The pressure was building. Seb was looking less and less certain.

'Not then, but I know it now. You're trying to trick me. I've done nothing wrong. Let me phone DCI Masters.'

'Not your lawyer?' Carlos asked.

'Do I need a lawyer?'

'I would say so, sir,' said Hugh.

'You see,' said Carlos, 'when Christina came here that night, she was wearing,' he reached for his notebook, 'a sky-blue business suit. The flower arranger remarked on how pretty she was and on her beautiful red hair. I expect even if you've wiped your own CCTV footage, there will be more in the locality, showing her driving her car towards the church, and later, the car leaving with somebody else in the driver's seat. No doubt the car's in some breaker's yard now, or burnt out in the middle of nowhere. Or perhaps it's at the farm.'

Seb's eyes widened in horror.

'I didn't kill her. It was Nicolae.' The priest put his head in his hands. 'When she called to arrange the meeting, she mentioned the illegal research. I swear I didn't know until that day what was going on. I called Nicolae to ask him about it, and he came here and threatened me. He told me it didn't concern me and no harm was coming to those taking part, and that they were happy.

'Christina arrived for our meeting. I thought Nicolae had already left the church, but he was listening in from outside my office. She told me how she had been posing as a homeless woman and some men had attacked her a few days earlier, warning her to stop asking questions, but it had made her more determined than ever. She was concerned about her friend, Simeon, but after the attack, she had stopped pretending to be homeless. Miss Sand wanted me to know what was going on, as if I could do something about it.' He held his hands out in despair before stroking the large crucifix like he'd done at his previous meeting with Carlos.

'Why did she come to you and not the police?' Hugh asked.

'She'd observed Nicolae having regular meetings with a detective.'

Hugh and Carlos exchanged a glance.

'After that, Nicolae came in and yelled at her, warning her not to repeat a word of what she'd said to me. She was braver than I and stood up to him, telling him that when her parents returned from their holiday, she'd get them to report what he was doing. Her parents know people in high places, just like—'

'Nicolae,' Carlos snapped.

'She raced towards the door. The church was empty by then and Nicolae caught up with her. He shoved her, and she fell backwards, hitting her head on concrete.' Seb rubbed his forehead. 'I was going to call an ambulance, but she was already dead.'

Like hell you were, thought Carlos. 'What happened next?'

'Nicolae knew the couple I'd married had invited me to their wedding reception. He told me to go and that he would deal with the body. I assume he took her car keys from her handbag, dressed her in what she was wearing when the body was found, or got someone else to do it, and then arranged for her body to be removed and placed at the museum.

'He called me at 4am to tell me he'd had a tip-off from one of his police contacts that the body had been discovered as planned, and to stick to the homeless story she had created. He told me to call DCI Masters, who would deal with the police side of things. I drove over to the museum and identified the body as Carrie Clark. I didn't know what else to do. Nicolae can be frightening.'

Carlos shook his head. 'You had numerous opportunities to come clean, Father Crane, but you only acted in your own interests, even involving Dr Andreeva in your cover up. He's dead now because, unlike you, he had a conscience and threatened to expose what was going on the minute he found out about it.'

Seb whimpered. 'I did it for the church and for God's work.'

'Don't you dare bring God into this. You did it for yourself,' Carlos had his fists clenched at his sides, not daring to go near the priest lest he do something he would regret.

Hugh ordered the priest to stand up and arrested him, reading him his rights.

'I think I will speak to a lawyer before I say anything else,' Seb replied.

Hugh called for a patrol car to take the priest away and asked the CSI team to visit the church once they were finished at Carlos's flat and the museum. Carlos opted to walk back to his office, phoning Harry and Rose Sand from a park bench on the way.

Chapter 34

Carlos pulled in at the pickup and drop-off bay outside of East Midlands Airport. He couldn't sit still. Climbing out of the car, he hopped from foot to foot, partly to keep warm from the freezing East wind and partly because of the anticipation of what lay ahead.

He knew her plane had landed and was pleased to see Fiona was one of the first to come through the doors. He grinned at the sight of her, stuffing a roll into her mouth. Carlos took her bag and placed it in the boot. He was relieved the guys who broke into his office hadn't touched his precious car.

'Welcome home.' Carlos gave her a brief hug.

'Sorry, I'm starving, hardly got time to eat in Edinburgh. DCI Shah's like a stick insect. I don't know how she survives,' Fiona muttered in between mouthfuls once inside the car. 'A formidable detective, though. I could see why the super likes her. You should have seen the way she handled Alastair *The Crooked* McTavish—'

'I can tell you had a successful day.'

His friend finished the egg and cress roll, turning to him with bright, shining eyes. 'And that's just the beginning, thanks to you. Did you do what I asked?'

Carlos pulled out of the airport and took the M1 back to Leicester. 'Yep. After you called your superintendent, I went to your headquarters and dropped off the memory card and memory stick as instructed.'

'Great. She didn't want to alert anyone else to what we know just yet. Take me to my base. That's where she'll be now. Where's Lady?'

'Keeping Julie company while she organises tradespeople to fix doors and windows, plus—'

'An alarm, I hope.'

'Precisely. Paul Brand's back in work today and Simeon's gone home to Herefordshire.'

'Good. I assume he'll give evidence?'

'Happily,' said Carlos.

'I reported your break-in first thing. Did CSI do their bit?'

'Yes, efficiently, and Barry King took all the details. He's good. I hope you get him on your team. Although the intruders wore gloves and masks, the idiots didn't cover the number plate of their van. Your team have picked it up on CCTV, speeding along the High Street and parked up on St Nicholas Circle for the half-hour it took the goons to dig up the body. With that and clear pictures of a trio of them killing Ray Sylvester, they'll be arrested for both crimes once you give the word. I'm sure it won't be long before they spill the beans on who gave the order to kill Ray.'

'And where Dr Andreeva's body is. Why do you think Nicolae met Dr Andreeva in such a public place?'

'It's quite well hidden at night. Not many brave that dark alleyway but I expect it was the GP who chose the meeting place. He was a member of St Nicholas Church apparently. Maybe it gave him a false sense of security.'

'Poor man should have come to us. We've got them, Carlos. We've finally got them.' A strong buzz filled the car, like a pulse of electricity generated by their joint anticipation.

Thirty minutes later, they were sitting in Superintendent Henley's office, waiting. Carlos sat on his hands to keep them from trembling. He was so excited.

Masters entered the room full of confidence, grinning at the superintendent. 'Ma'am, I guess you want an update on the Christina Sand murder. You'll be pleased to know—'

He stopped when he spied Carlos and Fiona.

'What's he doing here?' Masters's demeanour switched from friendly to undisguised aggression as he snarled, glowering at Carlos.

'Take a seat, Terry.' The superintendent's mouth formed a thin line. Her eyes were firm, but giving nothing away.

Masters reluctantly took the seat opposite her while Carlos and Fiona moved their chairs closer.

'You were saying?' Superintendent Henley said.

'Erm,' Masters averted his eyes from Carlos's scrutinising gaze, 'I'm not sure if I should speak about police matters in front of a civilian.' He plastered on a sarcastic smile.

'Don't be childish, DCI Masters.' The superintendent's formality wiped the grin off his face. 'You were about to give me an update on the Christina Sand case. Let's have it,' she commanded.

'Yes... I... er... we have reached the conclusion Henry Cutter killed her in a drunken rage, and then murdered Sylvester to make it look as if he'd done it, and to remove suspicion away from himself.'

Carlos suppressed a chortle, but Fiona couldn't. 'What about the men who beat Mr Cutter up?'

Ignoring Fiona, Masters looked at the superintendent. 'Acting DI Cook knows as well as I do, ma'am, that vagrants...' Masters wrinkled his nose in disgust, unable to conceal the obvious distaste he felt towards the homeless, '...are attacked by yobs from time to time. Uniform can deal with that. Our job is to investigate major crime.'

'I'm pleased you've pointed our duty to *investigate* out, DCI Masters. Fiona, perhaps you would like to give us your report. Please feel free to contribute, Mr Jacobi.'

Masters stared nervously at the superintendent, and then at Fiona, avoiding looking at Carlos.

'As you are aware, ma'am, I was in Edinburgh this morning, as per your instructions, working a joint operation with Edinburgh police. We arrested a defence lawyer for his crimes against the homeless in Leicester. Mr Alastair McTavish has been on Edinburgh's radar for some time because of his links with organised crime in Scotland and England. They've never had enough evidence to arrest him, but, like all criminals, his greed got the better of him.

'We believe he employs a man called Nicolae Romanescu to run his illegal operations. At first, we thought it was the other way around, and that McTavish was just a clever defence lawyer who made money protecting high-profile criminals, but after searching his home and offices, DCI Shah assures me McTavish is a leading career criminal hiding behind the law.'

Carlos watched Masters while Fiona spoke, enjoying the arrogant confidence being chipped away bit by bit. Even with his healthy suntan, the colour was draining from his face.

'It appears, DCI Masters, that this lawyer was a senior partner in the biotech company funding both the legitimate research Christina Sand was heading up, and the illegitimate she uncovered.'

Masters walked over to the water dispenser in the superintendent's office and filled a glass, taking a gulp.

'Mouth dry?' Carlos asked.

'Unlike you, Jacobi, I've already had a long day.' He turned to his superintendent. 'I take it the GP was doing something illegal on the side?'

'Not the GP, Terry,' she answered, gesturing back to the seat across her desk. He obeyed. 'Carry on, Fiona.'

'As soon as you give the go ahead, ma'am, the team can raid the farm and start gathering evidence over there.'

Henley picked up the phone and dialled. 'Go,' she said, before returning it to its receiver. 'Romanescu is already being held by border force after trying to leave the country. Somebody must have told him we were closing in on him.' Superintendent Henley's tone was scathing when she added, 'At least we know that leak came out of Edinburgh and not from here.'

Fiona continued, 'We will arrest him for the murders of Christina Sand and Dr Andreeva, and for his part in the illegal research and the murder of Mr Ray Sylvester.'

Masters spluttered. 'What? How do you reach that conclusion? I've just told you Cutter killed Sand and Sylvester, and then made up this story about seeing men holding Sylvester down and injecting him with heroin. It's a ridiculous story.'

'Mr Cutter,' snapped Fiona, glaring at Masters, 'was so battered he could hardly move when we spoke to him yesterday morning, and on top of that, I may have forgotten to mention he has a broken ankle. Pray, tell me how he got hold of a syringe full of opiates and managed to overpower a man in that state?'

'Well. I... erm... perhaps he had an accomplice.'

'Henry Cutter wasn't the witness to Sylvester's murder. It was someone else who saw the crime, although we might not need her testimony.'

Masters opened his mouth, but Carlos got in first.

'You don't seem surprised at the mention of Dr Andreeva's death, DCI Masters.' It was taking every ounce of self-control to temper the rage he still felt towards this man for causing the death of his best friend. But at last, Masters was being brought to justice for something.

'The GP? Is he dead? How did he die? And why hasn't it been reported?' Masters returned to his pretentious mask, but his hands were shaking as he took another drink of water.

'Mr Romanescu stabbed him before burying him, aided by an accomplice. The five men who abducted Henry Cutter and killed Mr Sylvester later moved the body.'

Beads of sweat were forming on Masters's forehead. Carlos leaned forward and stage whispered, 'You were the accomplice.'

'This is absurd, even for you, Jacobi. See what I have to deal with, ma'am? This man is a neurotic waste of space. He couldn't hack the special forces, so he goes around blaming other people for his failures. He's a coward and a traitor with no loyalty to his fellow officers. Do you know he tried to get my team to turn on me then? And it seems he's doing it again with unsubstantiated allegations.' Masters's voice had risen, and he looked like he might leap out of his seat and attack Carlos any minute. If he did, Carlos was ready.

'DCI Masters!' Superintendent Henley's voice was raised – firm, but controlled. 'Remember where you are.'

Masters slumped back in his chair. 'Sorry, ma'am, but he's lying. And now he's got Fiona believing his fairy tales.'

Superintendent Henley turned her computer screen towards her DCI. 'Then perhaps you would care to explain this.'

Masters crumpled as the video played of three men entering the museum grounds before one – Dr Andreeva – fell to the ground. The other two men carried him between them and threw him into a hole, burying him. Finally, the footage moved to show a different camera angle and the faces of the two men.

The DCI's eyes moved wildly from the screen to his superintendent, and then to Fiona. His mouth opened, but he couldn't speak.

'Fiona,' Henley's voice broke the silence.

Fiona opened the door to the office to let two uniformed officers inside. She then returned to face Masters.

'Terry Masters, please stand.'

Masters pushed himself from the chair to his full height, towering over Fiona. The uniformed officers stepped forward, but Fiona motioned for them to stay where they were.

'Terry Masters, I'm arresting you for the murder of Dr Mishka Andreeva, and for assisting an offender in relation to the deaths of Mr Ray Sylvester and Miss Christina Sand. I'm also arresting you for malfeasance in a public office. You do not have to say anything. But it may harm your defence if you do not mention when questioned something that you later rely on in court. Anything you say may be given in evidence. Do you understand?'

'Yes,' Masters mumbled.

Superintendent Henley moved around from behind her desk, holding her hand out. A dejected Masters handed over his warrant card and other official items from his pockets.

'You have brought your office into disrepute and, by association, this team's reputation, Terry. As is my duty when we find a corrupt officer, I've had to refer your case to the Independent Office for Police Conduct, who will look into all of your past investigations. I hate to say it, but I fear more bad apples will be discovered. I only hope that real criminals aren't released on the streets because of your wrongdoing.'

Masters didn't look at her but stared over her shoulder. The superintendent turned to the uniformed officers.

'Take him away.'

Masters shrugged free of the officers, turning to Carlos. 'Satisfied? You—' He lunged forward, but Fiona tripped him up. The officers pulled him from the floor, cuffing him so he couldn't do any more damage.

Carlos looked him in the eyes. 'Very satisfied.'

After they left the room, Carlos excused himself. Fiona stayed behind to discuss the farm operation with her superintendent. He had no doubt she would be made a permanent DI after her work here and that her DC, Gary

Munro would turn out to be one of the bad apples her super had referred to.

Finding a coffee machine, Carlos used his card to buy a lemon and ginger tea, his fallen friend and comrade's favourite drink. He held the cardboard cup up in salute.

'Cheers, Don. We finally got him, mate.'

He downed the drink and left the building.

Epilogue

The gravel crunched under Carlos's shoes as he stepped out of his classic Ford Capri. Lady bounded out after him, tail wagging eagerly. She loved Rachel's parents' home.

The immense vicarage was a welcome sight. Carlos inhaled a deep breath, taking in the fresh fragrance of the countryside.

'Carlos, I've been looking out for you!' His heart missed a beat as Rachel approached. Her beauty took his breath away. She embraced him warmly. Carlos felt himself relax into her arms, and when they kissed, he knew there was no place he'd rather be.

Lady ran around their feet, tail swirling. Rachel stepped away from Carlos, laughing as she bent down to embrace his dog.

'It's good to see you, Lady! Thank you for keeping him safe.'

Footsteps sounded behind Rachel, and her parents appeared in the doorway. 'Welcome, welcome!' The Reverend Brendan Prince beckoned Carlos forward. His wife Susan opened her arms to embrace him.

'It's wonderful to have you both to stay,' said Susan, her voice soothing. She leaned down to pat Lady. 'I understand you've been busy.'

Carlos smiled gratefully. He hadn't told them too much about his work, but had explained to Brendan a little of what had been happening. Rachel was a detective in London and they regularly shared information about cases.

'Thank you for having us. Lady loves it here.' He inhaled again, taking in the timeless beauty surrounding him. For now, the past week's chaos was a million miles away.

Rachel took his arm as they walked inside.

'Where's Henry?' Carlos asked.

'He's in the conservatory,' said Brendan. 'Thank you for trusting us to look after him. He's an interesting man.'

'Thanks for having him. I couldn't think of anywhere safer.' By the looks on Brendan and Susan's faces, he guessed they had genuinely got on well with Henry. He'd hoped, rather than believed, they might be able to help Henry in more ways than just providing shelter.

'When did you arrive?' Carlos asked Rachel.

'About an hour ago. Your new friend is getting on really well with David.'

Carlos raised an eyebrow. Rachel's brother was so different to her; reserved and almost aloof. They got on well enough, but not as well as Carlos would like.

'That's great news.'

'Come on through,' said Susan. 'I've just made tea and we've got cake left over from our Girl Guides' bake-off last night.'

Feeling happy and content with one huge weight of his army days lifted from his shoulders, Carlos caught Brendan's arm while the women walked ahead.

'There's something I'd like to ask you this weekend.' His mouth felt dry as he spoke.

Brendan's eyes crinkled as his face broke into a warm smile. 'Whenever you're ready, Carlos.'

The men entered the conservatory as tea was being poured. Henry was a different man to the one Carlos had seen only a few days ago.

'Carlos!' Henry's eyes were warm and honest.

'I love the haircut,' Carlos said, taking a seat next to his new friend.

'Couldn't stay in a place like this and not look my best. Susan did it herself. I've trimmed the beard, and when I'm feeling stronger, I'll shave it off. Time to get my life back.'

Carlos gripped his shoulder. 'I couldn't be happier for you.'

'It's you I've got to thank for this. I heard you got the baddies, but I'm going to stay down here, if it's all the same to you. David here's offered me a job in his garage once I'm on my feet.'

Carlos smiled at Rachel's brother. 'That's good of you.'

'Not at all. Henry's got more experience with car engines than all my apprentices put together.'

'That's what you did in the army,' Carlos said to Henry.

'Yep. There's not an engine in existence I don't know how to fix.'

Carlos spotted the leg plaster and the signatures on it. 'Room for one more?'

'I'll say.' Henry leaned forward and whispered in Carlos's ear, 'If I were you, I'd get a ring on that one's finger before someone like me snaps her up.'

'I'm working on it,' said Carlos, looking over at Brendan, hoping to catch him as early as possible after tea. Brendan would give permission, he had no doubt about that, but Rachel had been burned in the past.

I just hope she'll have me.

THE END

Author's Note

Thank you for reading *The Museum Murders*, the third book in the current Carlos Jacobi series. If you have enjoyed it, **please leave an honest review on Amazon** and/or any other platform you may use. I love receiving feedback from readers and can assure you that I read every review.

Want to know more about Carlos's girlfriend? Why not check out my Rachel Prince Mystery series?

Keep in touch:

Sign up for my no-spam newsletter for news of new releases, offers and competitions at:

https://www.dawnbrookespublishing.com

Follow me on Facebook:

https://www.facebook.com/dawnbrookespublishing/

Follow me on Pinterest:

https://www.pinterest.co.uk/dawnbrookespublishing

Books by Dawn Brookes

Rachel Prince Mysteries

A Cruise to Murder

Deadly Cruise

Killer Cruise

Dying to Cruise

A Christmas Cruise Murder

Murderous Cruise Habit

Honeymoon Cruise Murder

A Murder Mystery Cruise

Hazardous Cruise

Captain's Dinner Cruise Murder

Corporate Cruise Murder

Treacherous Cruise Flirtation

Toxic Cruise Cocktail

Carlos Jacobi

Body in the Woods (Winner of Readers' Favorite Gold Medal Award for Crime fiction)

The Bradgate Park Murders

The Museum Murders

Lady Marjorie Snellthorpe Mysteries

Death of a Blogger (Prequel novella)
Murder at the Opera House
Murder in the Highlands
Murder at the Christmas Market
Murder at a Wimbledon Mansion
Murder in the Care Home

Memoirs

Hurry up Nurse: Memoirs of nurse training in the 1970s
Hurry up Nurse 2: London calling
Hurry up Nurse 3: More adventures in the life of a student nurse

Picture Books for Children

Ava & Oliver's Bonfire Night Adventure
Ava & Oliver's Christmas Nativity Adventure
Danny the Caterpillar
Gerry the One-Eared Cat
Suki Seal and the Plastic Ring

Acknowledgements

Thank you to my editor Alison Jack, as always, for her kind comments about the book and for suggestions, corrections and amendments that make it a more polished read. Thanks to Alex Davis for the final proofread, corrections and suggestions.

A huge thanks to beta readers for comments and suggestions.

A special thank you to readers Kerry Gray and Hazel Jarvis for volunteering to have their names used for characters in this book.

Thanks to my immediate circle of friends, who are so patient with me when I'm absorbed in my fictional world, for your continued support in all my endeavours.

About the Author

Dawn Brookes is an award-winning author who holds an MA in creative writing with distinction. She is author of the *Rachel Prince Mystery* series, combining a unique blend of murder, cruising and medicine with a touch of romance. The Carlos Jacobi books are based on a tenacious PI who is joined by Fiona Cook, a troubled but likeable detective sergeant, and his beloved ex-police dog, Lady. Dawn also writes the *Lady Marjorie Snellthorpe Mysteries* where four octogenarians solve crime with sharp wits and humour.

Dawn has a 39-year nursing pedigree and takes regular cruise holidays, which she says are for research purposes! She brings these passions together with a love of clean crime to her writing.

Dawn is also author of a series of nursing memoirs: the *Hurry up Nurse* series. Dawn worked as a hospital nurse, a midwife, district nurse and community matron across her career. Before turning her hand to writing for a living, she had multiple articles published in professional journals and co-edited a nursing textbook.

She grew up in Leicester, later moved to London and Berkshire, but now lives in Derbyshire. Dawn holds a Bachelor's degree with Honours and a Master's degree in education. Writing across genres, she also writes for children. Dawn has a passion for nature and loves animals, especially dogs. Animals will continue to feature in her children's books, as she believes caring for animals and nature helps children to become kinder human beings.